THE CRIT CLUB

YOU DON'T KNOW JACKALOPE

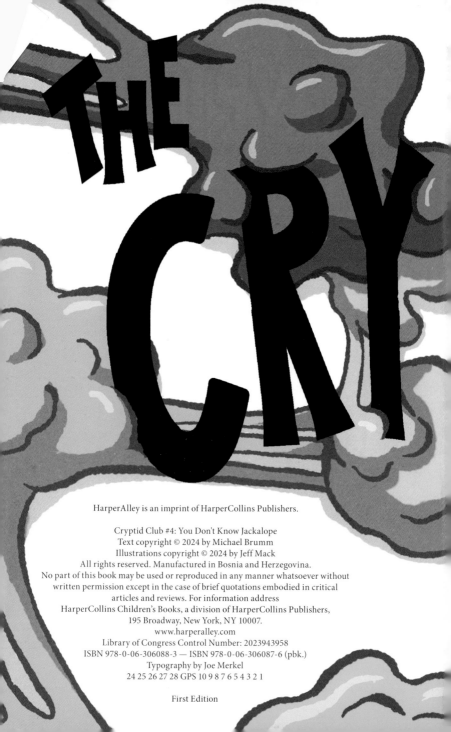

THE CRY

HarperAlley is an imprint of HarperCollins Publishers.

Cryptid Club #4: You Don't Know Jackalope
Text copyright © 2024 by Michael Brumm
Illustrations copyright © 2024 by Jeff Mack
All rights reserved. Manufactured in Bosnia and Herzegovina.
HarperCollins Children's Books, a division of HarperCollins Publishers,
195 Broadway, New York, NY 10007.
www.harperalley.com
Library of Congress Control Number: 2023943958
ISBN 978-0-06-306088-3 — ISBN 978-0-06-306087-6 (pbk.)
Typography by Joe Merkel
24 25 26 27 28 GPS 10 9 8 7 6 5 4 3 2 1

First Edition

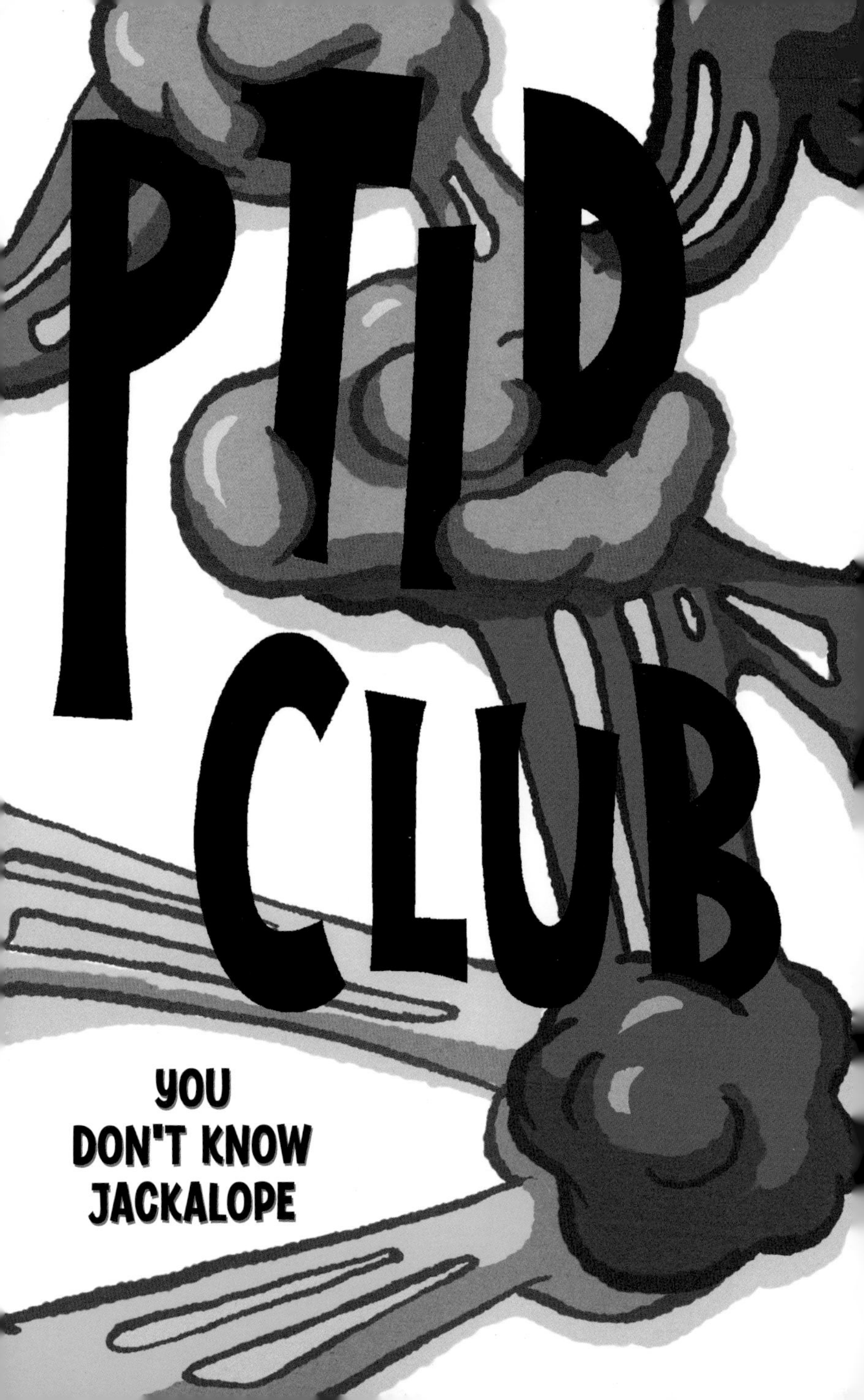
PTLD CLUB
YOU
DON'T KNOW
JACKALOPE

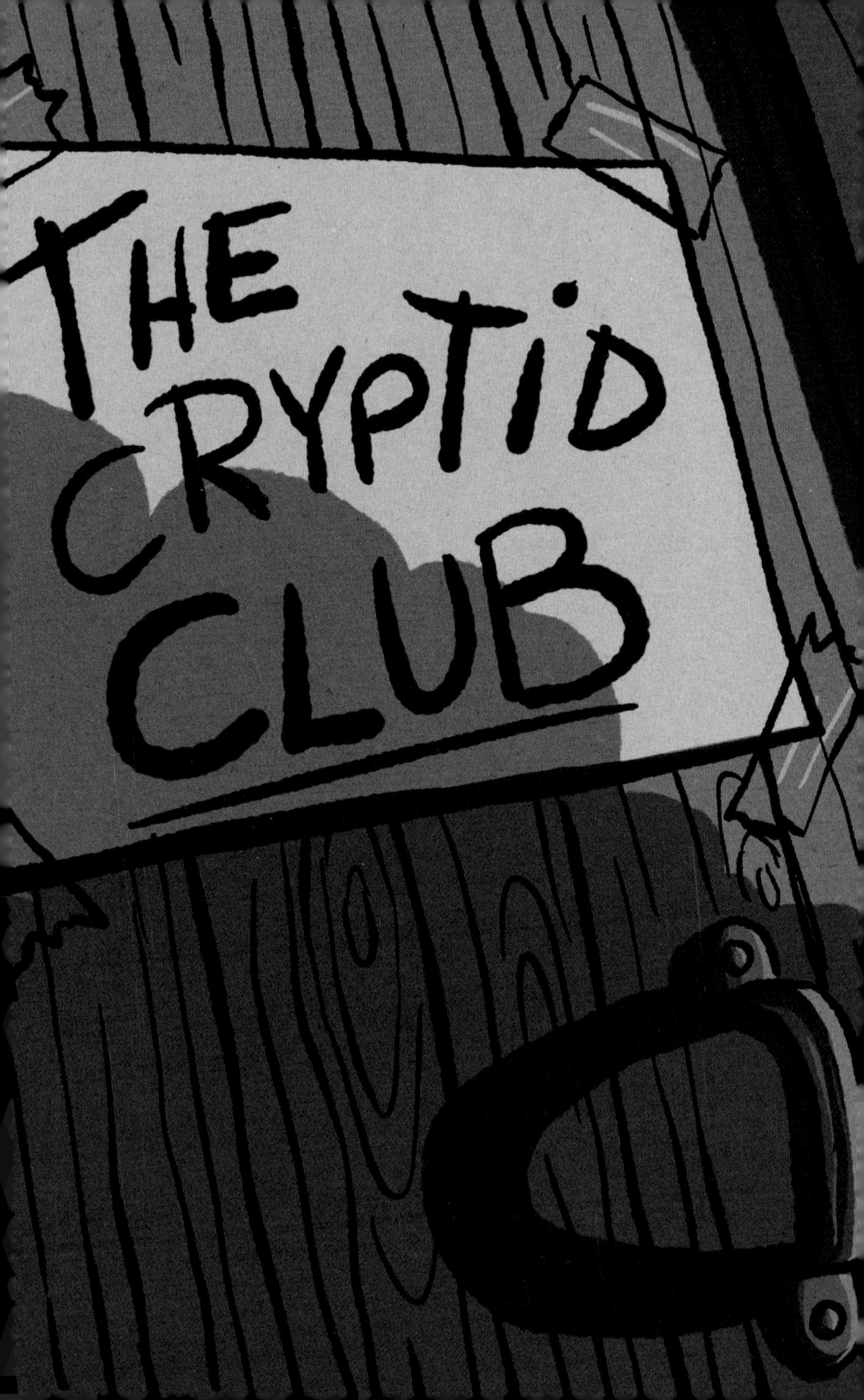
THE CRYPTID CLUB

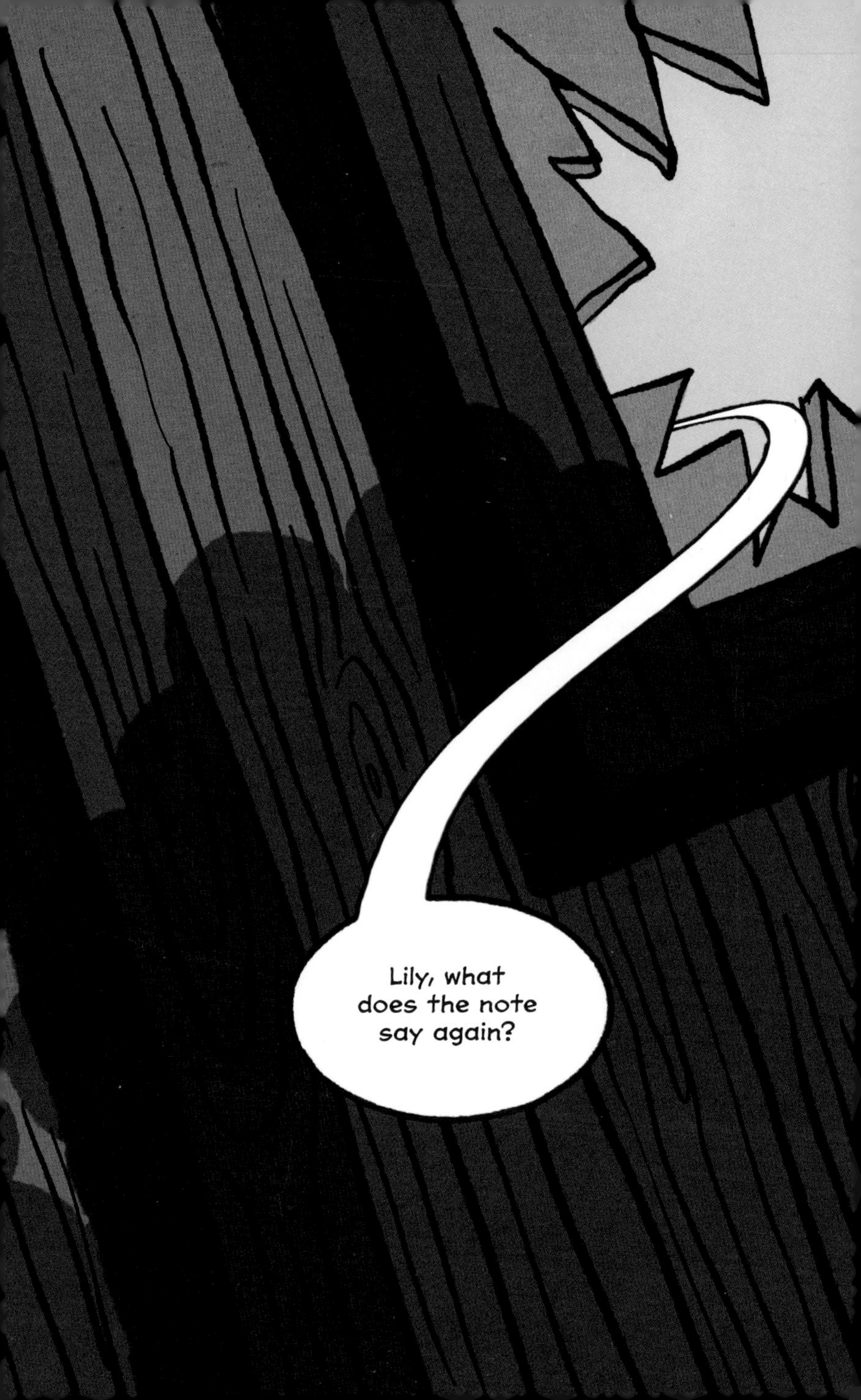
Lily, what does the note say again?

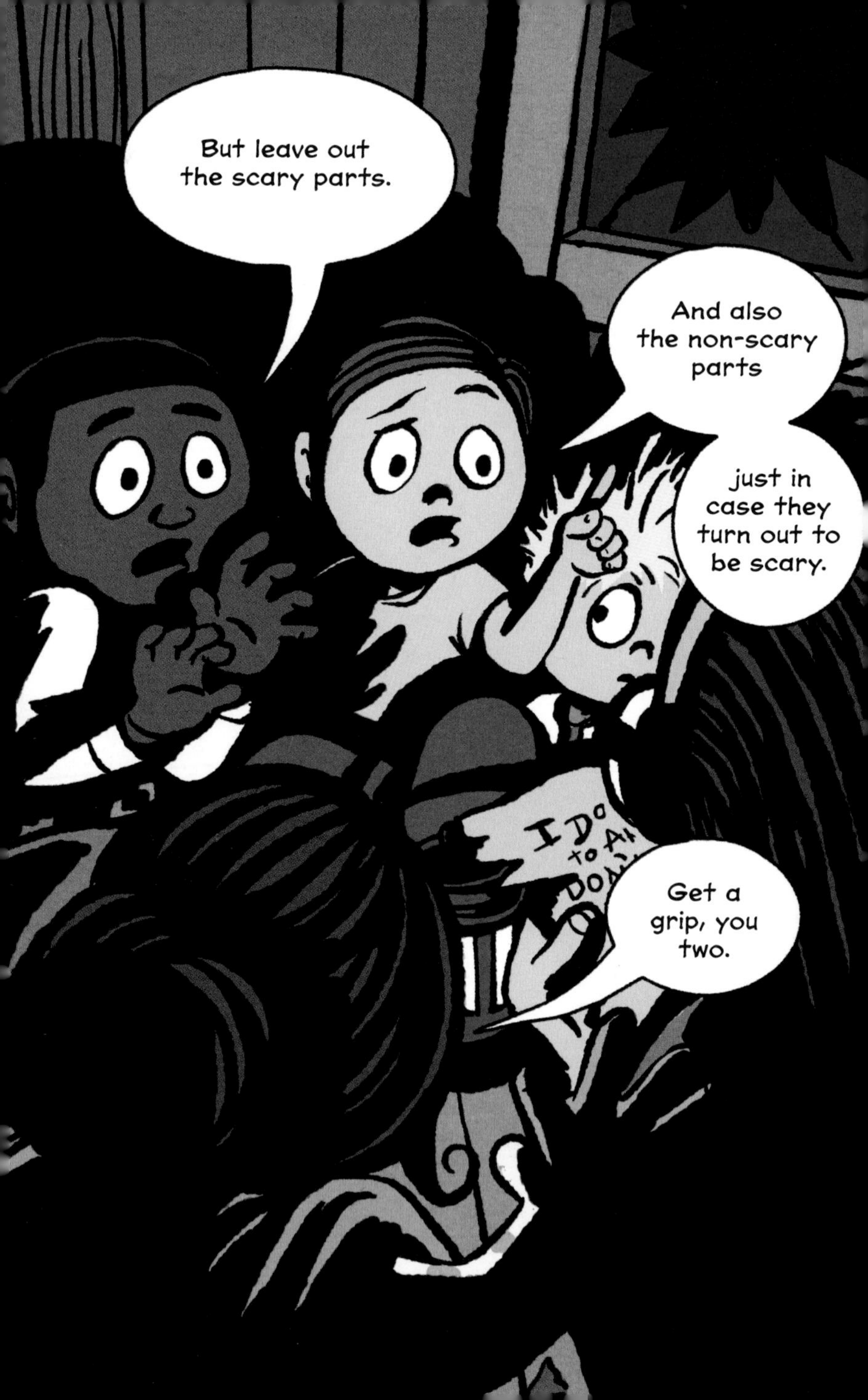
But leave out the scary parts.
And also the non-scary parts
just in case they turn out to be scary.
Get a grip, you two.

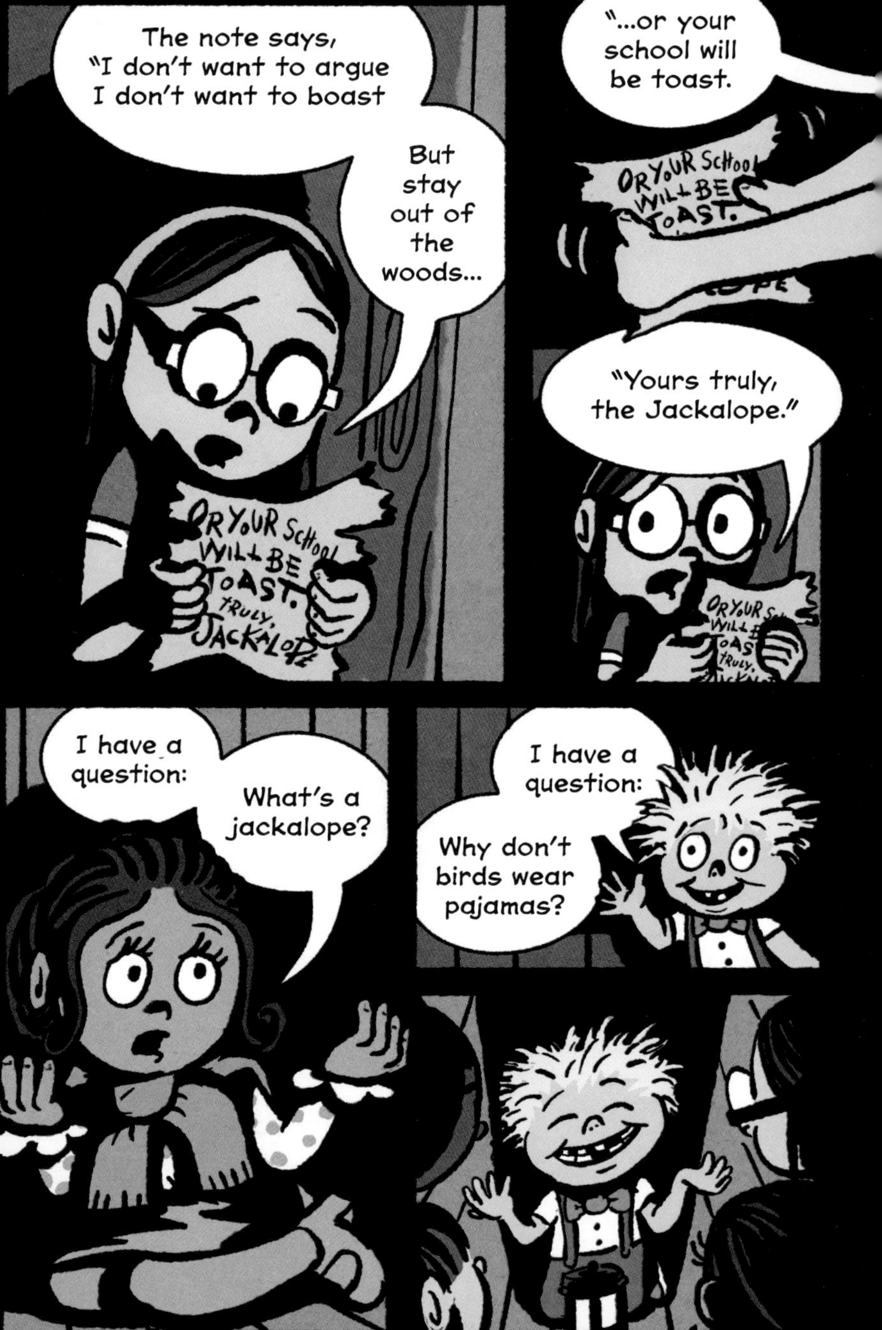
The note says, "I don't want to argue I don't want to boast
But stay out of the woods...
OR YOUR SCHOOL WILL BE TOAST. TRULY, JACKALOPE
"...or your school will be toast.
OR YOUR SCHOOL WILL BE TOAST.
"Yours truly, the Jackalope."
I have a question:
What's a jackalope?
I have a question:
Why don't birds wear pajamas?

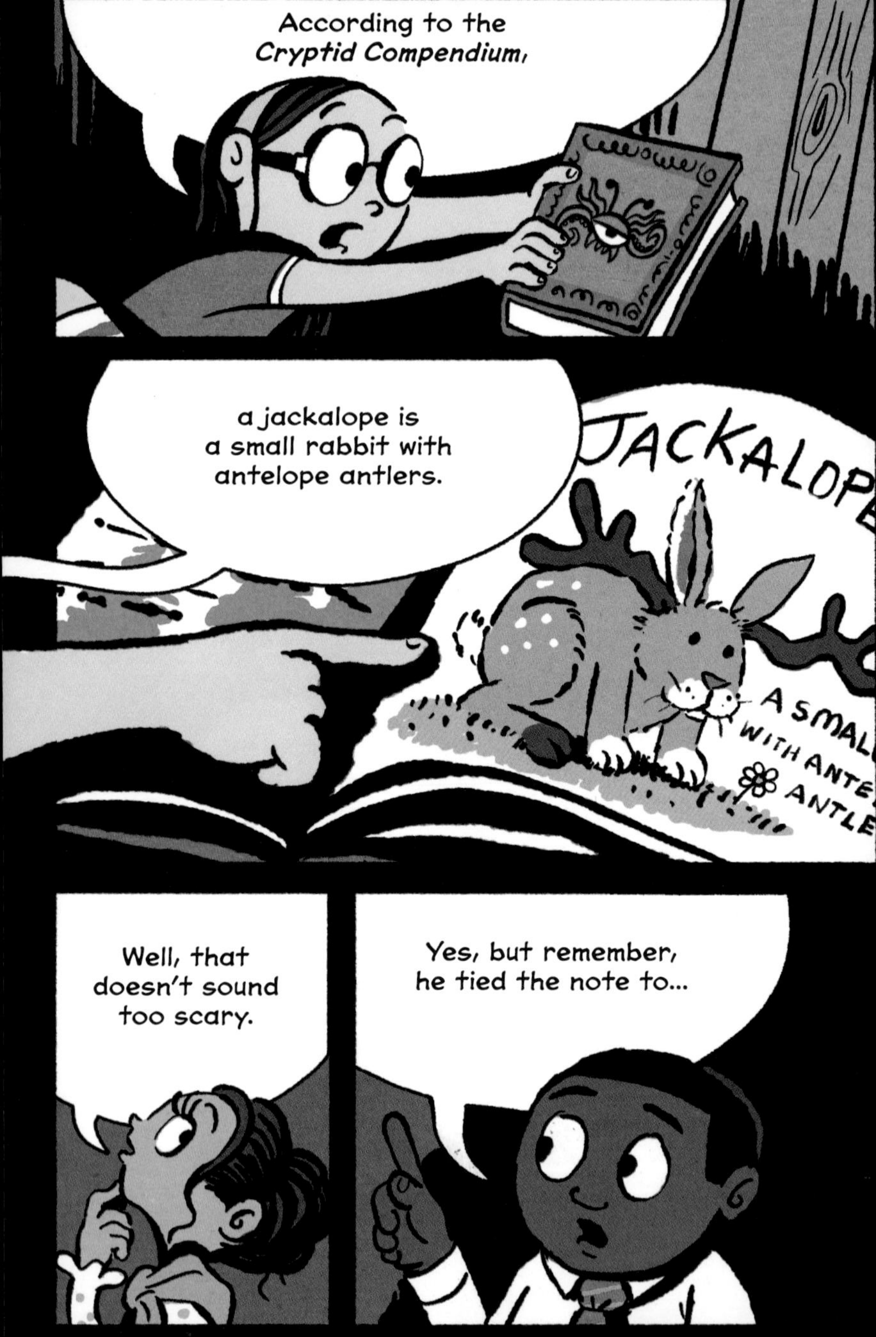
According to the *Cryptid Compendium*,
a jackalope is a small rabbit with antelope antlers.
JACKALOPE
A SMALL WITH ANTE ANTLE
Well, that doesn't sound too scary.
Yes, but remember, he tied the note to...

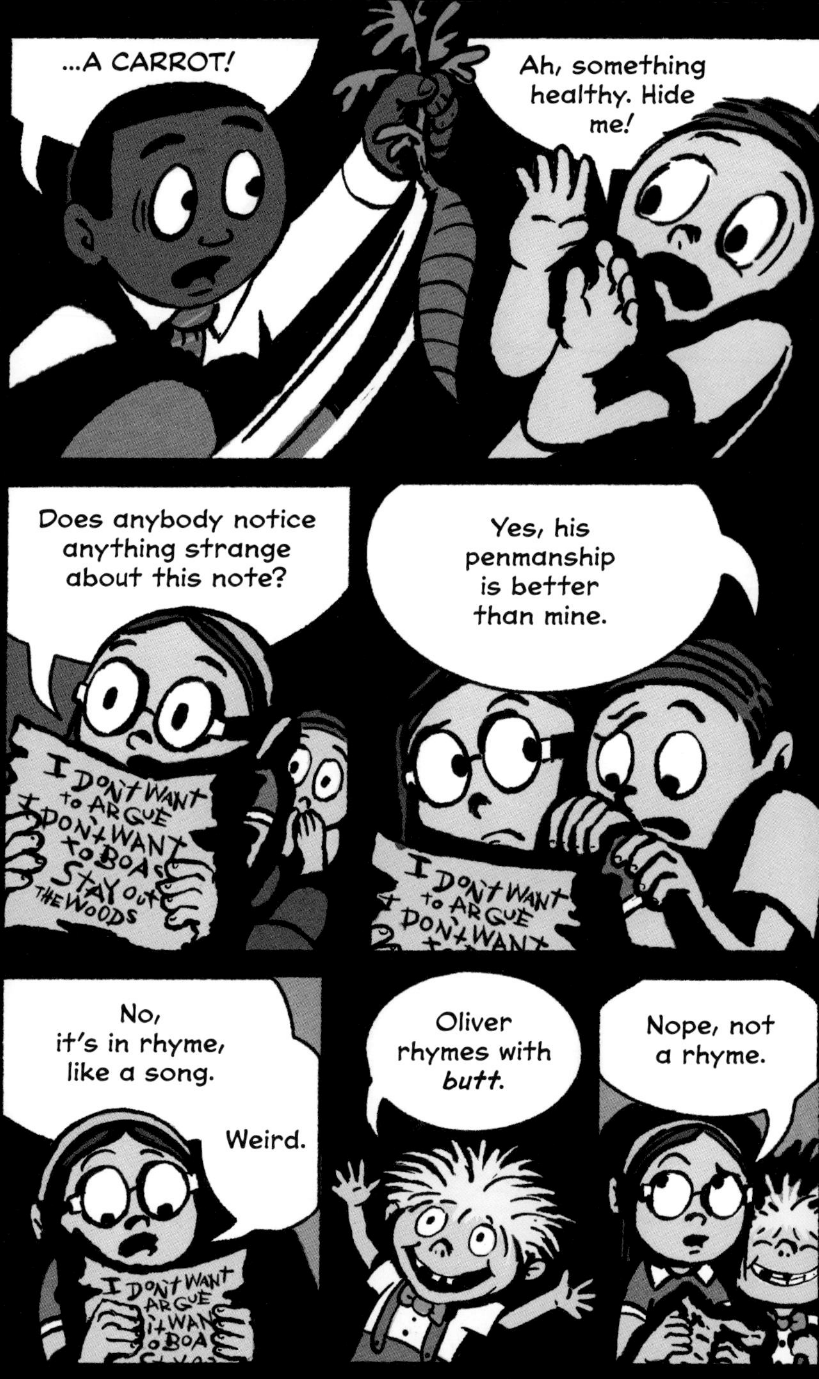
...A CARROT!
Ah, something healthy. Hide me!
Does anybody notice anything strange about this note?
I DON'T WANT to ARGUE + DON'T WANT to BOAS STAY OUT THE WOODS
Yes, his penmanship is better than mine.
No, it's in rhyme, like a song.
Weird.
Oliver rhymes with *butt*.
Nope, not a rhyme.

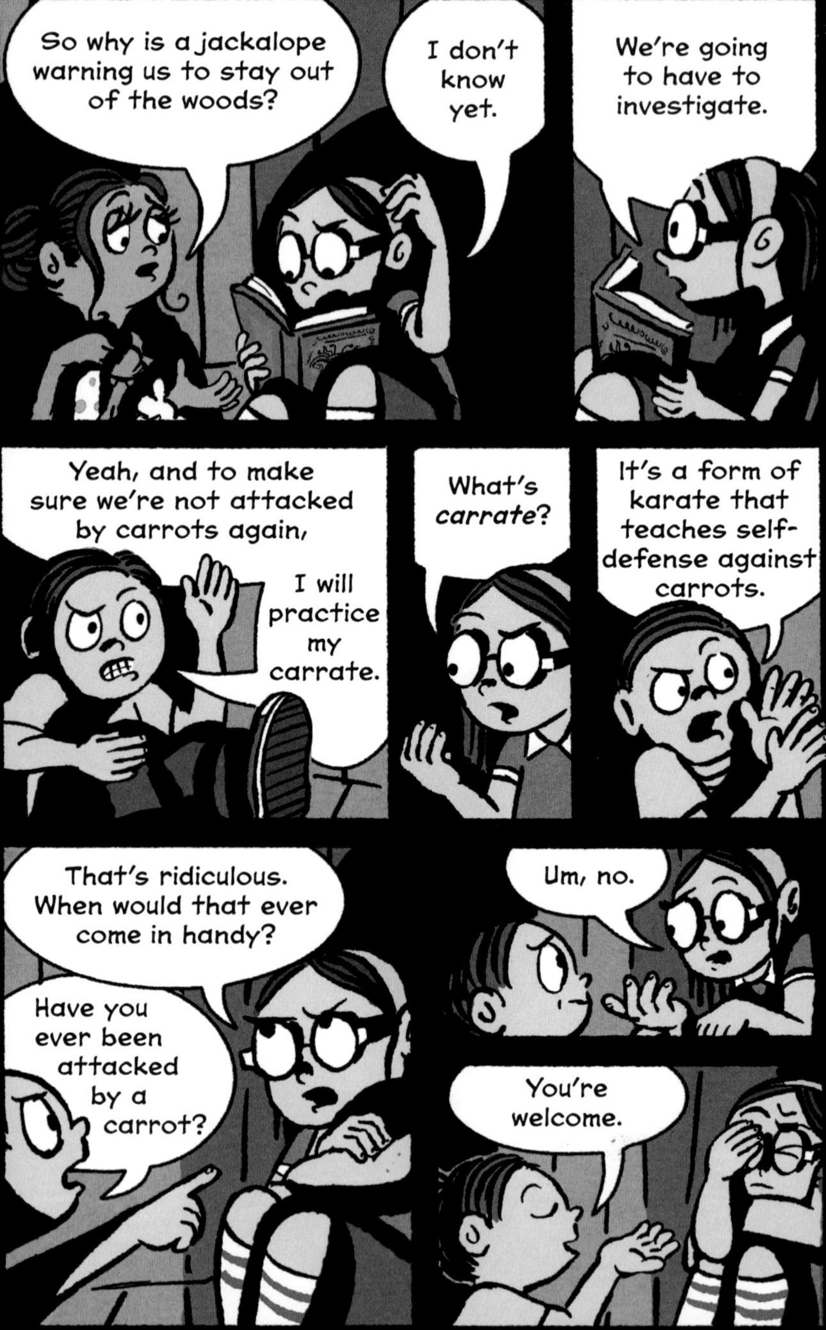
So why is a jackalope warning us to stay out of the woods?
I don't know yet.
We're going to have to investigate.
Yeah, and to make sure we're not attacked by carrots again,
I will practice my carrate.
What's *carrate*?
It's a form of karate that teaches self-defense against carrots.
That's ridiculous. When would that ever come in handy?
Have you ever been attacked by a carrot?
Um, no.
You're welcome.

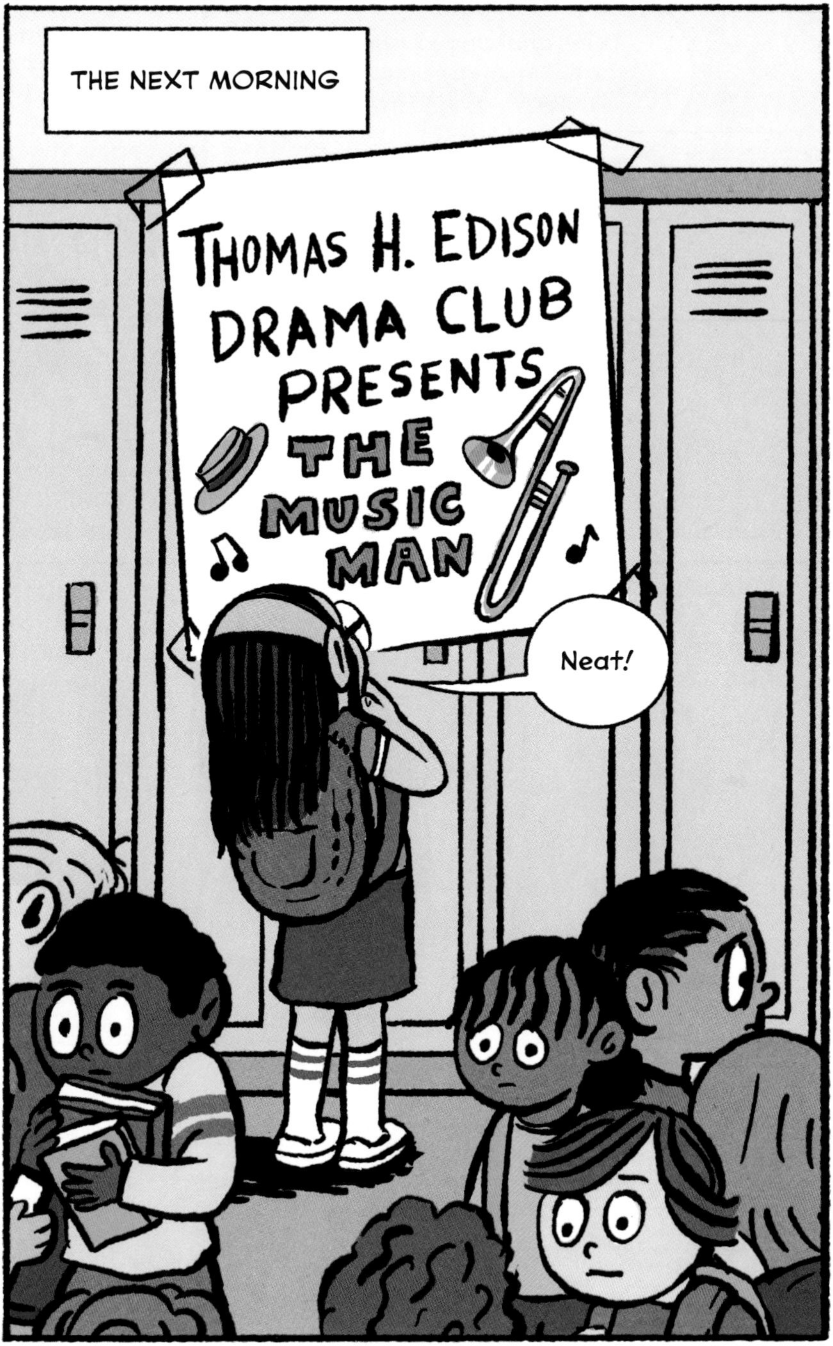
THE NEXT MORNING
THOMAS H. EDISON DRAMA CLUB PRESENTS THE MUSIC MAN
Neat!

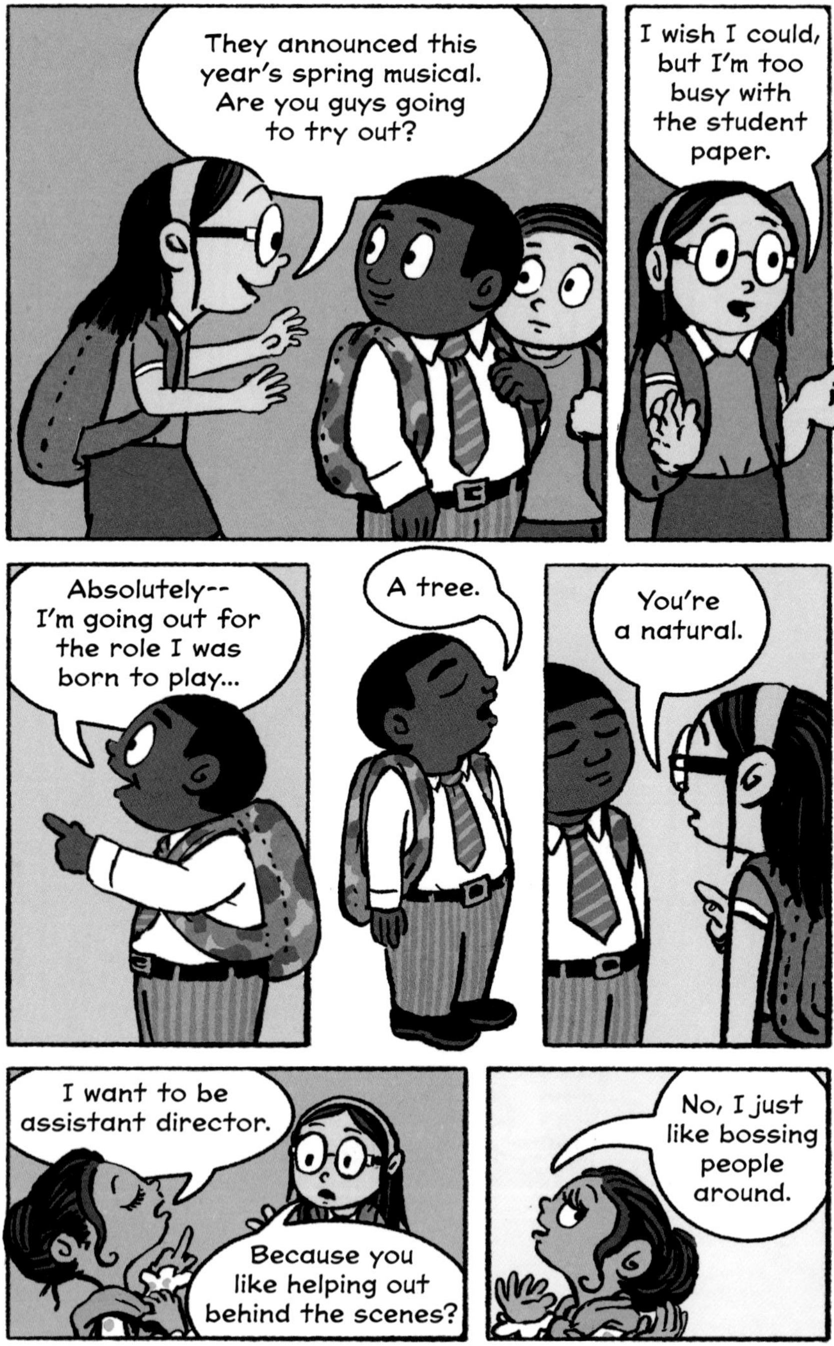
They announced this year's spring musical. Are you guys going to try out?
I wish I could, but I'm too busy with the student paper.
Absolutely-- I'm going out for the role I was born to play...
A tree.
You're a natural.
I want to be assistant director.
Because you like helping out behind the scenes?
No, I just like bossing people around.

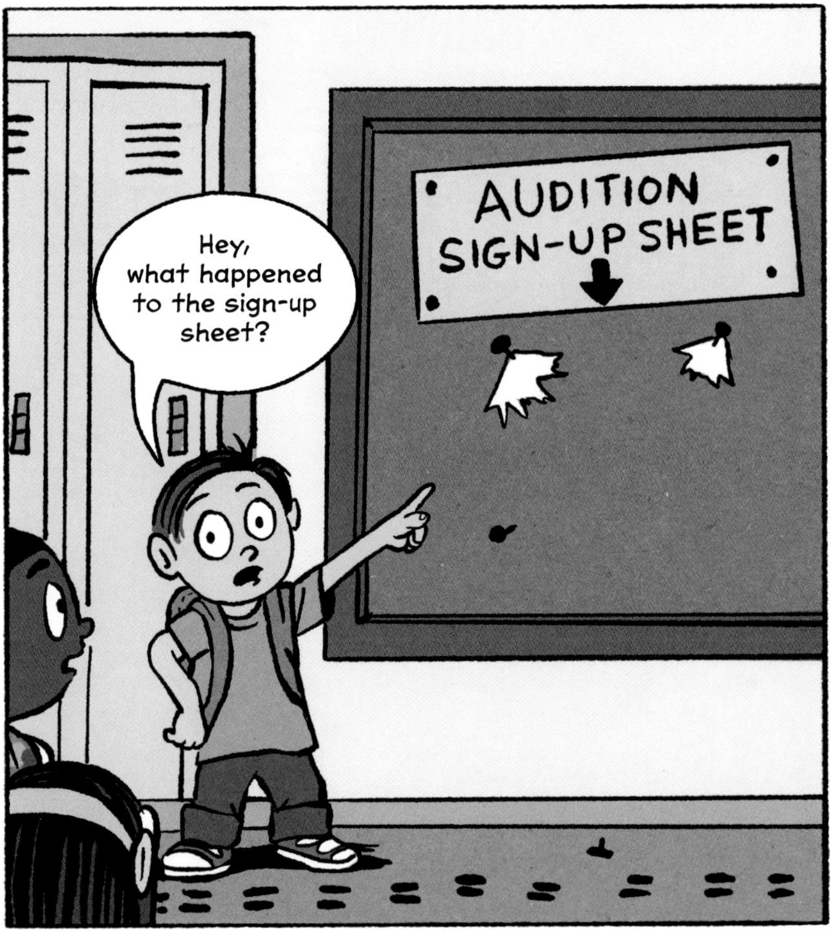
AUDITION
SIGN-UP SHEET
Hey, what happened to the sign-up sheet?

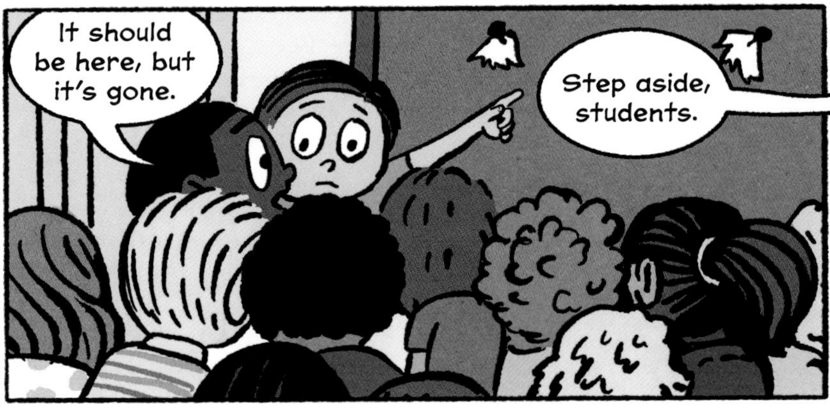
It should be here, but it's gone.
Step aside, students.

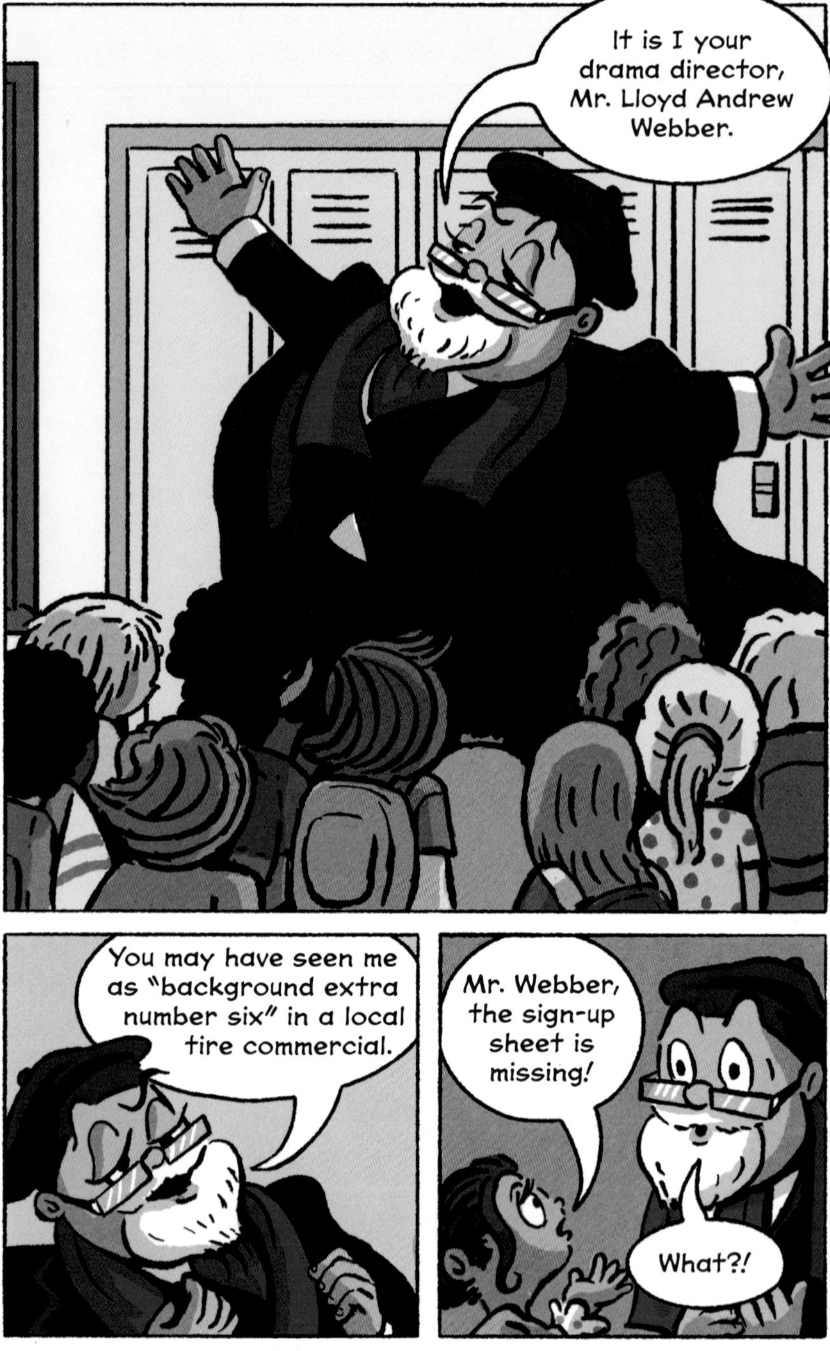
It is I your drama director, Mr. Lloyd Andrew Webber.
You may have seen me as "background extra number six" in a local tire commercial.
Mr. Webber, the sign-up sheet is missing!
What?!

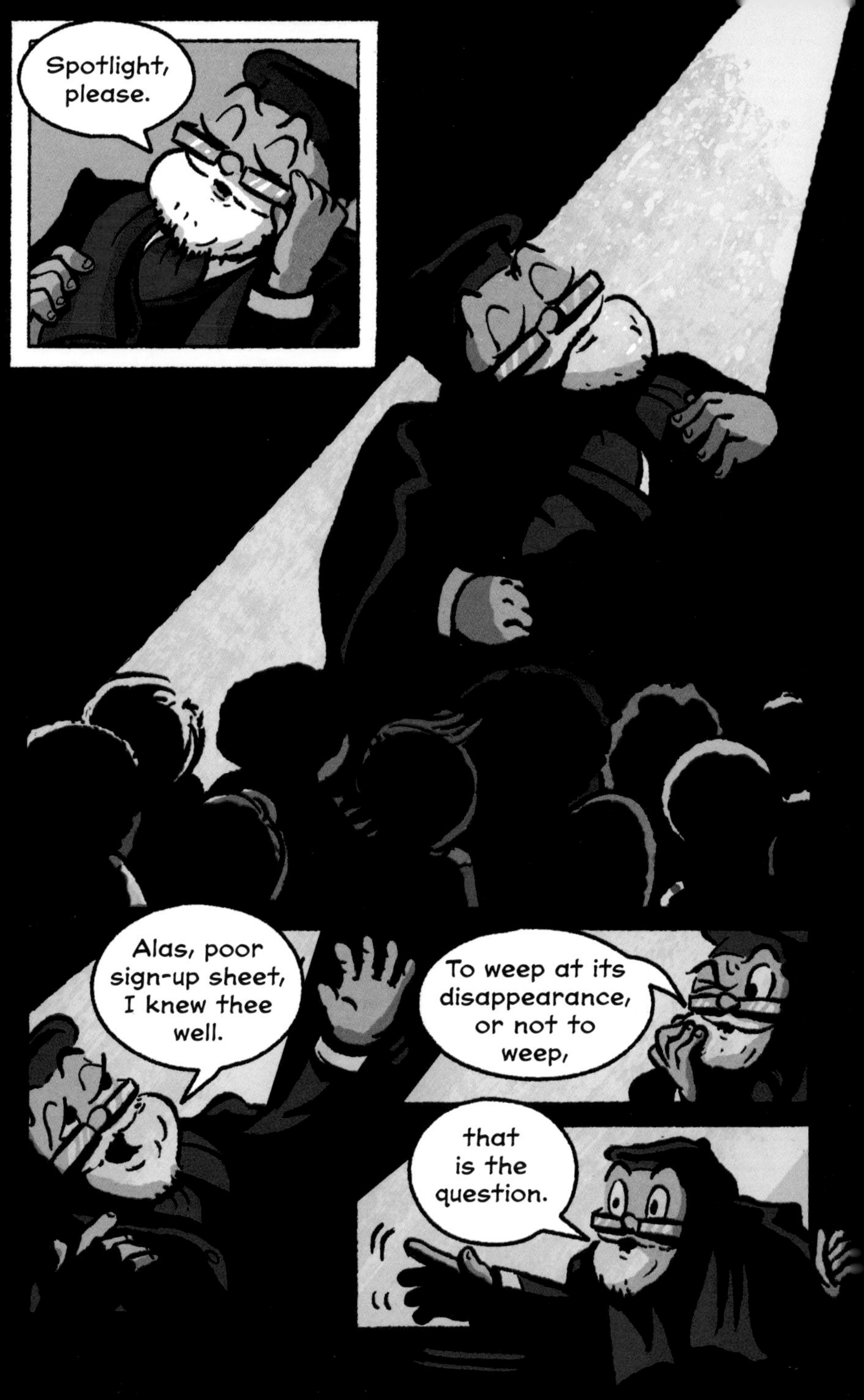

Spotlight, please.
Alas, poor sign-up sheet, I knew thee well.
To weep at its disappearance, or not to weep,
that is the question.

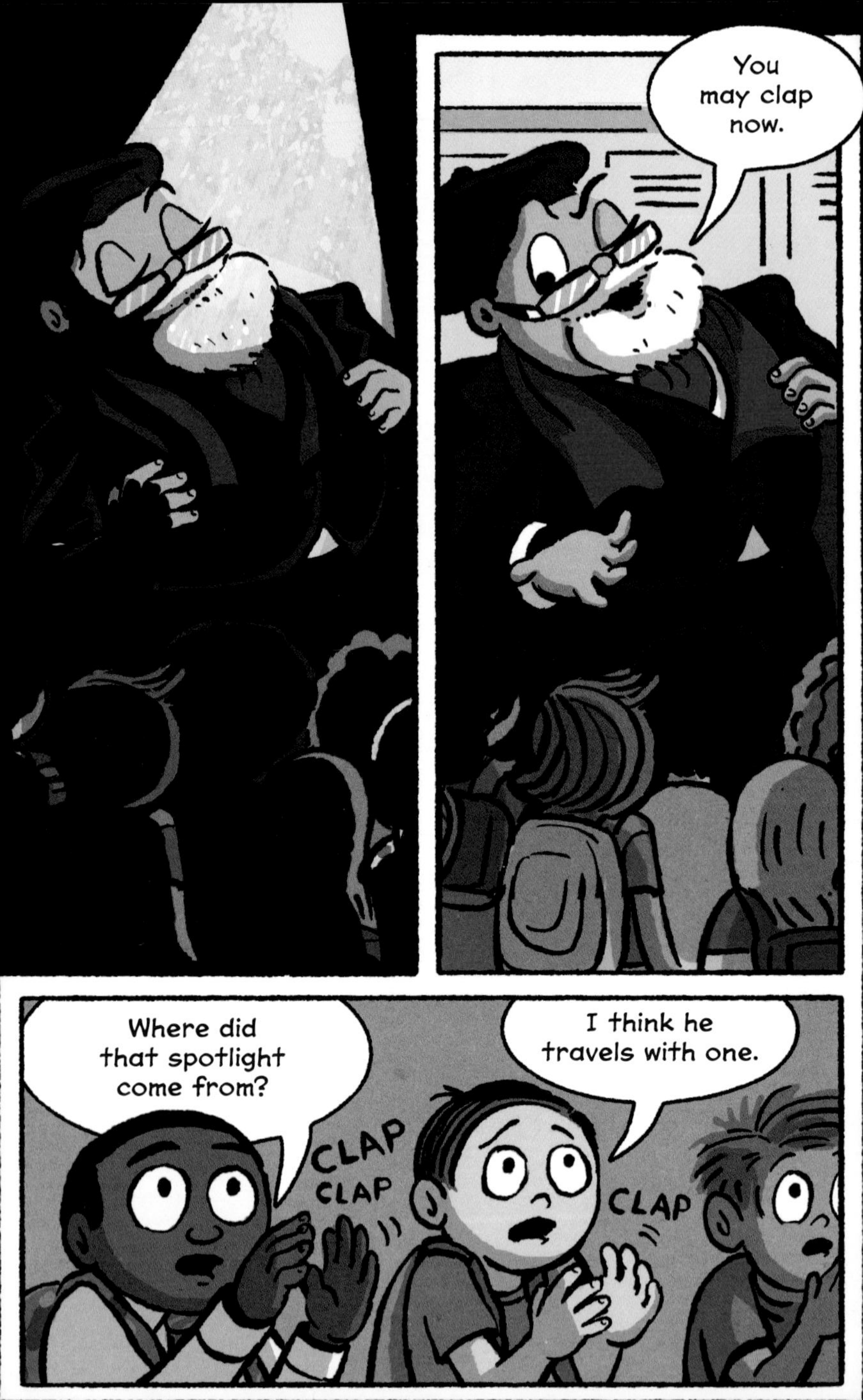
You may clap now.
Where did that spotlight come from?
CLAP
CLAP
I think he travels with one.
CLAP

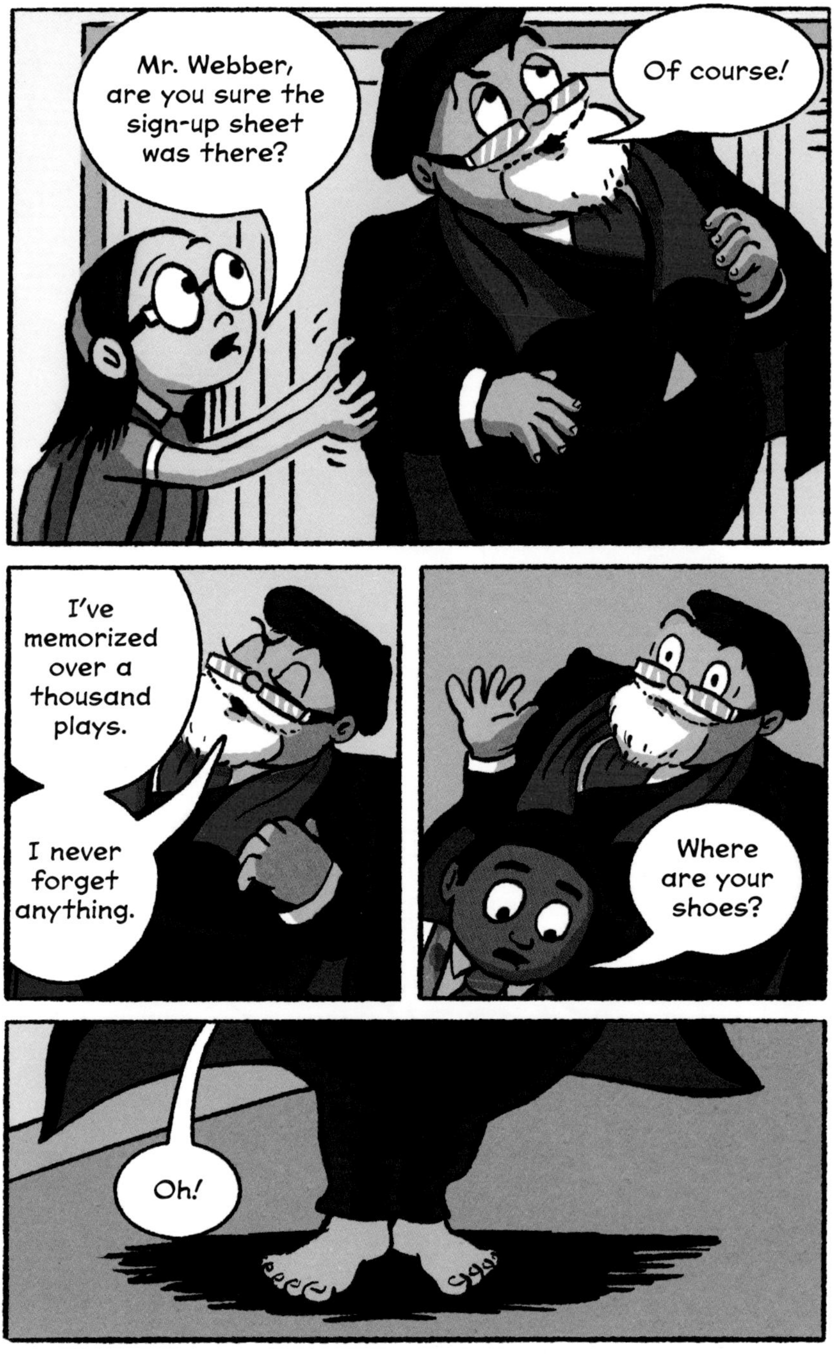
Mr. Webber, are you sure the sign-up sheet was there?
Of course!
I've memorized over a thousand plays.
I never forget anything.
Where are your shoes?
Oh!

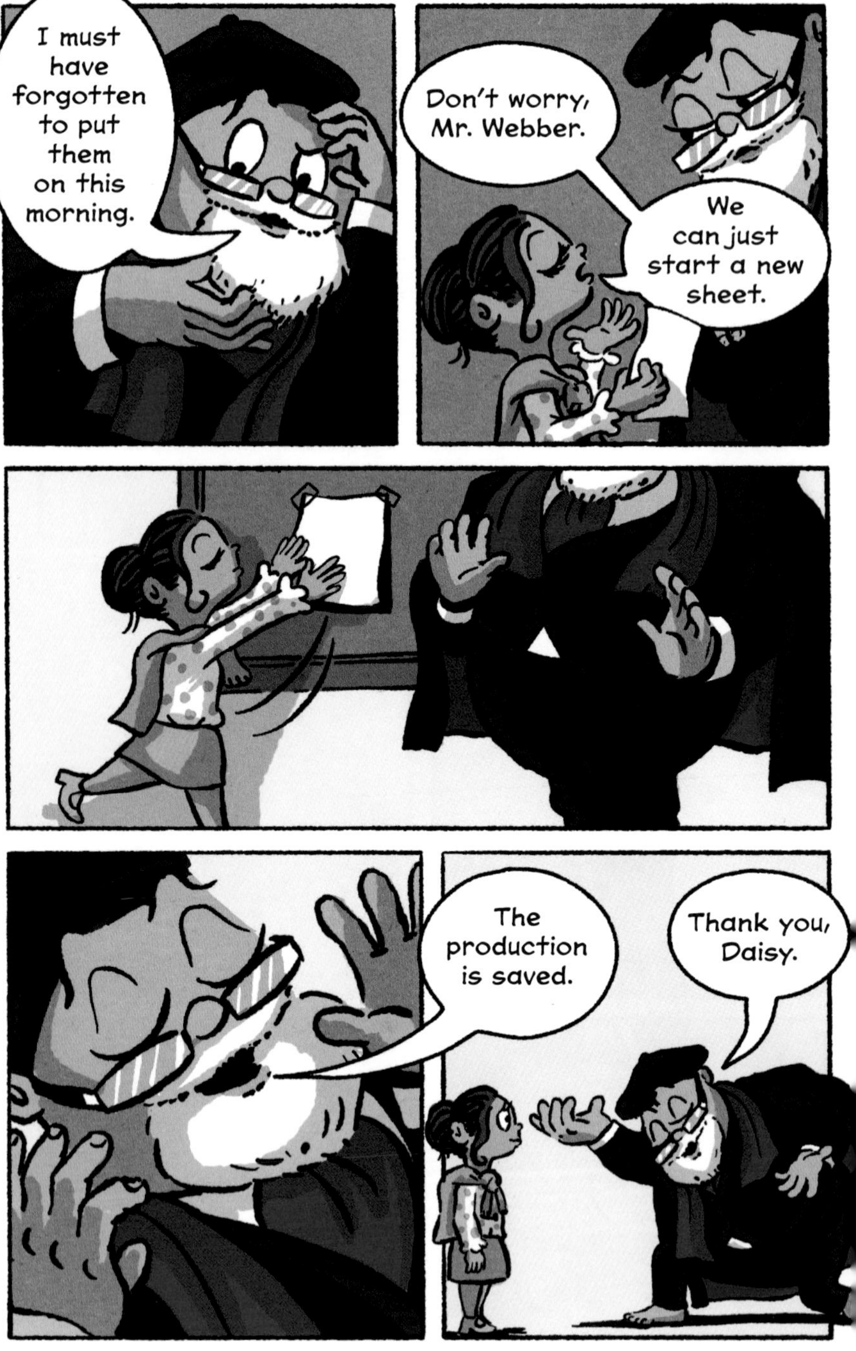
I must have forgotten to put them on this morning.
Don't worry, Mr. Webber.
We can just start a new sheet.
The production is saved.
Thank you, Daisy.

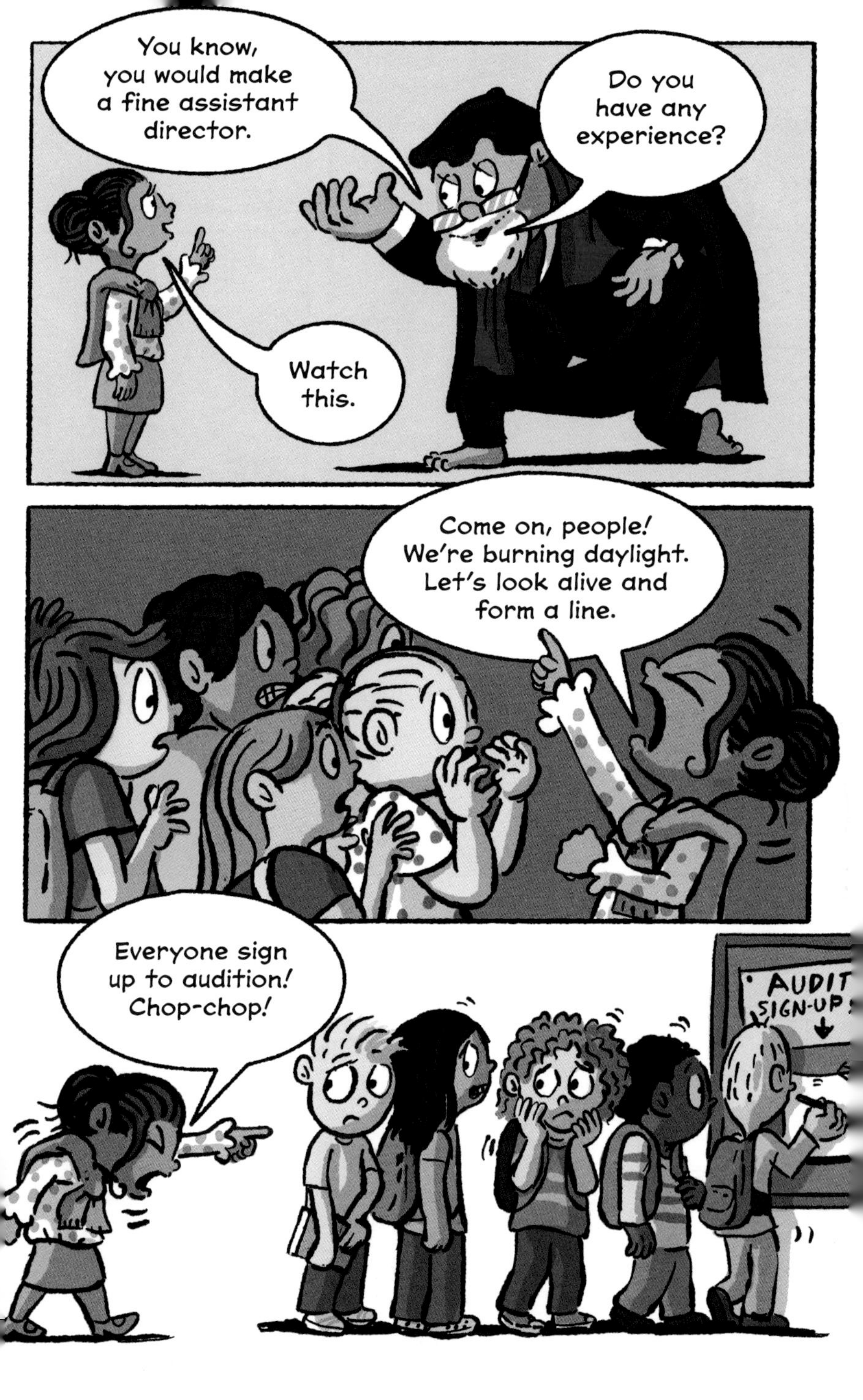
You know, you would make a fine assistant director.
Do you have any experience?
Watch this.
Come on, people! We're burning daylight. Let's look alive and form a line.
Everyone sign up to audition! Chop-chop!
SIGN-UP

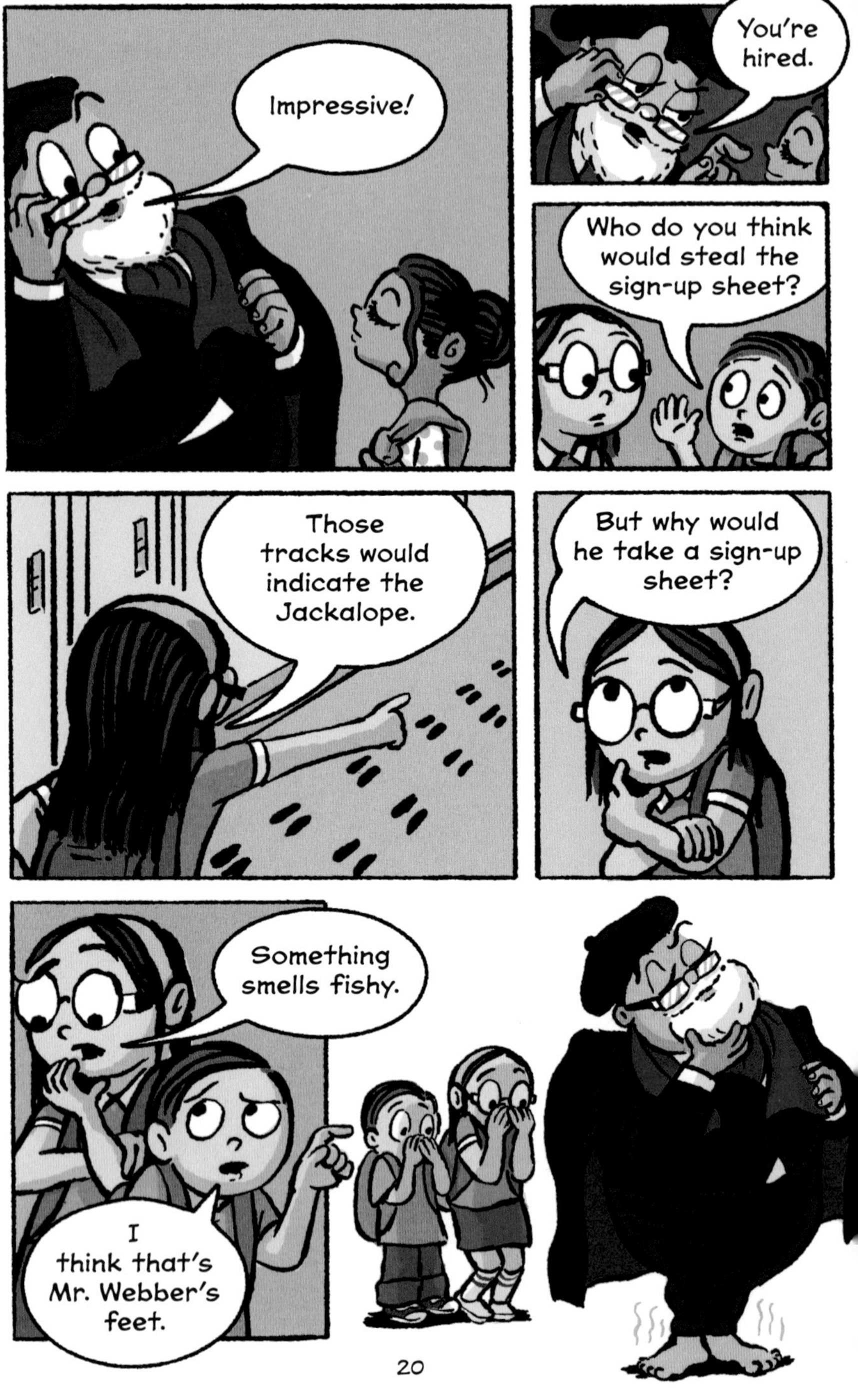
Impressive!
You're hired.
Who do you think would steal the sign-up sheet?
Those tracks would indicate the Jackalope.
But why would he take a sign-up sheet?
Something smells fishy.
I think that's Mr. Webber's feet.

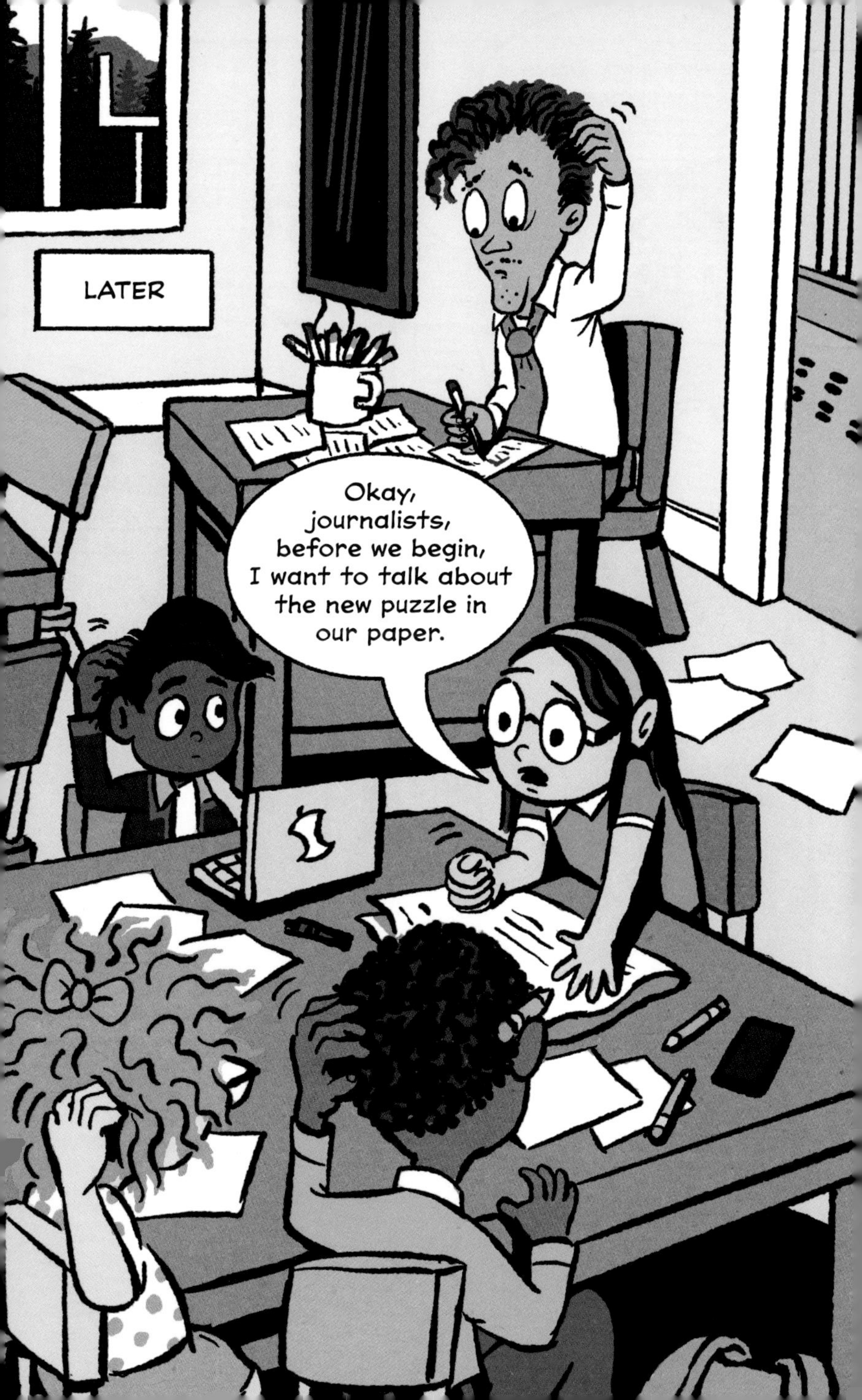
LATER
Okay, journalists, before we begin, I want to talk about the new puzzle in our paper.

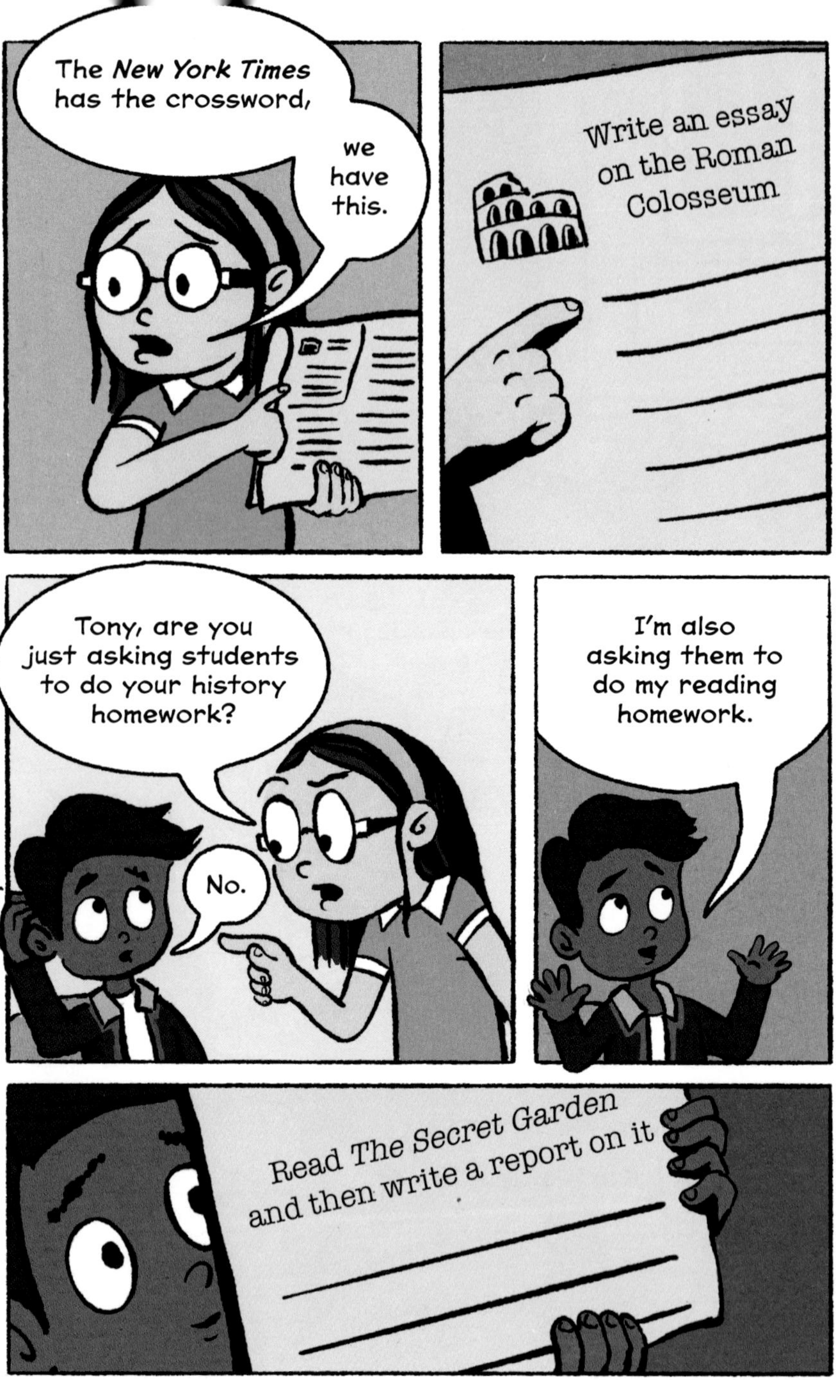
The New York Times has the crossword,
we have this.
Write an essay on the Roman Colosseum
Tony, are you just asking students to do your history homework?
No.
I'm also asking them to do my reading homework.
Read The Secret Garden and then write a report on it

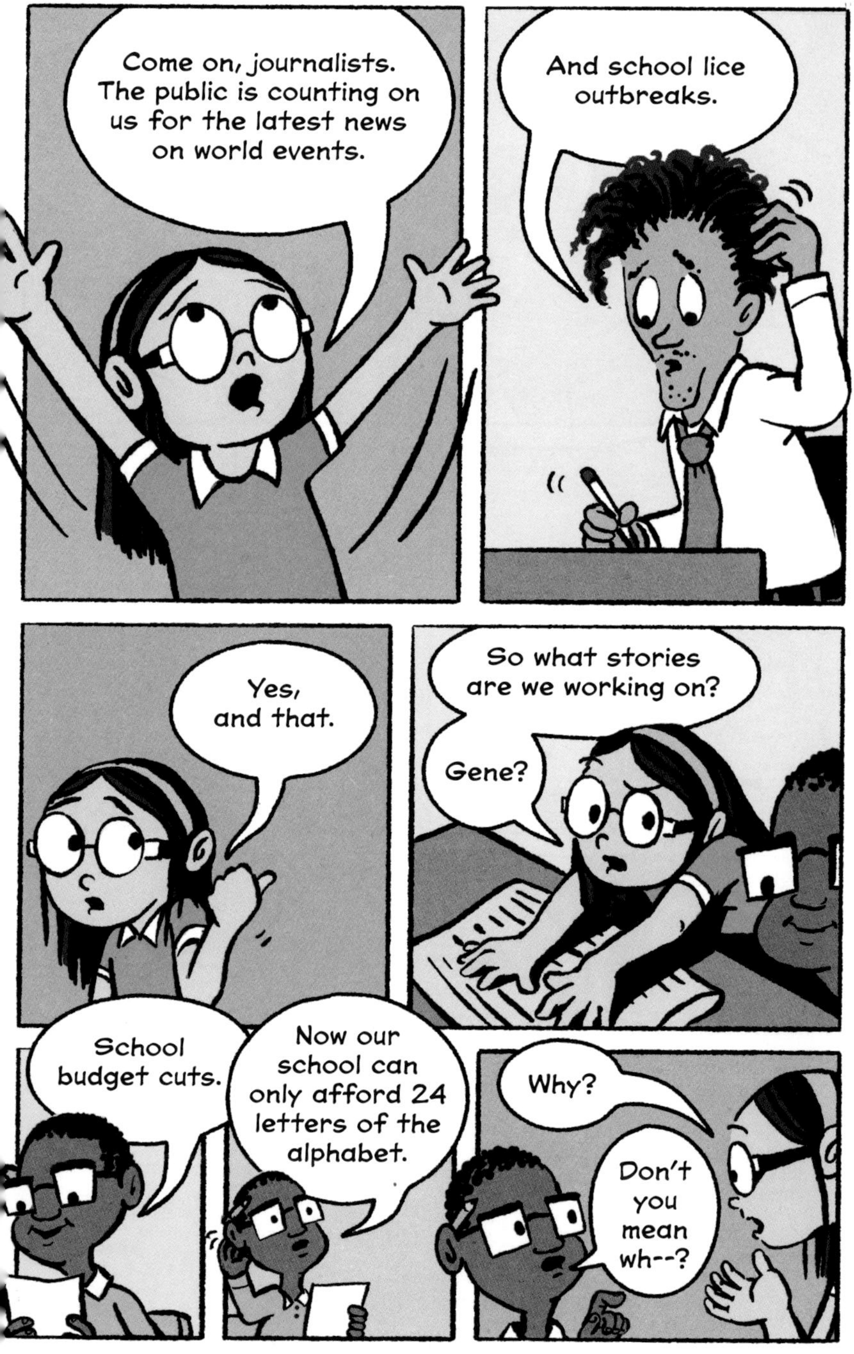
Come on, journalists. The public is counting on us for the latest news on world events.
And school lice outbreaks.
Yes, and that.
So what stories are we working on?
Gene?
School budget cuts.
Now our school can only afford 24 letters of the alphabet.
Why?
Don't you mean wh--?

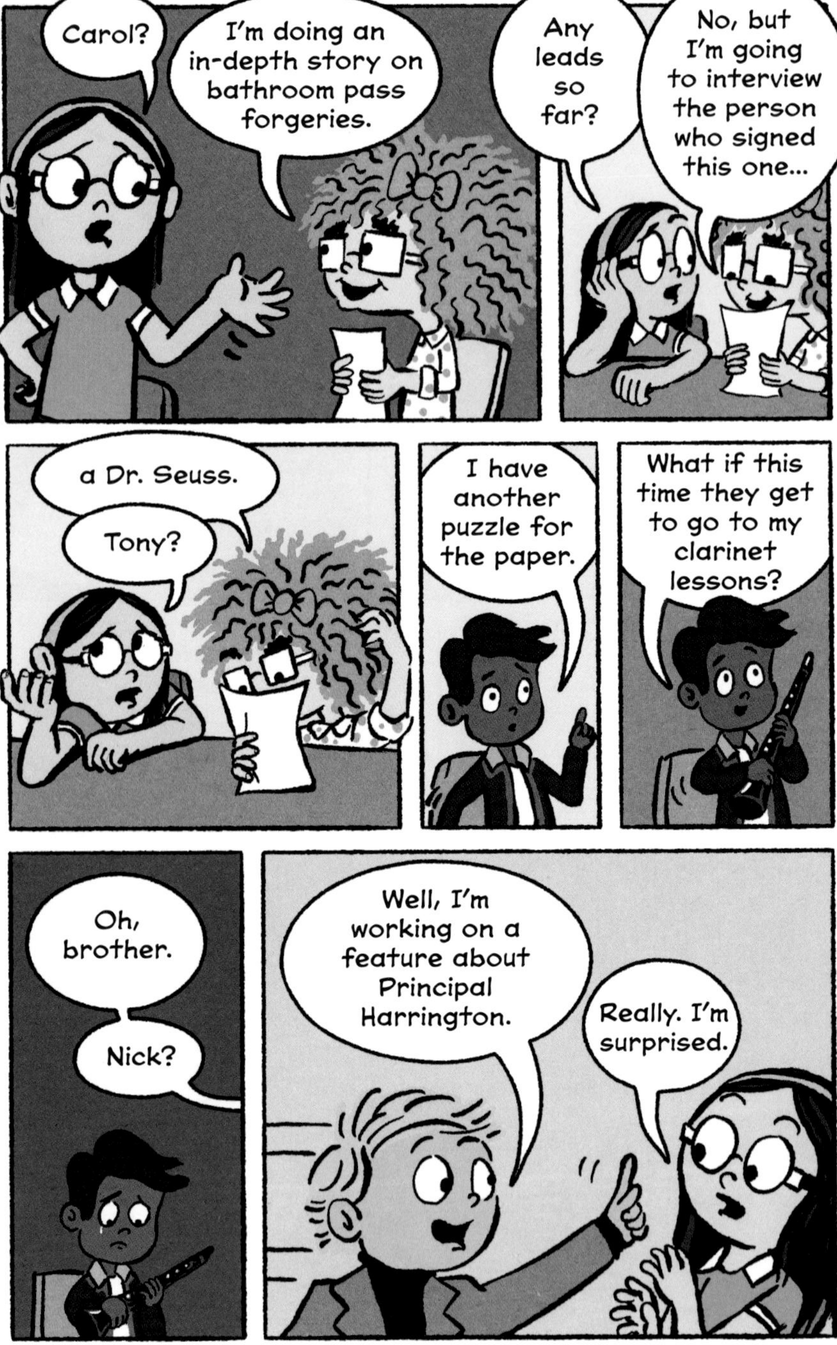
Carol?
I'm doing an in-depth story on bathroom pass forgeries.
Any leads so far?
No, but I'm going to interview the person who signed this one...
a Dr. Seuss.
Tony?
I have another puzzle for the paper.
What if this time they get to go to my clarinet lessons?
Oh, brother.
Nick?
Well, I'm working on a feature about Principal Harrington.
Really. I'm surprised.

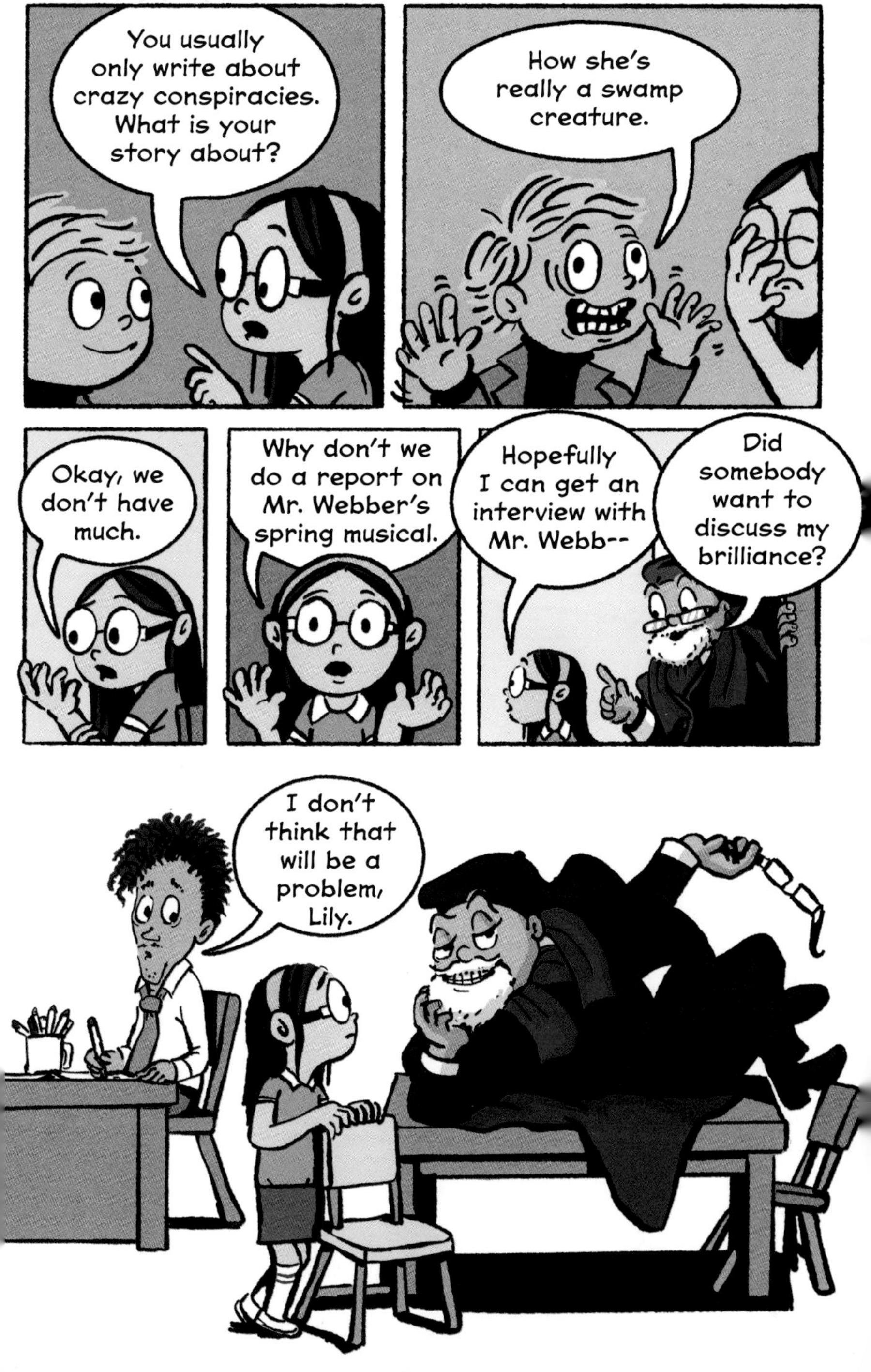
You usually only write about crazy conspiracies. What is your story about?
How she's really a swamp creature.
Okay, we don't have much.
Why don't we do a report on Mr. Webber's spring musical.
Hopefully I can get an interview with Mr. Webb--
Did somebody want to discuss my brilliance?
I don't think that will be a problem, Lily.

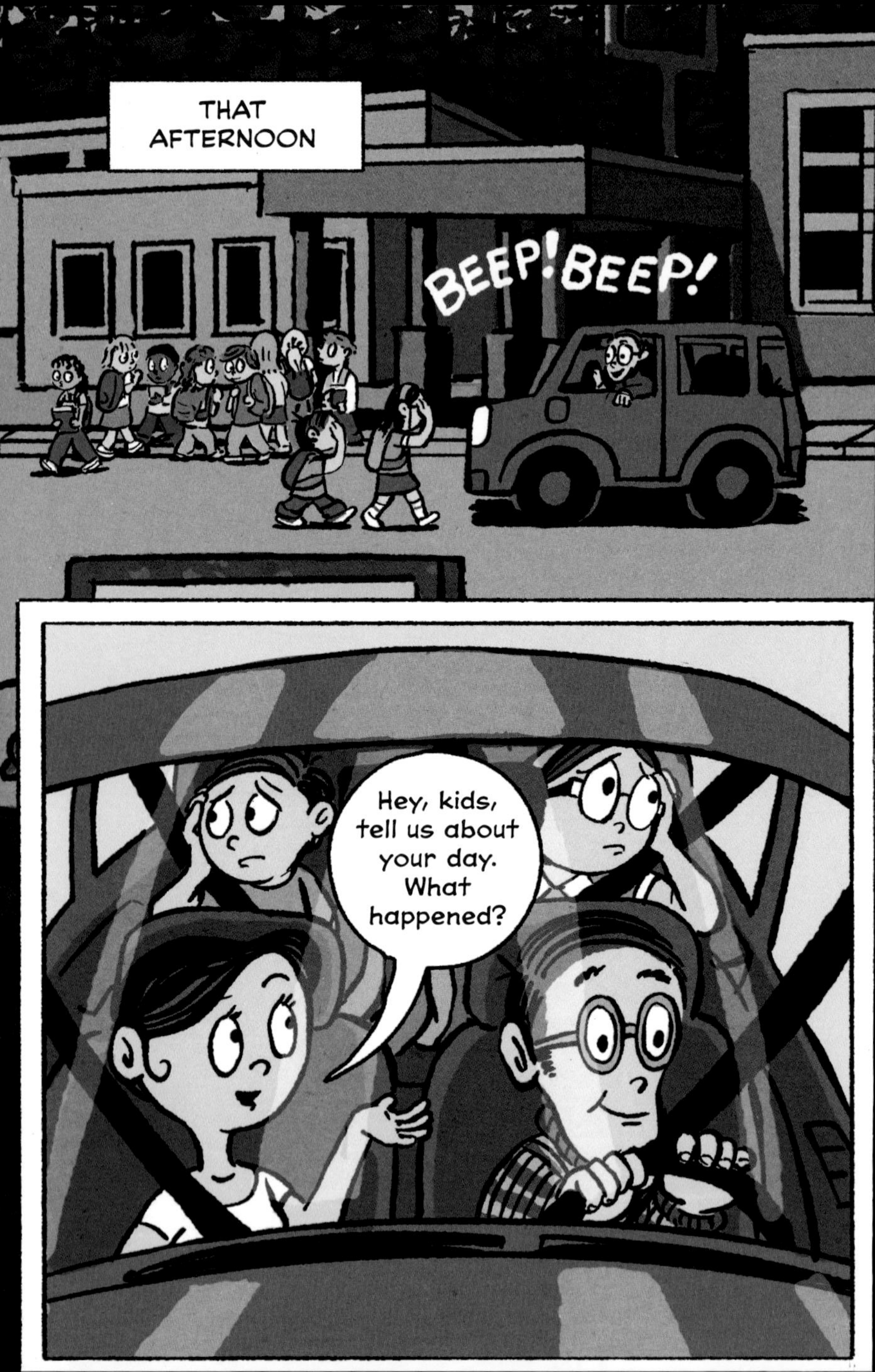
THAT AFTERNOON
BEEP! BEEP!
Hey, kids, tell us about your day. What happened?

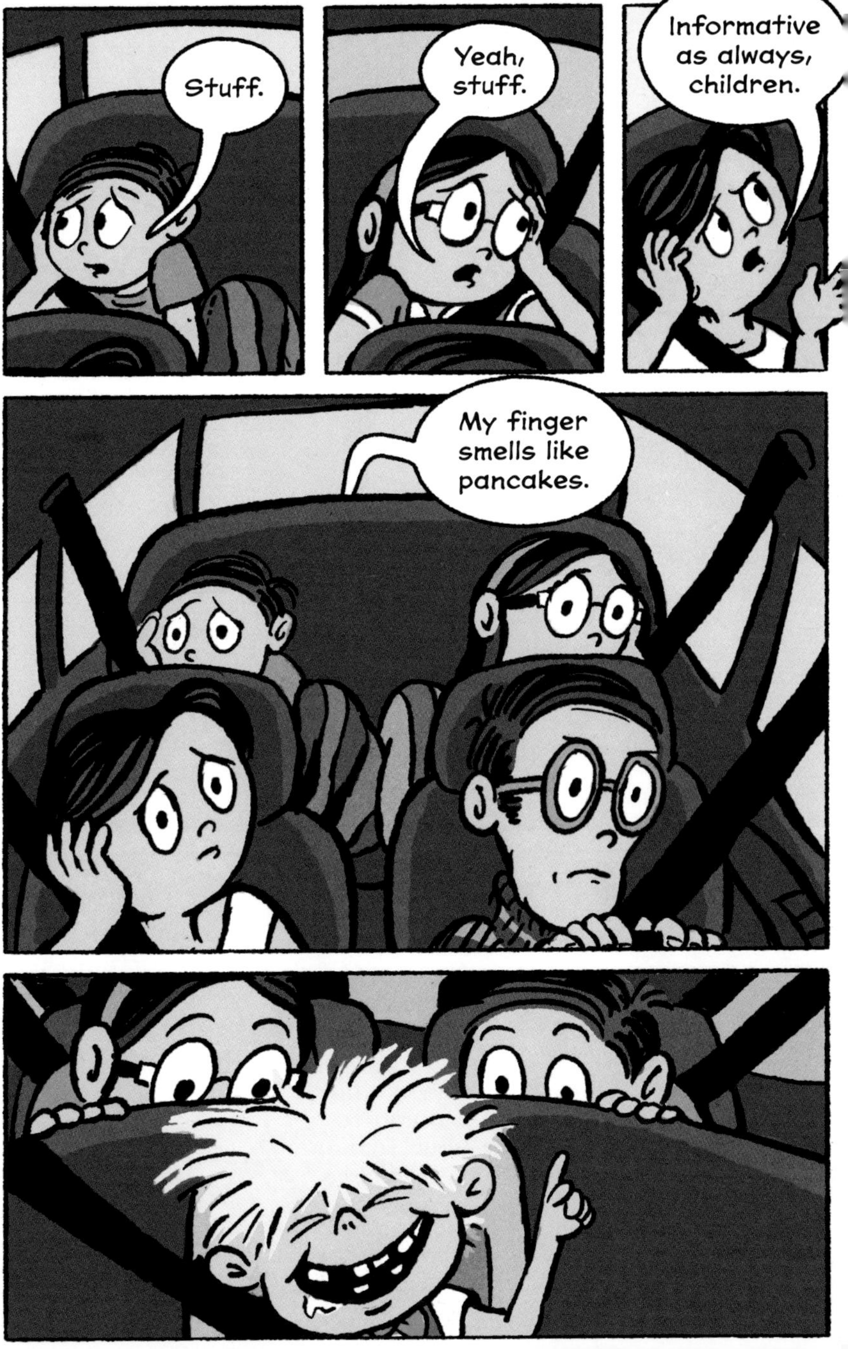
Stuff.
Yeah, stuff.
Informative as always, children.
My finger smells like pancakes.

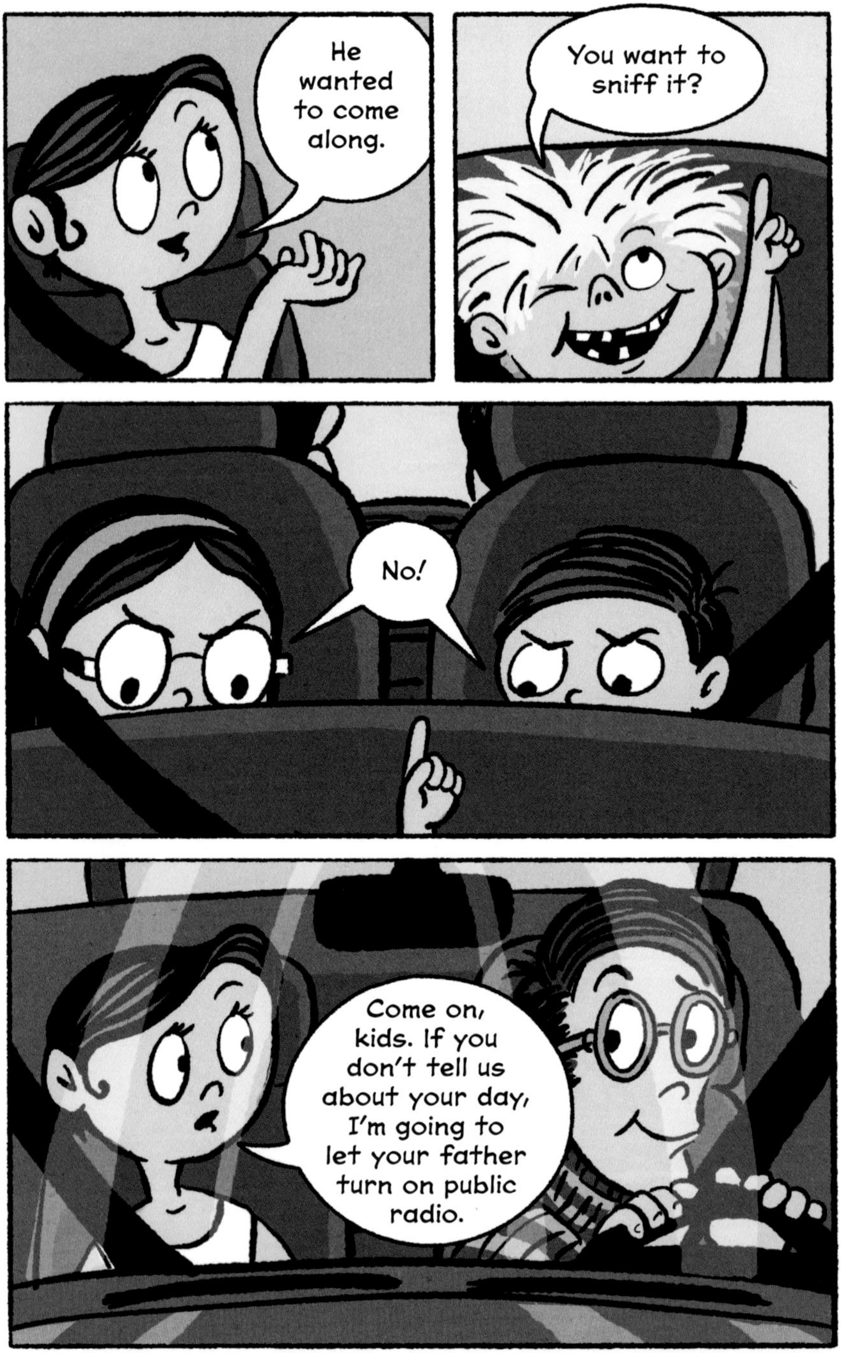
He wanted to come along.
You want to sniff it?
No!
Come on, kids. If you don't tell us about your day, I'm going to let your father turn on public radio.

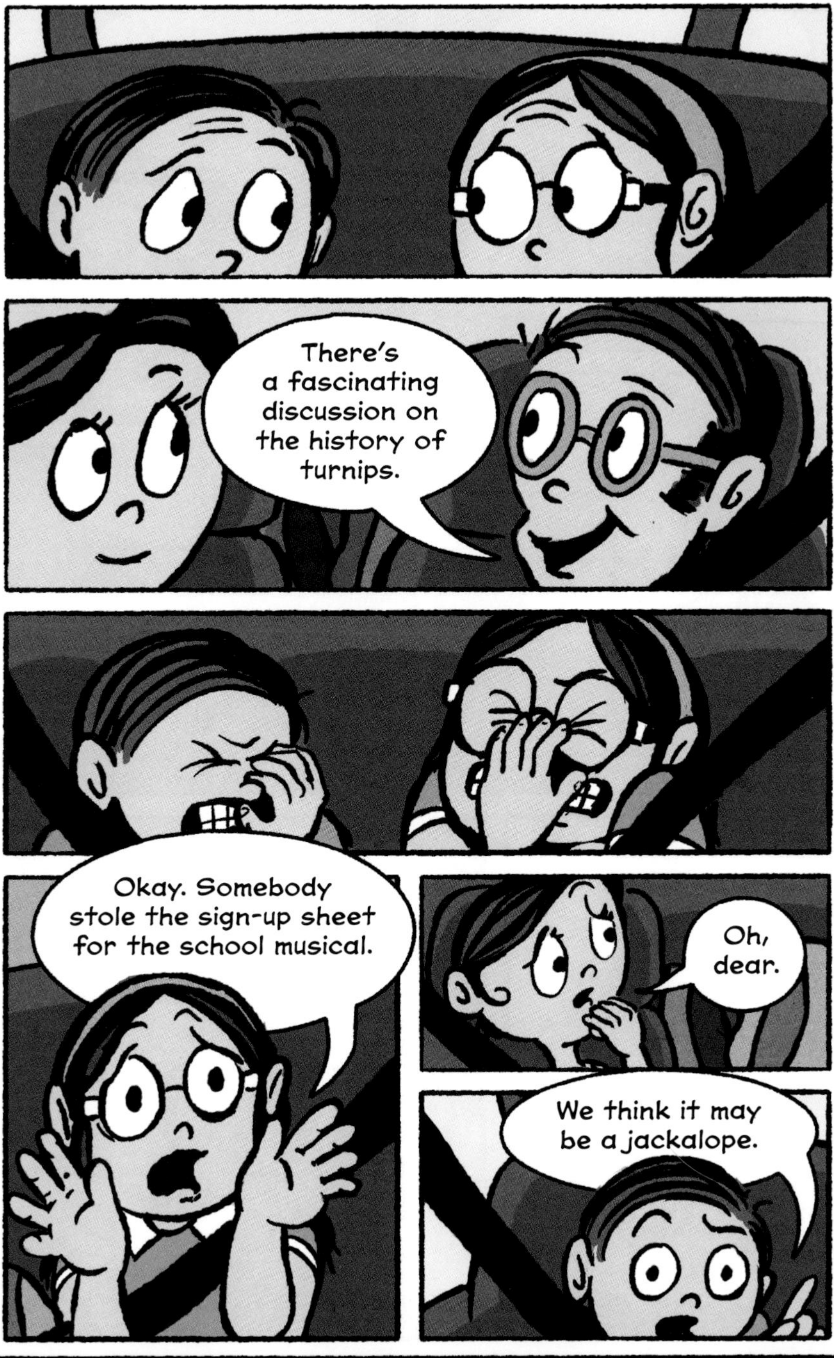
There's a fascinating discussion on the history of turnips.
Okay. Somebody stole the sign-up sheet for the school musical.
Oh, dear.
We think it may be a jackalope.

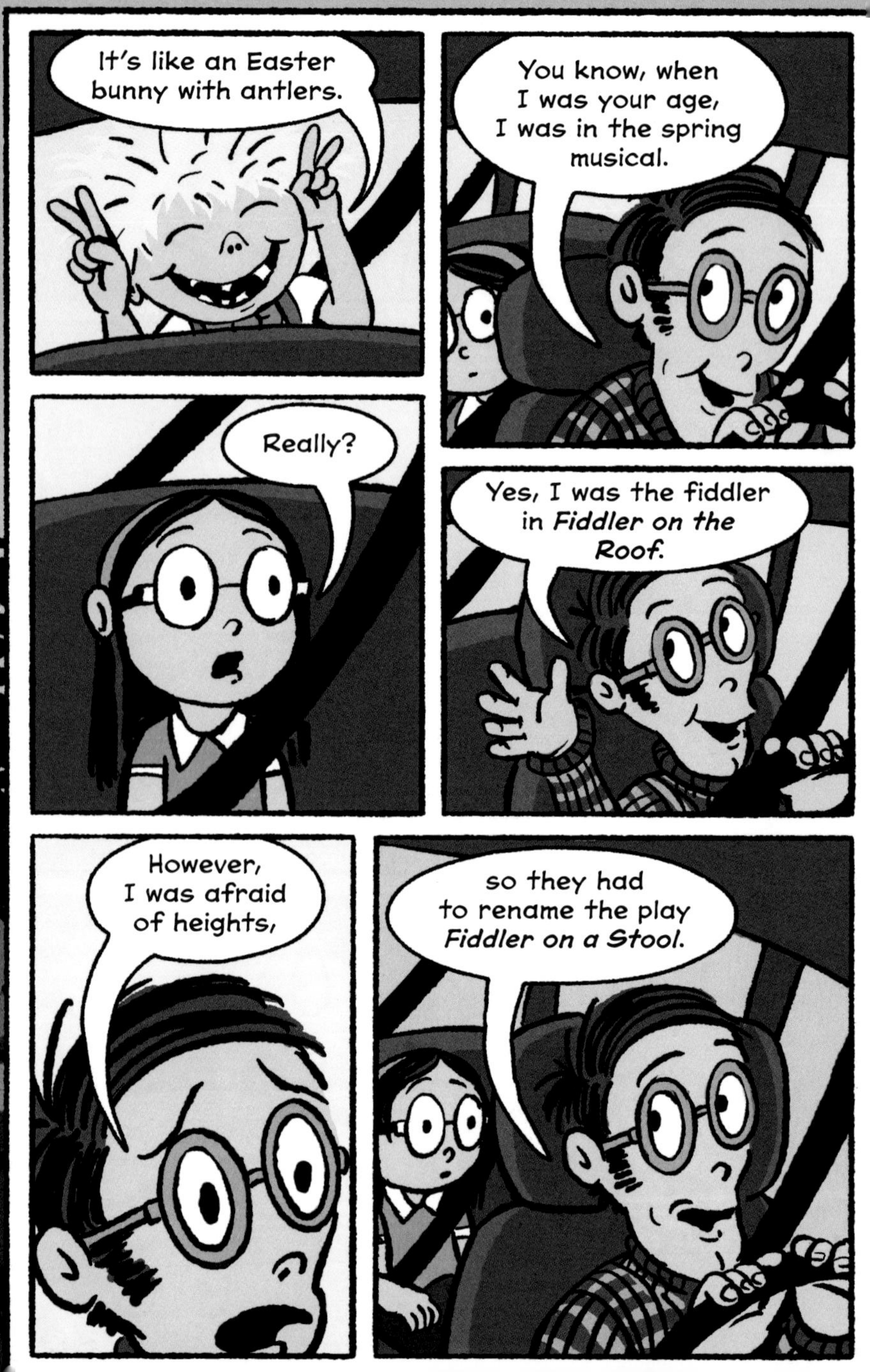
It's like an Easter bunny with antlers.
You know, when I was your age, I was in the spring musical.
Really?
Yes, I was the fiddler in *Fiddler on the Roof.*
However, I was afraid of heights,
so they had to rename the play *Fiddler on a Stool.*

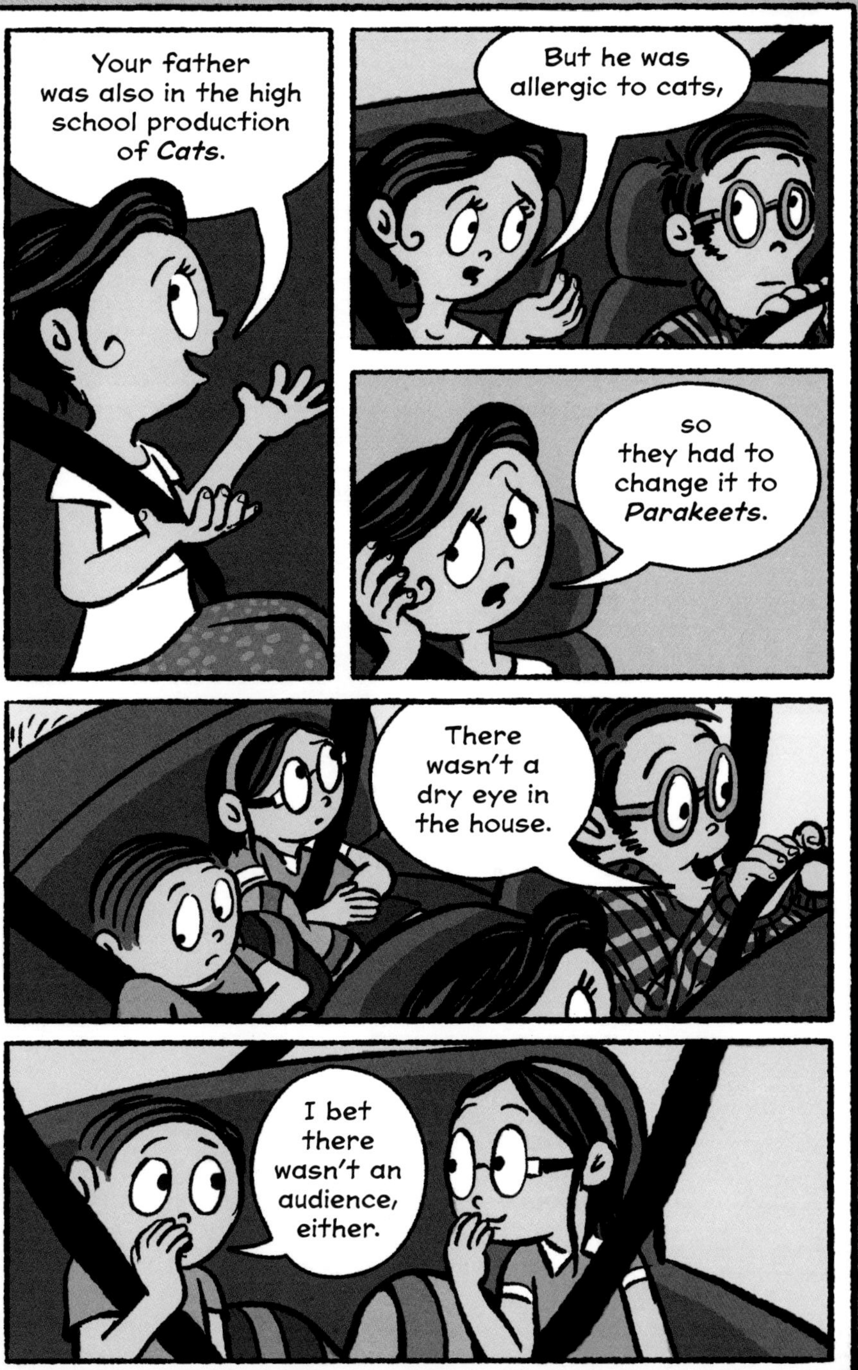
Your father was also in the high school production of *Cats*.
But he was allergic to cats,
so they had to change it to *Parakeets*.
There wasn't a dry eye in the house.
I bet there wasn't an audience, either.

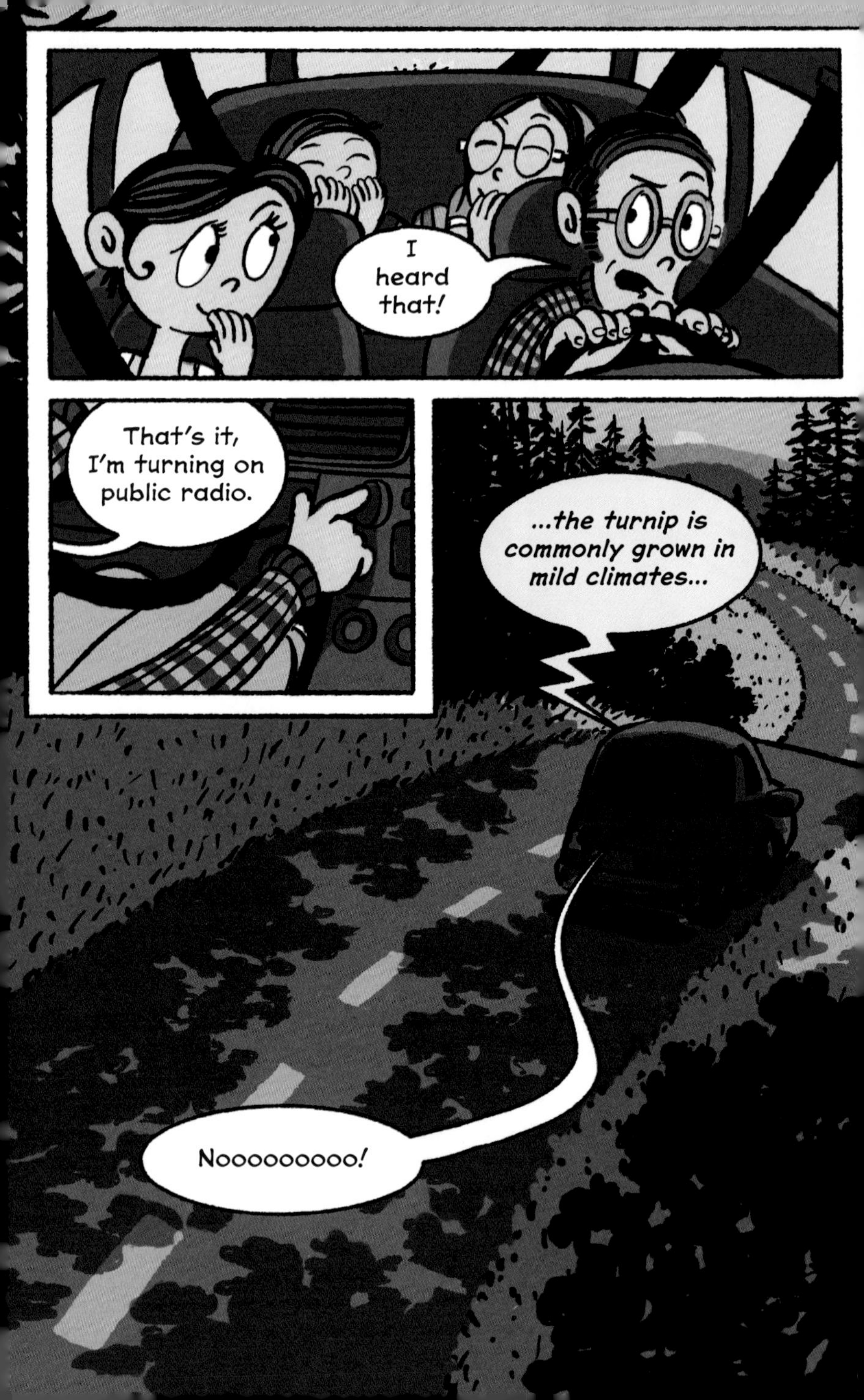
I heard that!
That's it, I'm turning on public radio.
...the turnip is commonly grown in mild climates...
Noooooooooo!

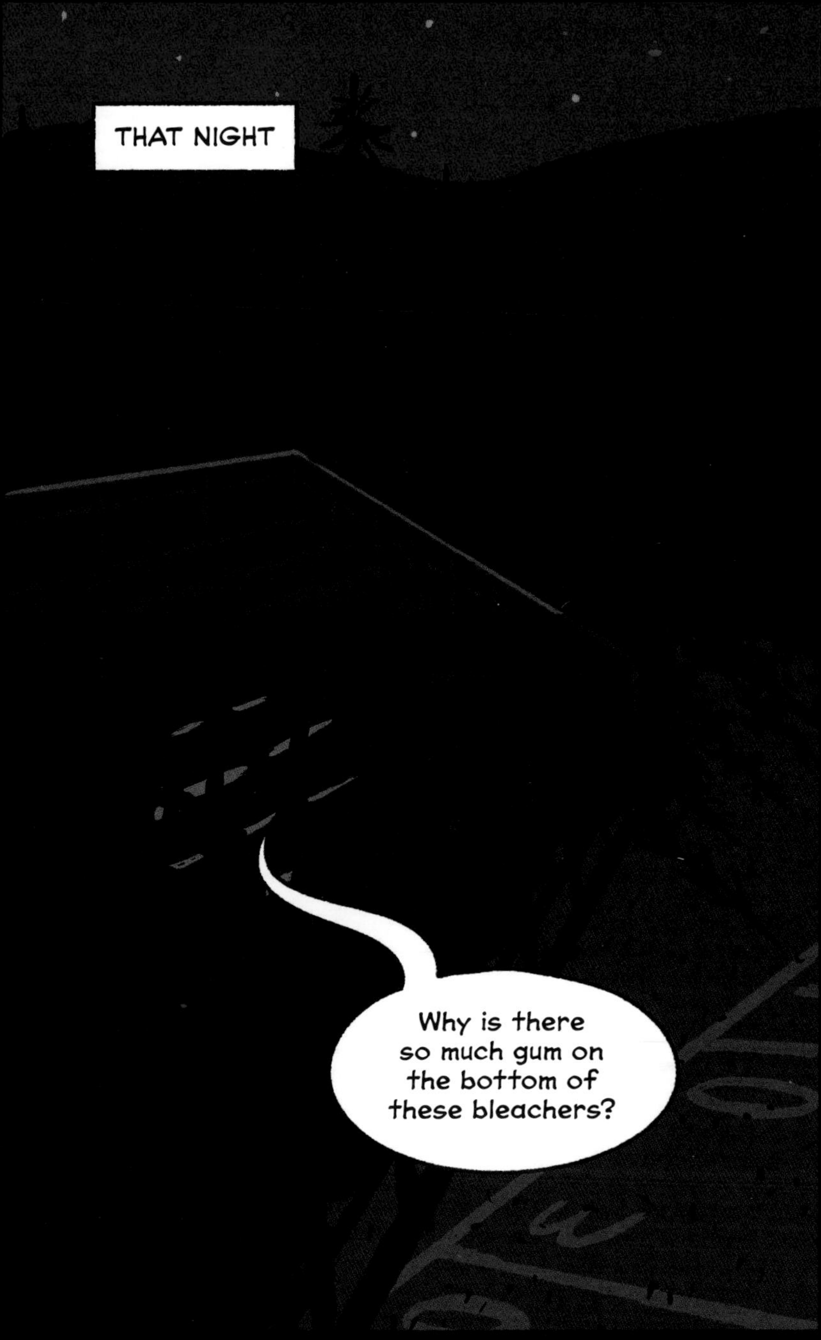
THAT NIGHT
Why is there so much gum on the bottom of these bleachers?

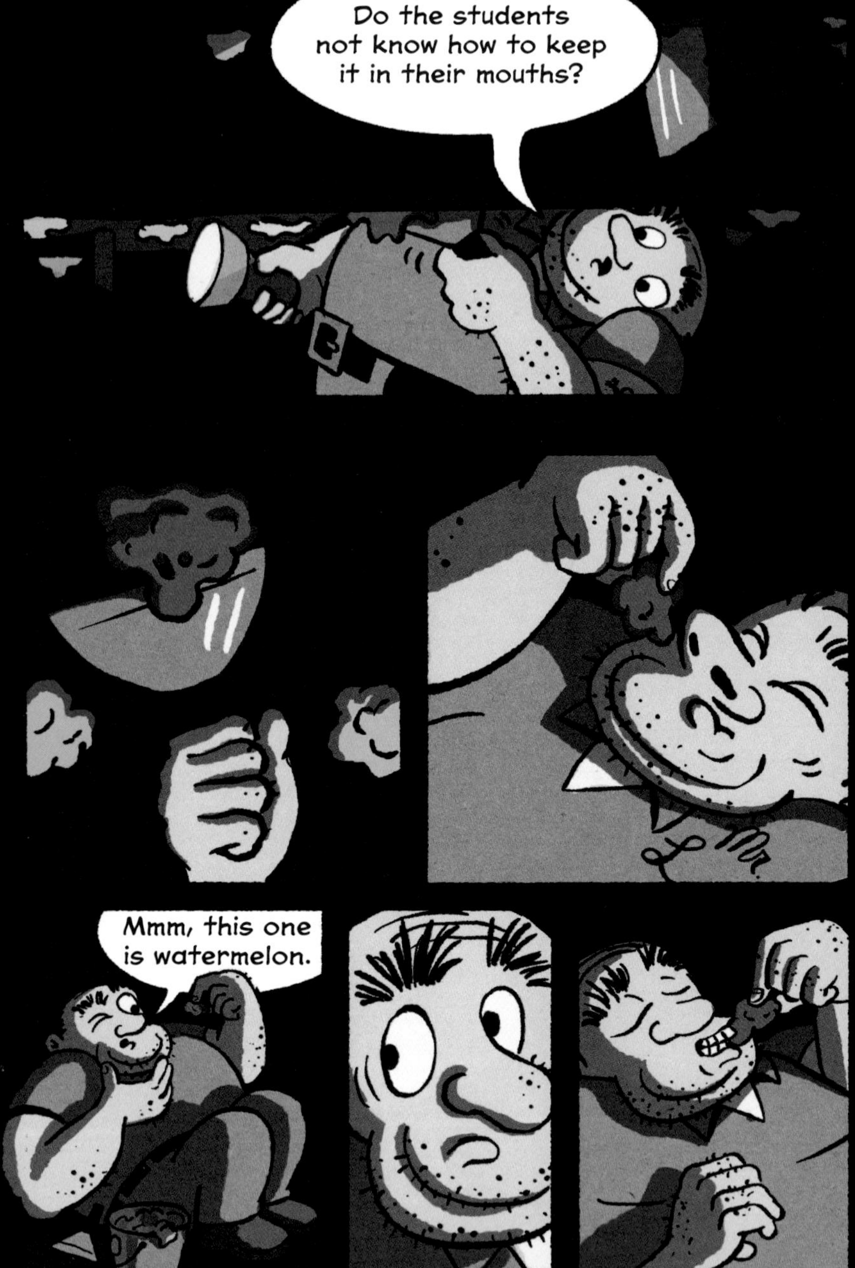
Do the students not know how to keep it in their mouths?
Mmm, this one is watermelon.

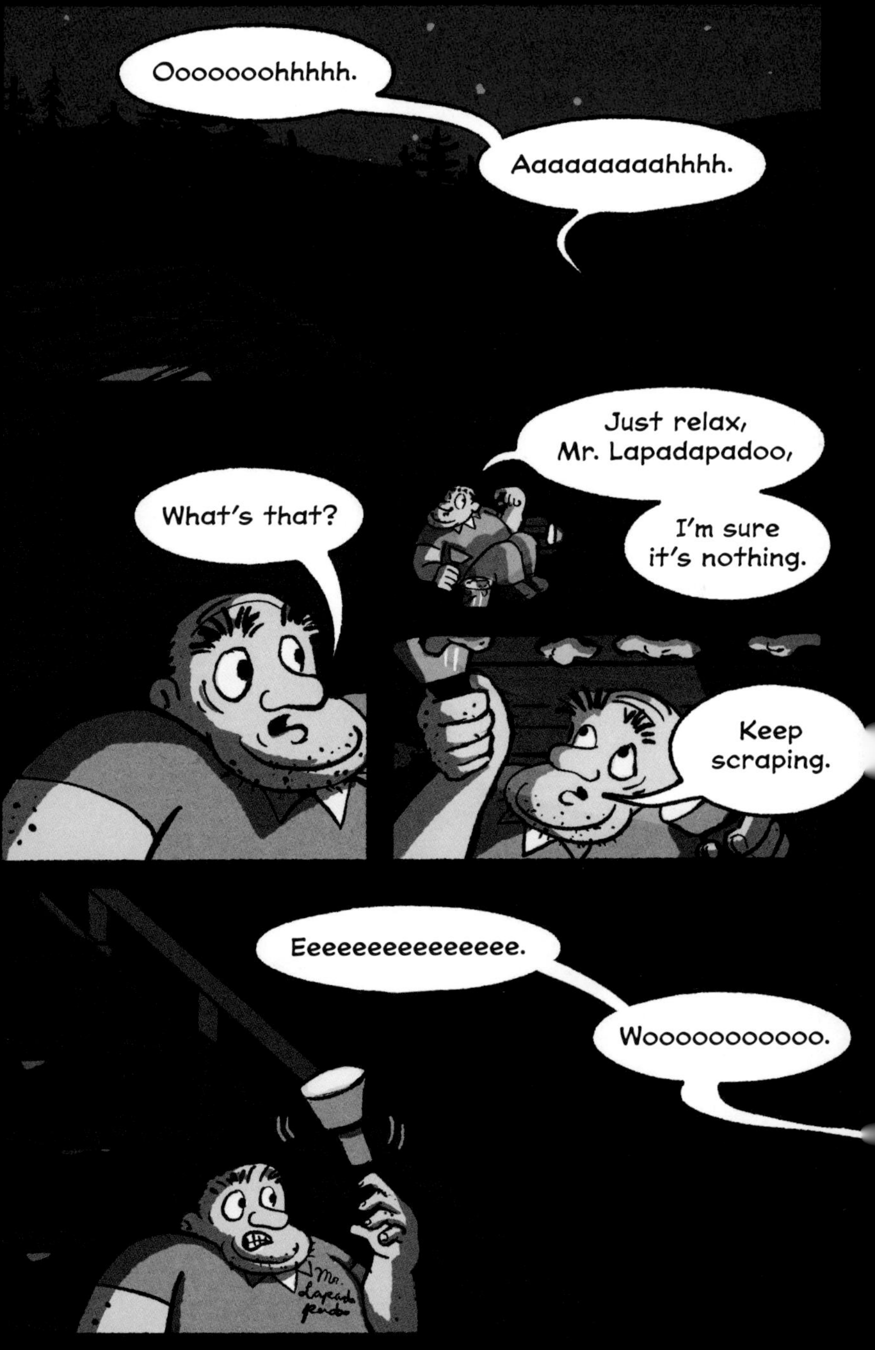
Oooooooohhhhh.
Aaaaaaaaahhhh.
What's that?
Just relax, Mr. Lapadapadoo,
I'm sure it's nothing.
Keep scraping.
Eeeeeeeeeeeeeee.
Wooooooooooo.

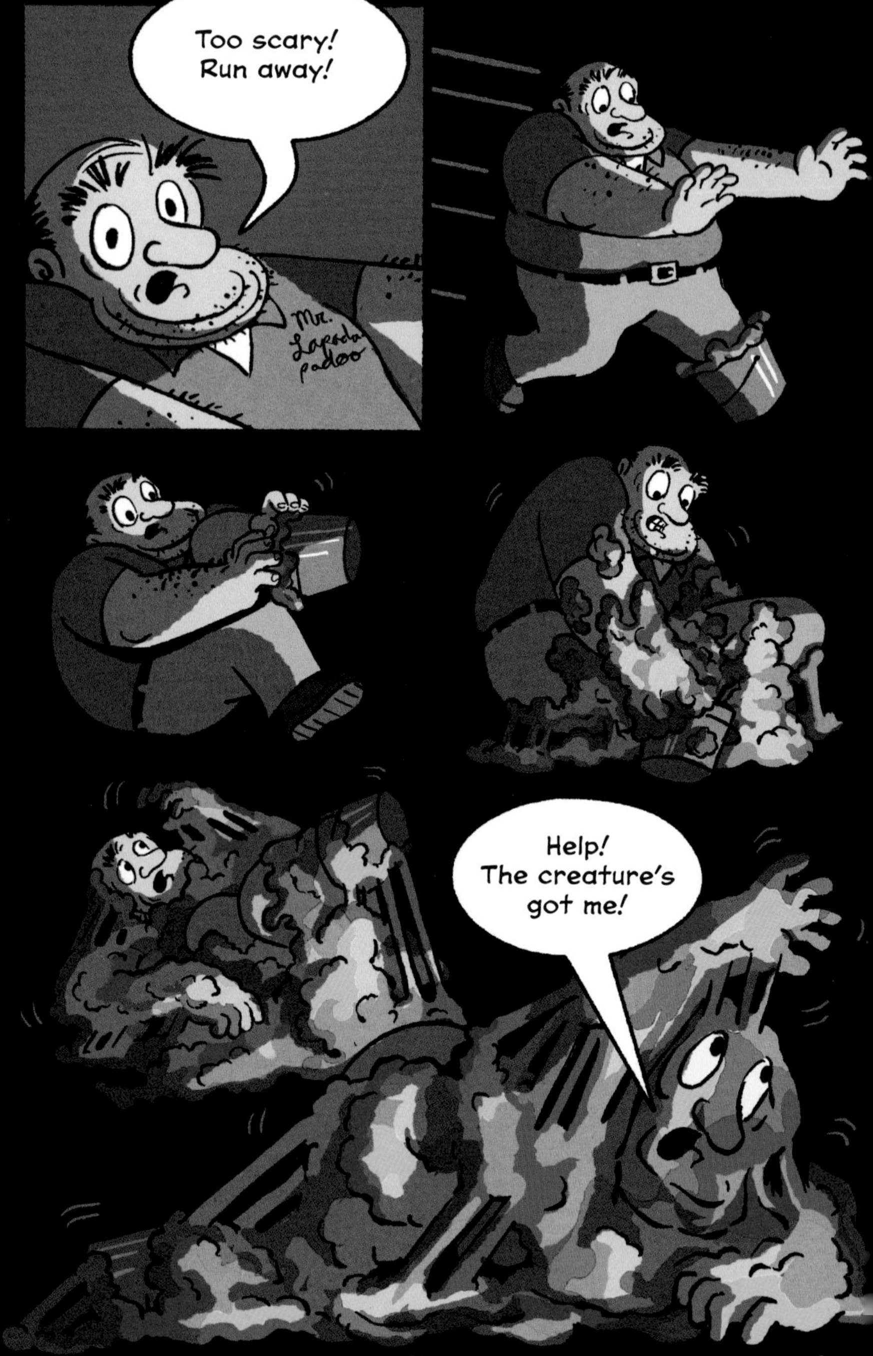
Too scary!
Run away!
Mr. Laroda padoo
Help!
The creature's
got me!

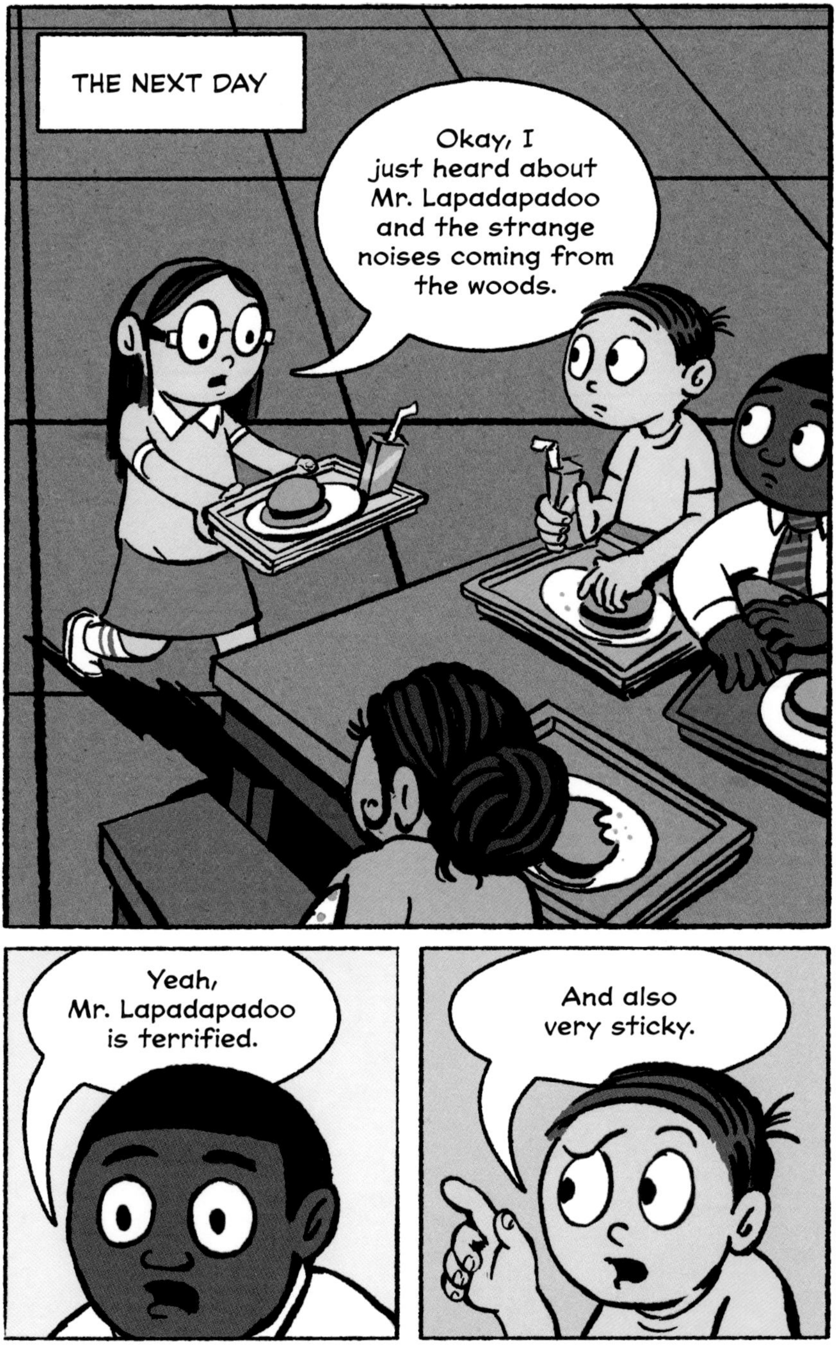
THE NEXT DAY
Okay, I just heard about Mr. Lapadapadoo and the strange noises coming from the woods.
Yeah, Mr. Lapadapadoo is terrified.
And also very sticky.

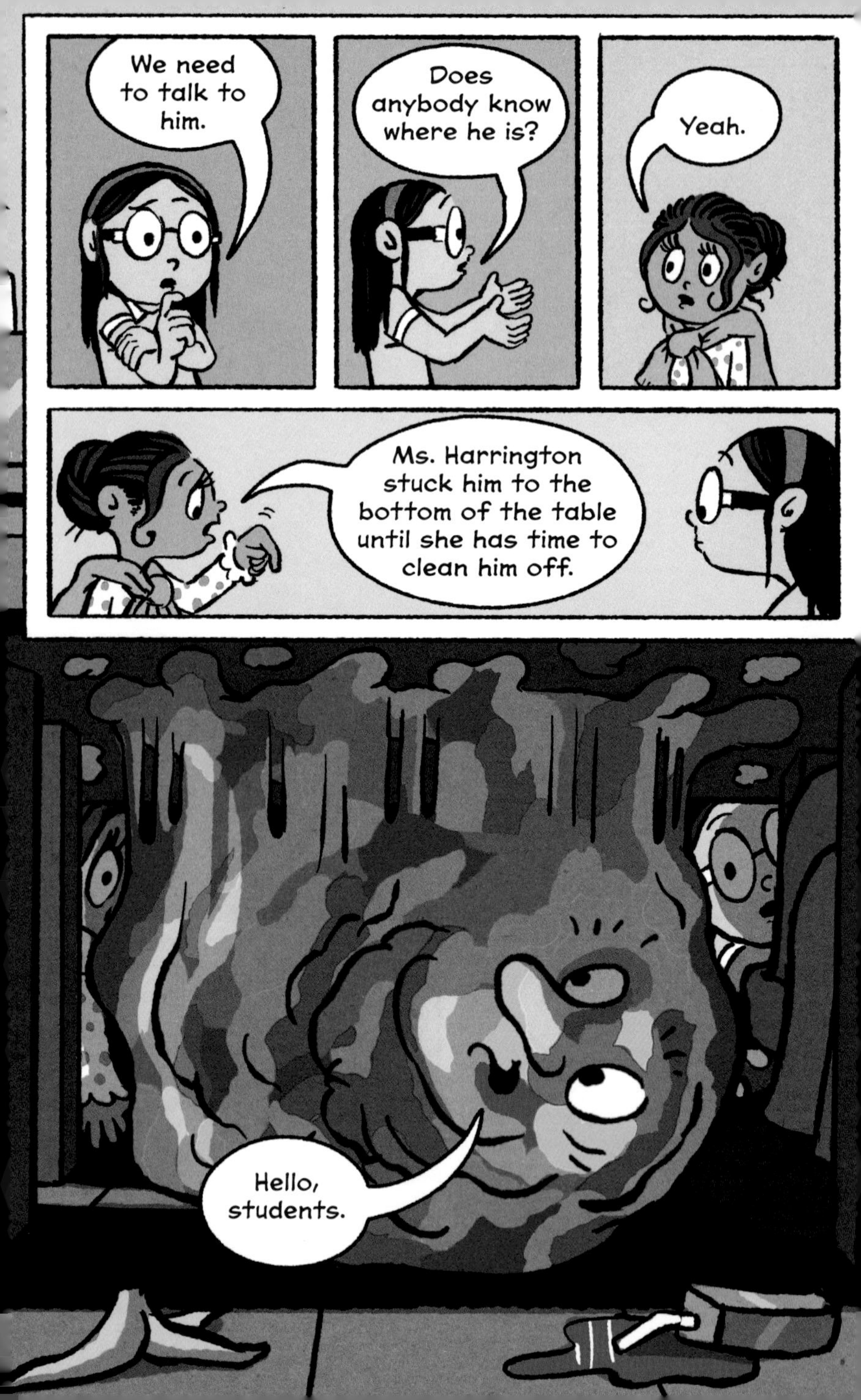
We need to talk to him.
Does anybody know where he is?
Yeah.
Ms. Harrington stuck him to the bottom of the table until she has time to clean him off.
Hello, students.

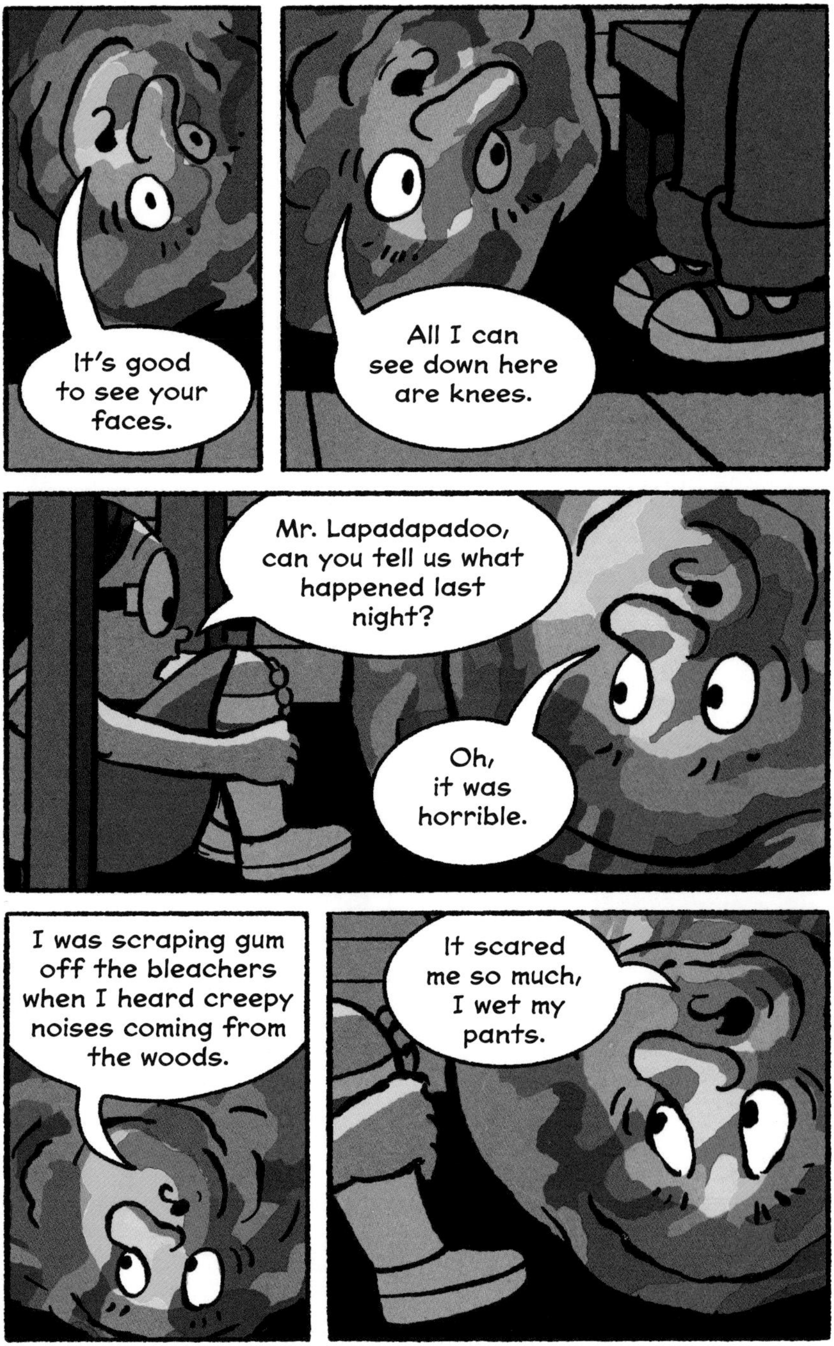
It's good to see your faces.
All I can see down here are knees.
Mr. Lapadapadoo, can you tell us what happened last night?
Oh, it was horrible.
I was scraping gum off the bleachers when I heard creepy noises coming from the woods.
It scared me so much, I wet my pants.

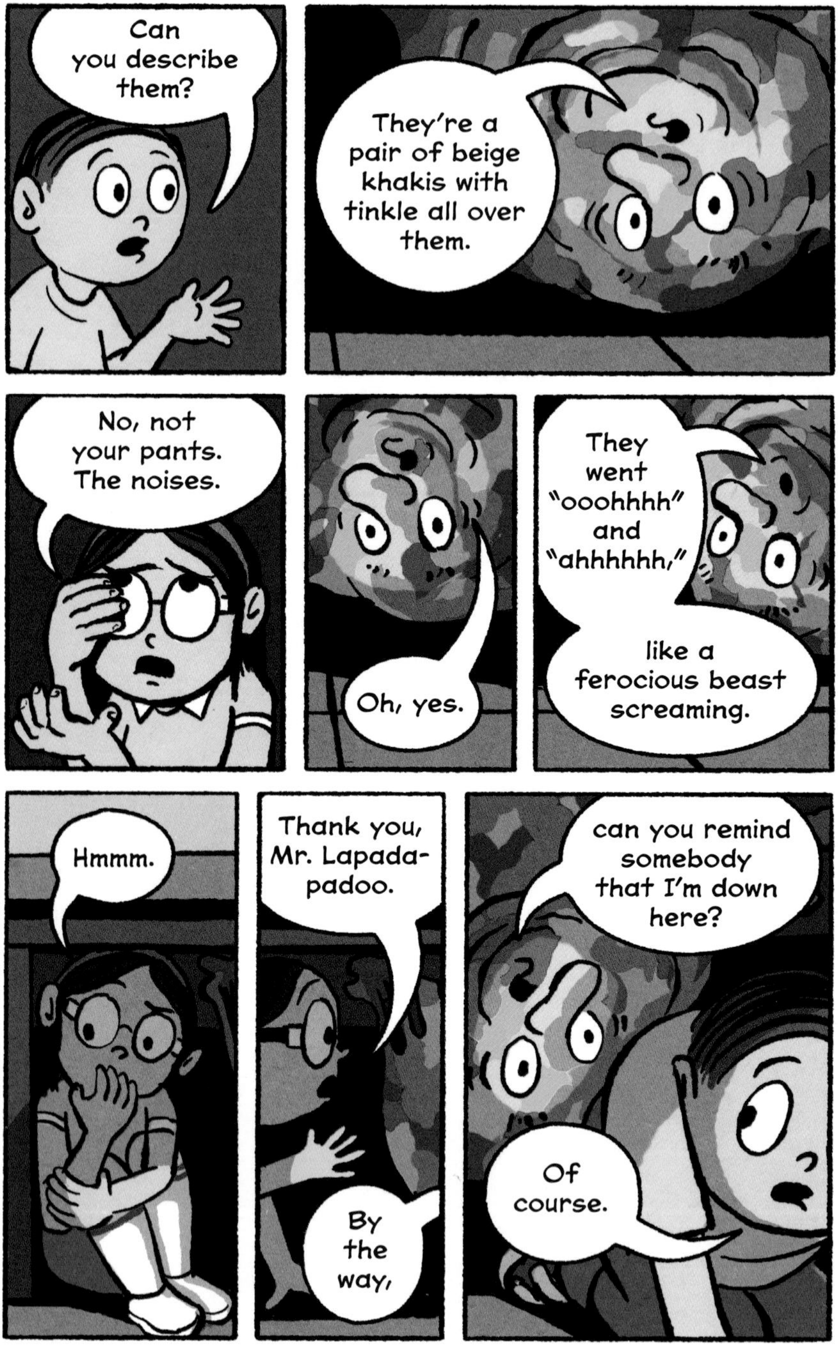
Can you describe them?
They're a pair of beige khakis with tinkle all over them.
No, not your pants. The noises.
Oh, yes.
They went "ooohhhh" and "ahhhhhh,"
like a ferocious beast screaming.
Hmmm.
Thank you, Mr. Lapada-padoo.
By the way,
can you remind somebody that I'm down here?
Of course.

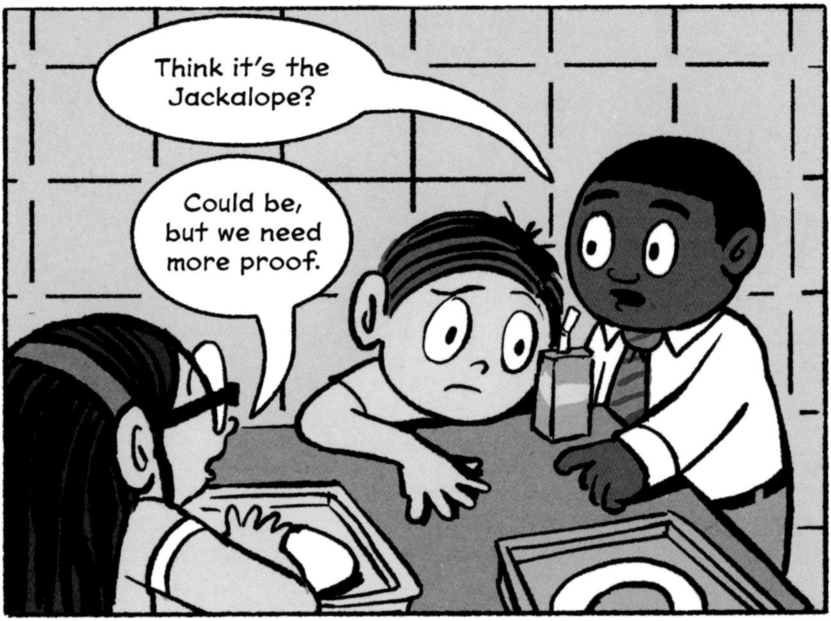
Think it's the Jackalope?
Could be, but we need more proof.

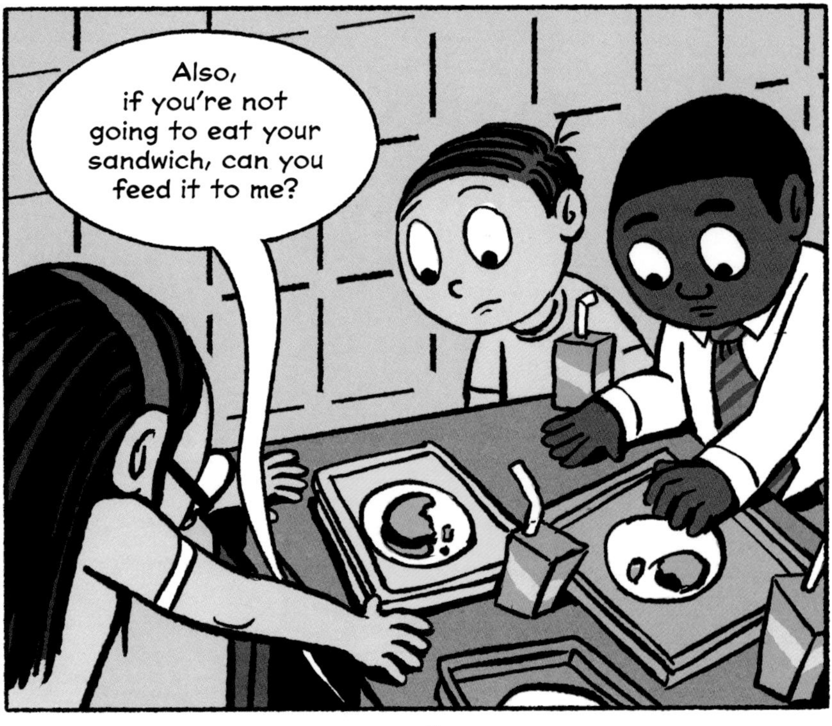
Also, if you're not going to eat your sandwich, can you feed it to me?

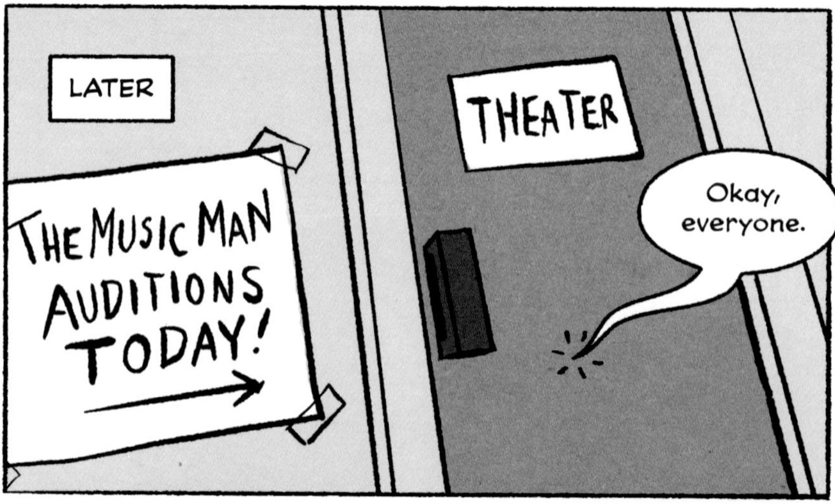
LATER
THEATER
THE MUSIC MAN AUDITIONS TODAY!
Okay, everyone.

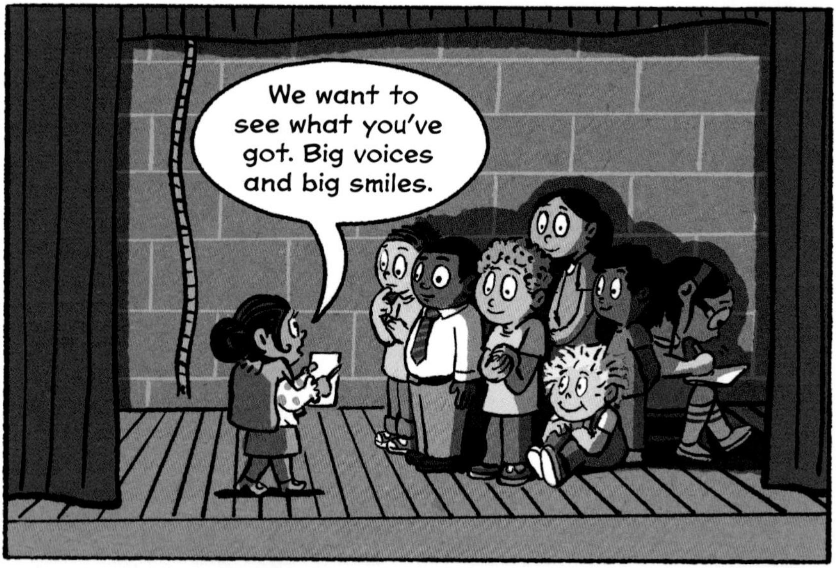
We want to see what you've got. Big voices and big smiles.

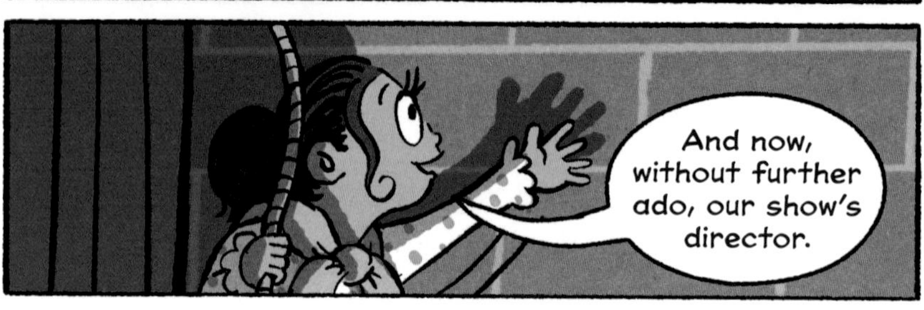
And now, without further ado, our show's director.

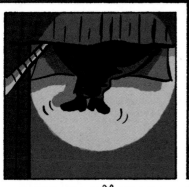

I do love a dramatic entrance.

Greetings, students. I am your director.

You may recognize me from my work as "before photo" in a regional hair transplant ad.

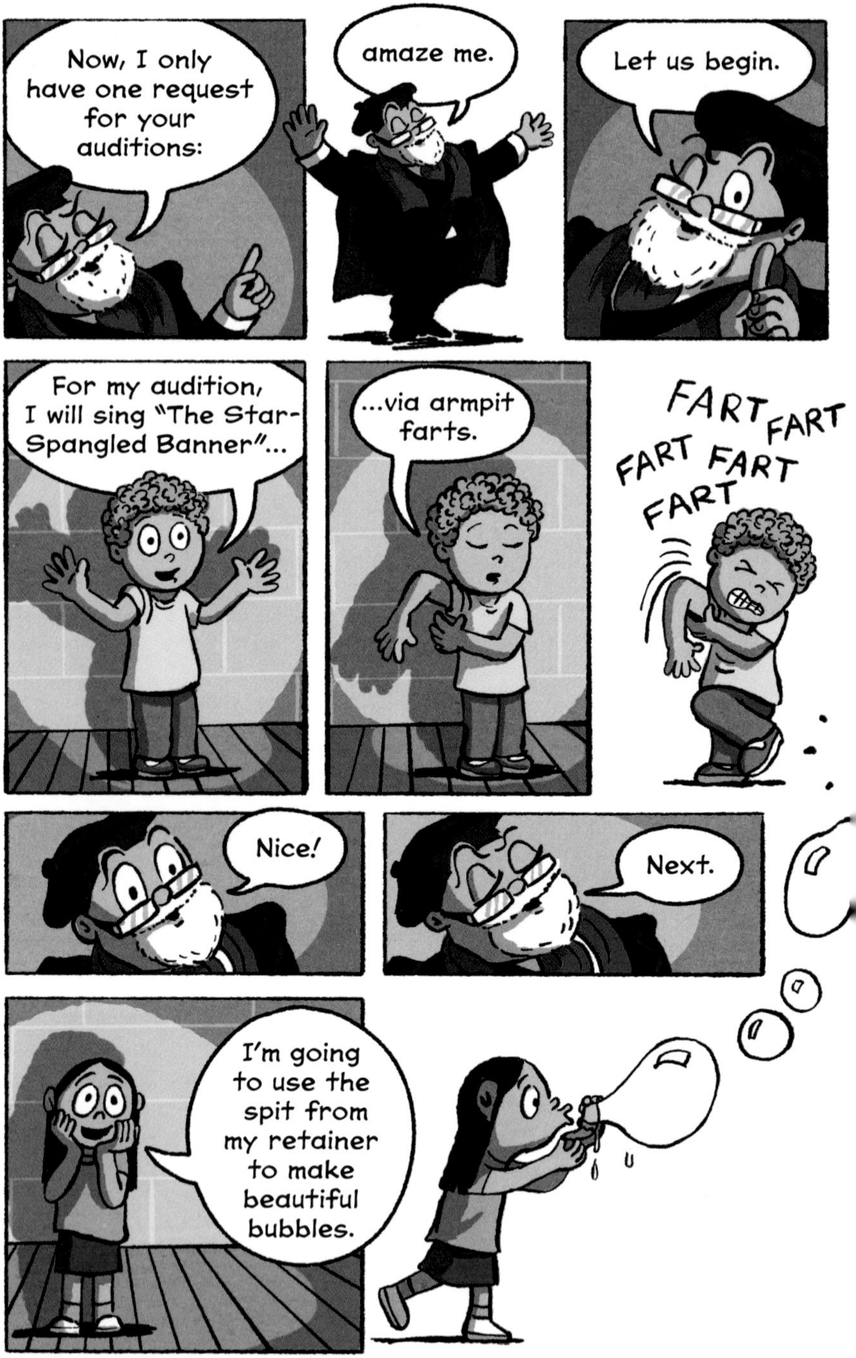
Now, I only have one request for your auditions:
amaze me.
Let us begin.
For my audition, I will sing "The Star-Spangled Banner"...
...via armpit farts.
FART FART
FART FART
FART
Nice!
Next.
I'm going to use the spit from my retainer to make beautiful bubbles.

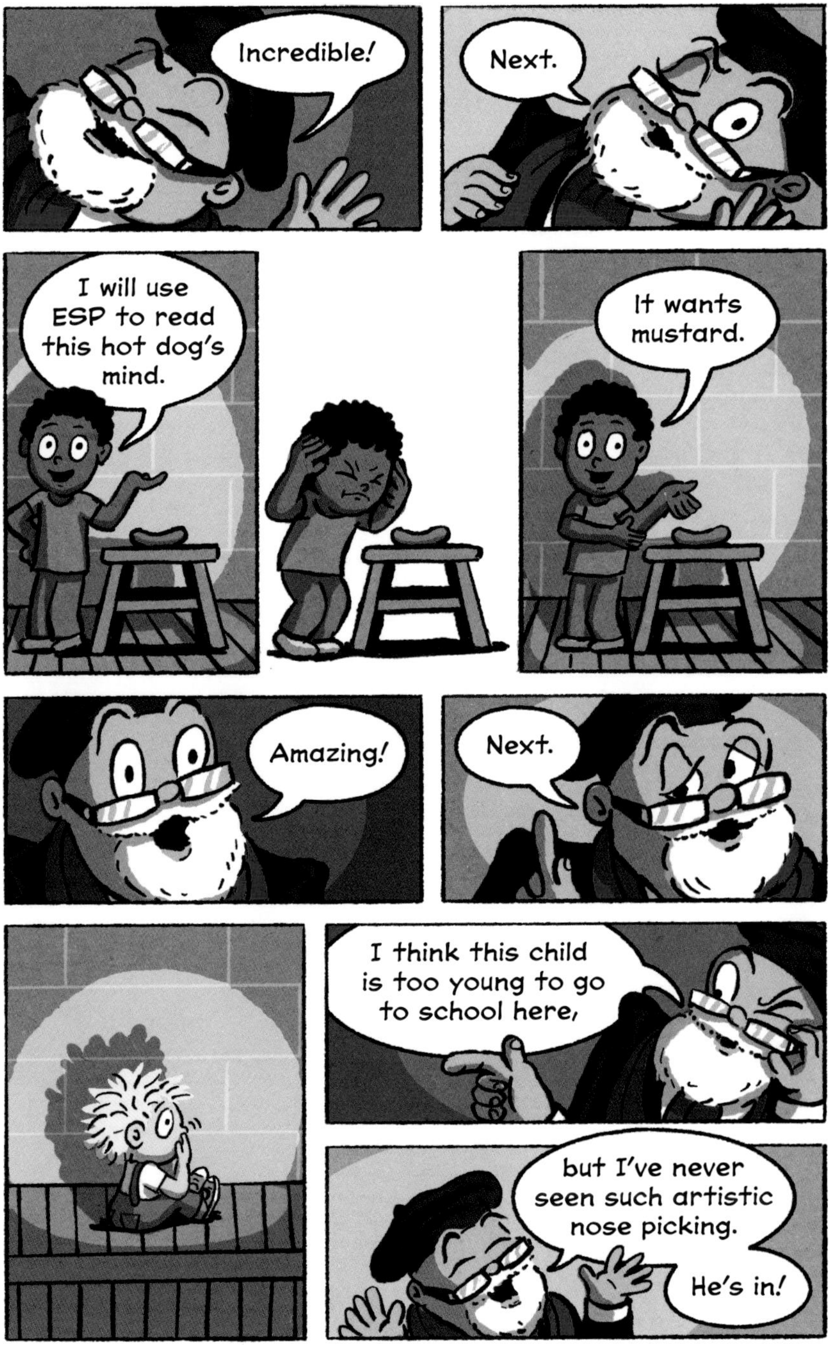
Incredible!
Next.
I will use ESP to read this hot dog's mind.
It wants mustard.
Amazing!
Next.
I think this child is too young to go to school here,
but I've never seen such artistic nose picking.
He's in!

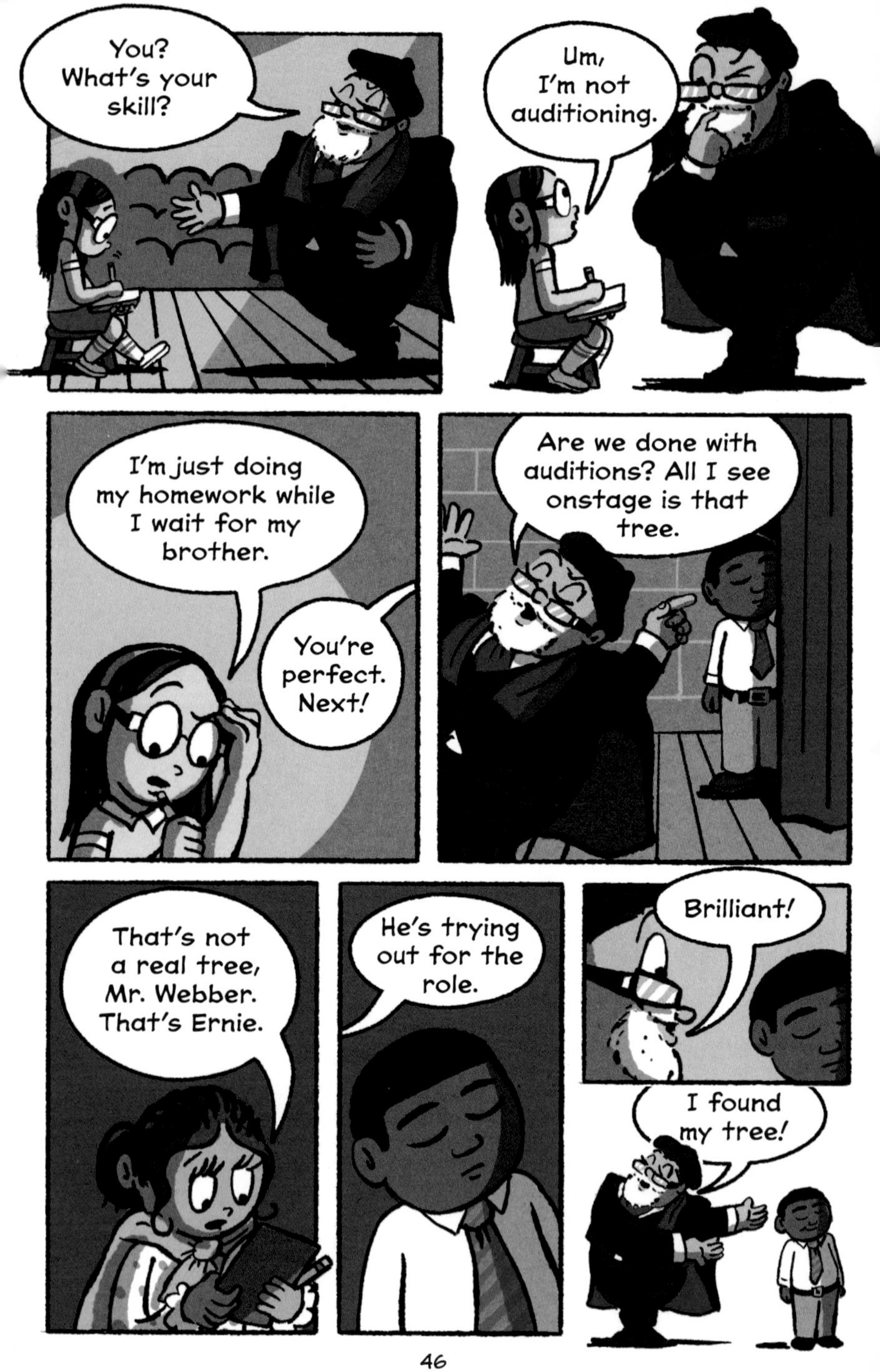
You? What's your skill?
Um, I'm not auditioning.
I'm just doing my homework while I wait for my brother.
You're perfect. Next!
Are we done with auditions? All I see onstage is that tree.
That's not a real tree, Mr. Webber. That's Ernie.
He's trying out for the role.
Brilliant!
I found my tree!

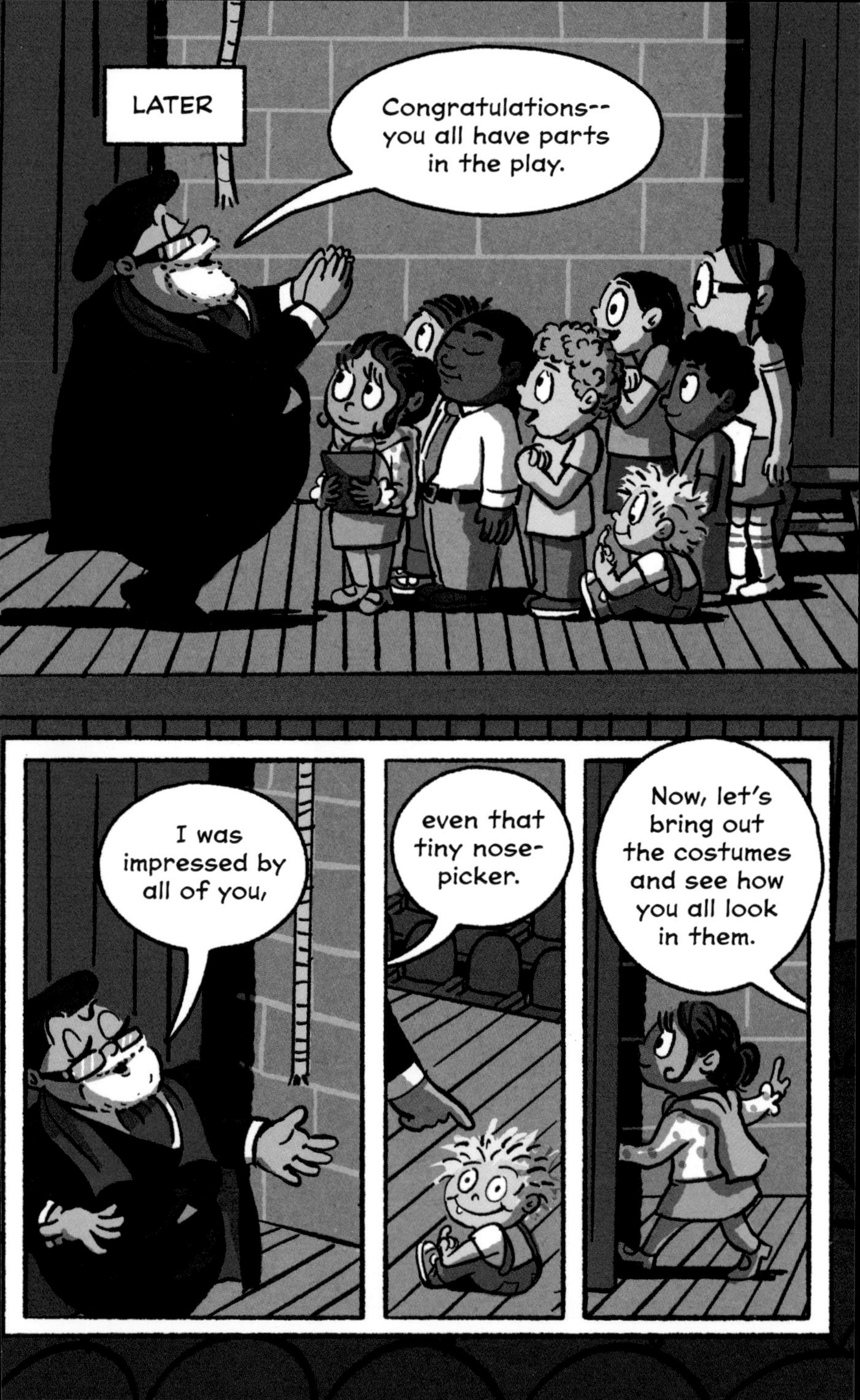
LATER
Congratulations--you all have parts in the play.
I was impressed by all of you,
even that tiny nose-picker.
Now, let's bring out the costumes and see how you all look in them.

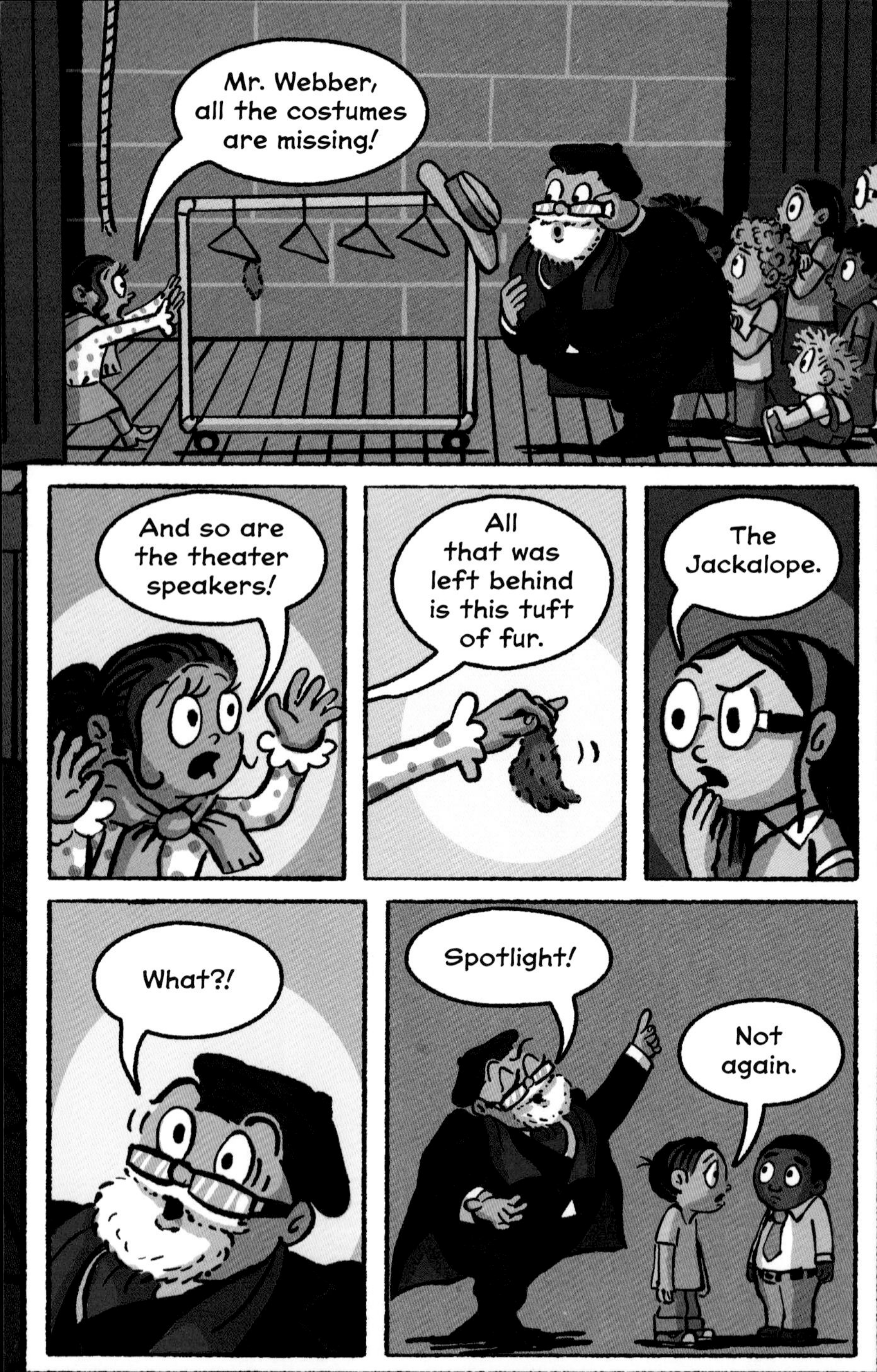
Mr. Webber, all the costumes are missing!
And so are the theater speakers!
All that was left behind is this tuft of fur.
The Jackalope.
What?!
Spotlight!
Not again.

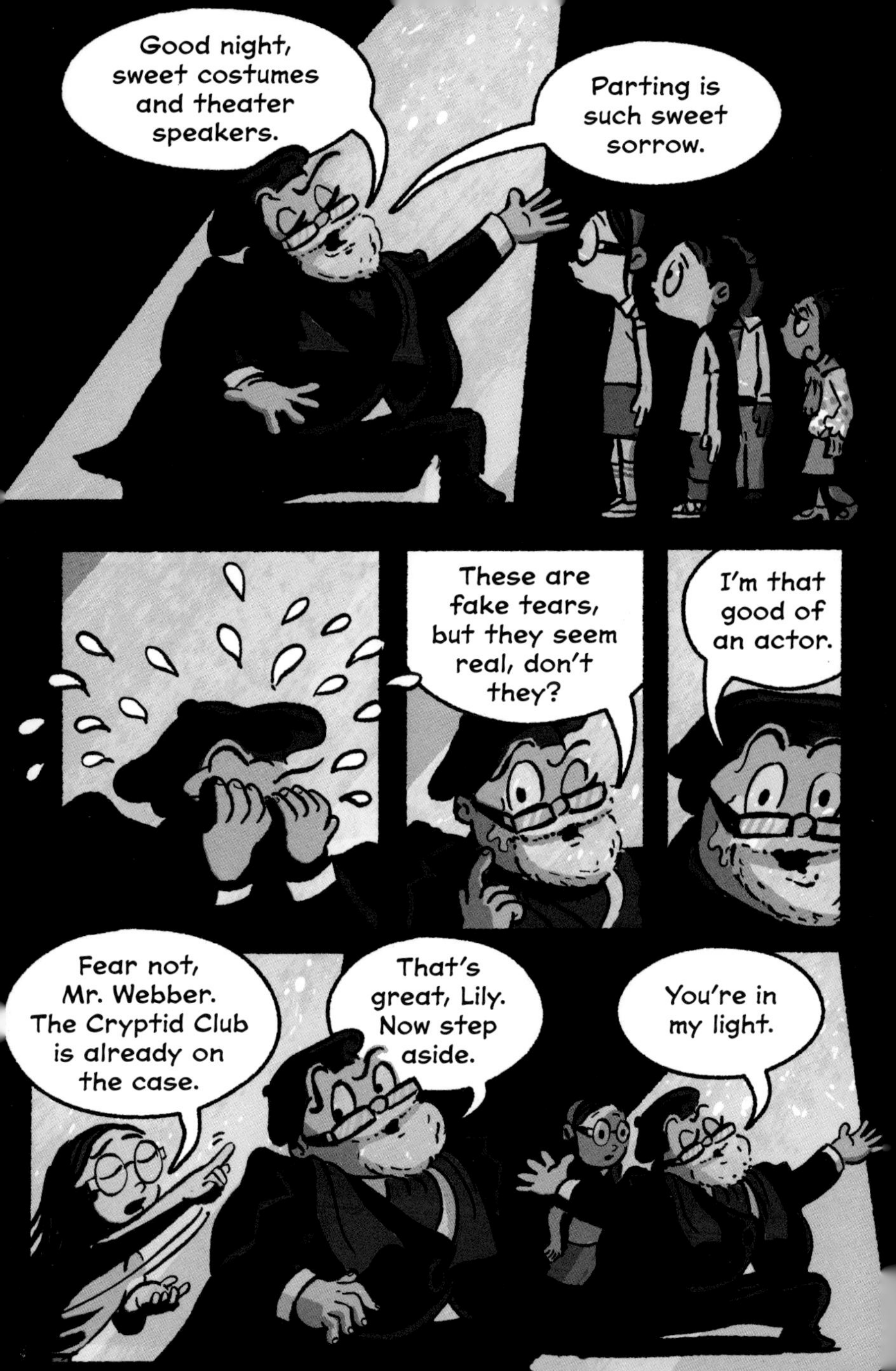
Good night, sweet costumes and theater speakers.
Parting is such sweet sorrow.
These are fake tears, but they seem real, don't they?
I'm that good of an actor.
Fear not, Mr. Webber. The Cryptid Club is already on the case.
That's great, Lily. Now step aside.
You're in my light.

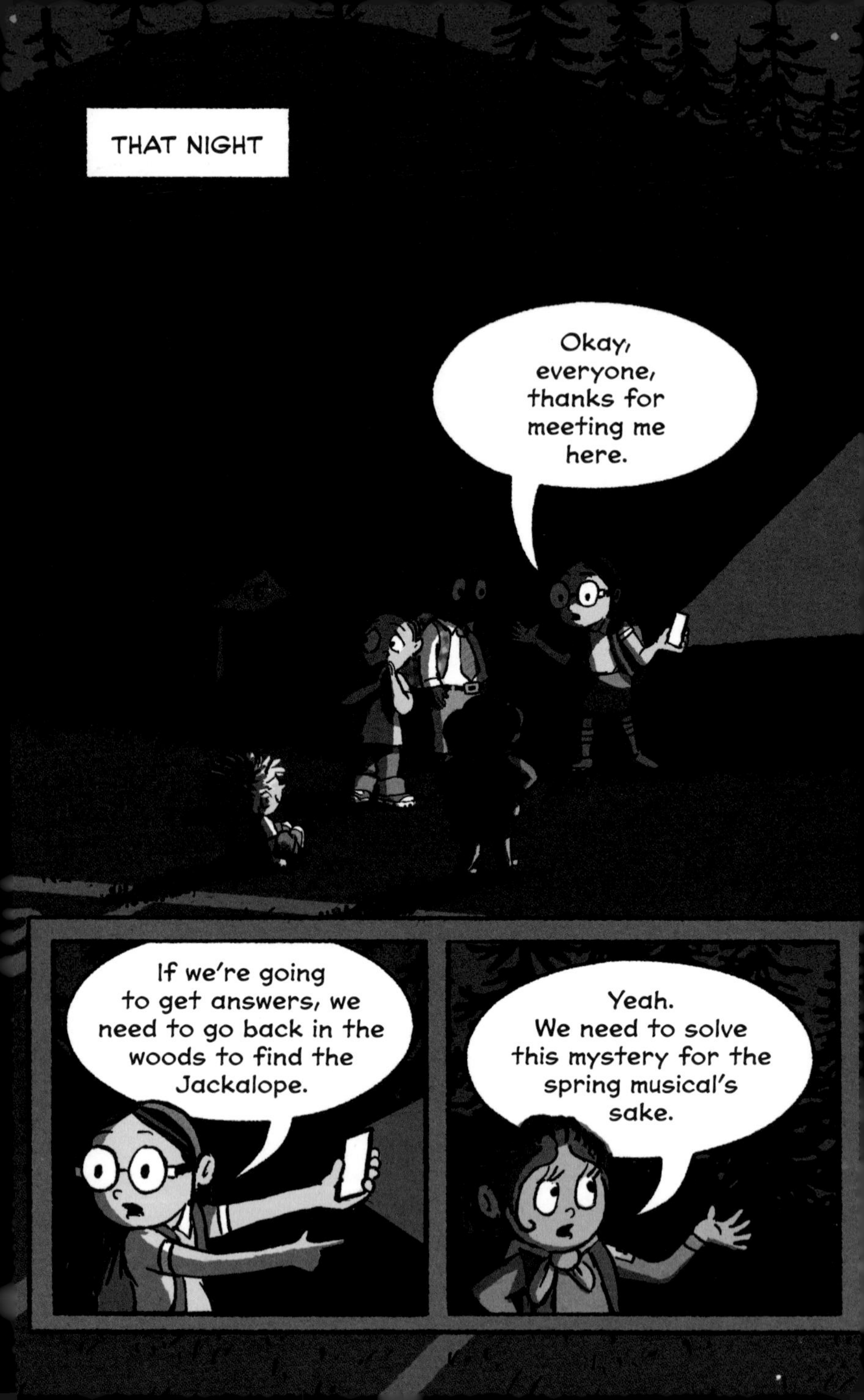
THAT NIGHT
Okay, everyone, thanks for meeting me here.
If we're going to get answers, we need to go back in the woods to find the Jackalope.
Yeah. We need to solve this mystery for the spring musical's sake.

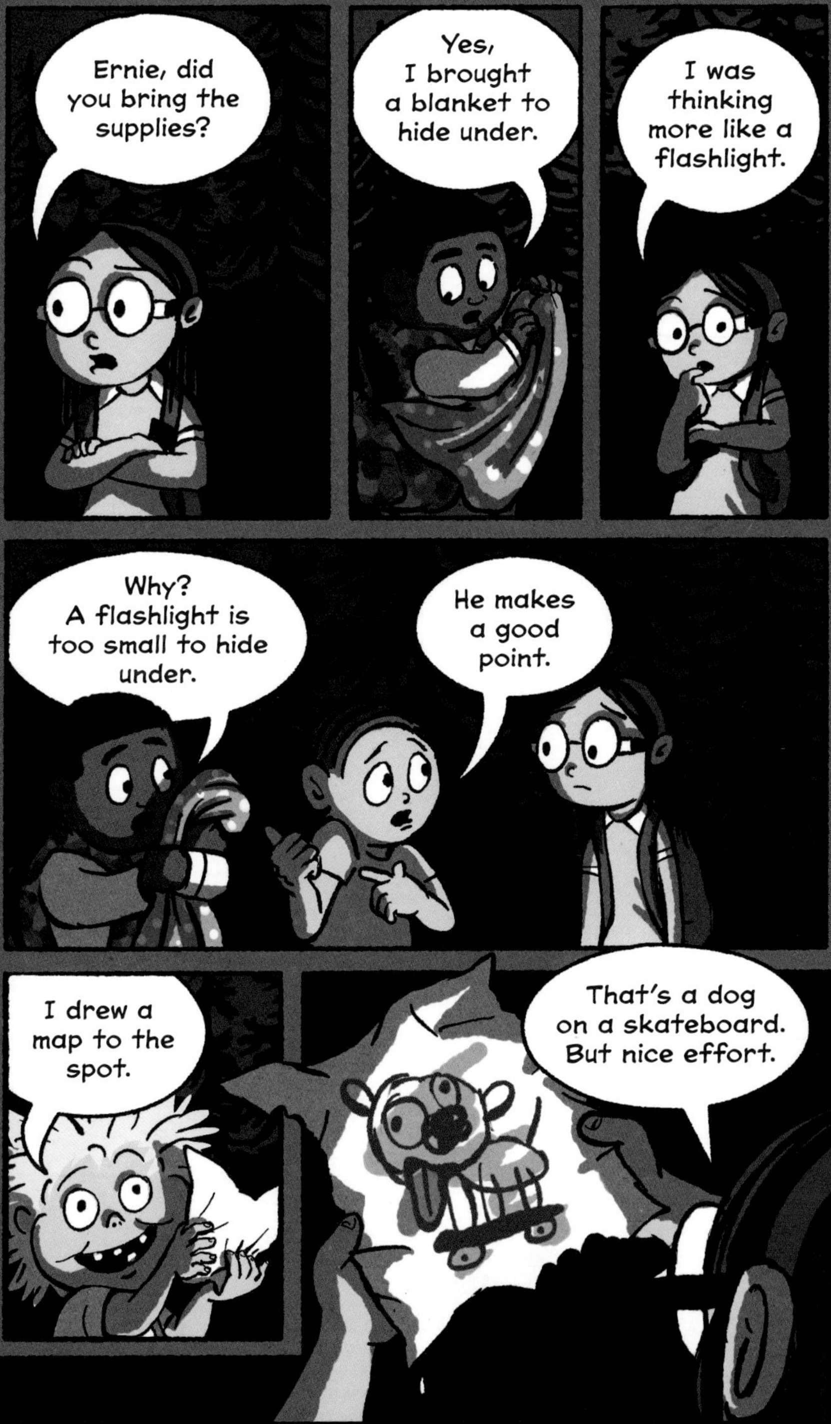
Ernie, did you bring the supplies?
Yes, I brought a blanket to hide under.
I was thinking more like a flashlight.
Why? A flashlight is too small to hide under.
He makes a good point.
I drew a map to the spot.
That's a dog on a skateboard. But nice effort.

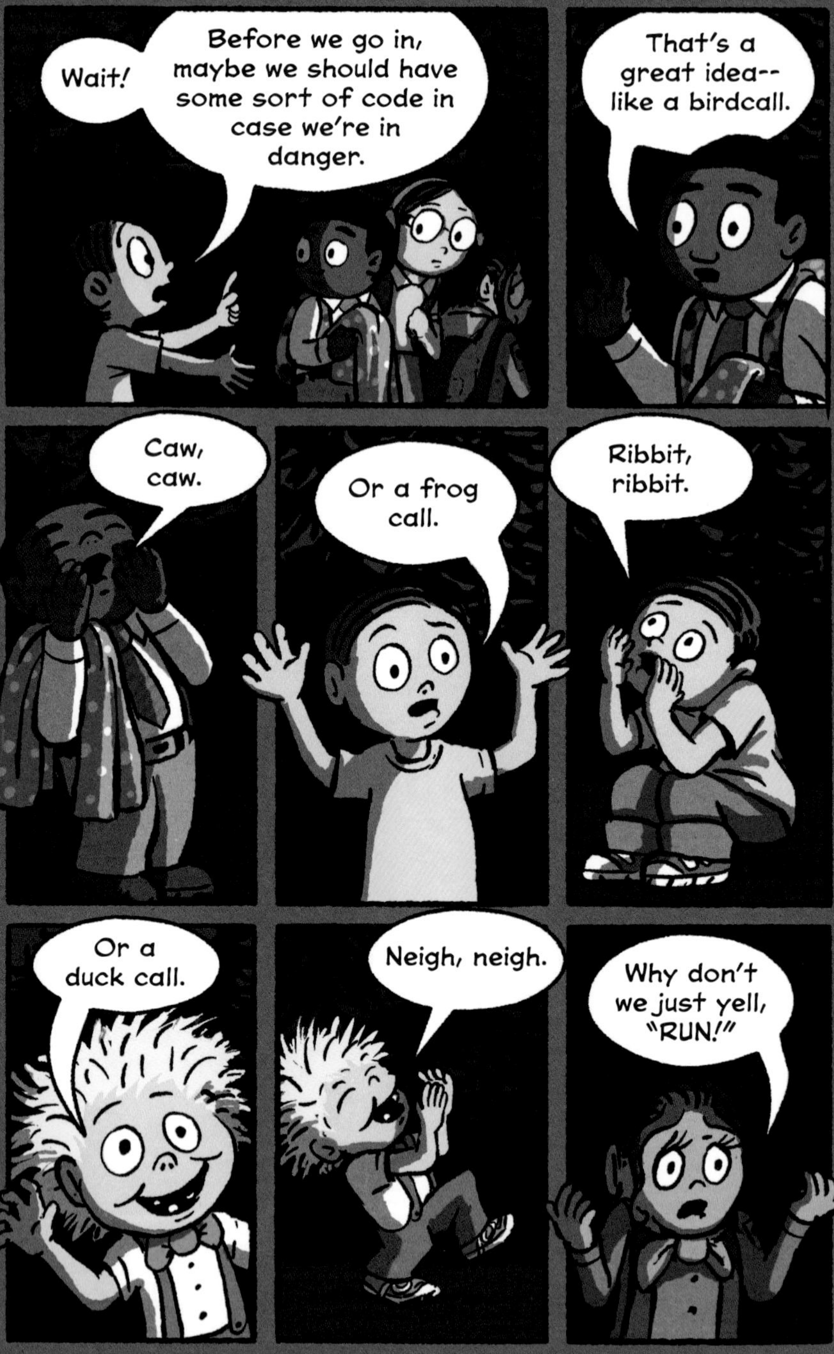
Wait!
Before we go in, maybe we should have some sort of code in case we're in danger.
That's a great idea-- like a birdcall.
Caw, caw.
Or a frog call.
Ribbit, ribbit.
Or a duck call.
Neigh, neigh.
Why don't we just yell, "RUN!"

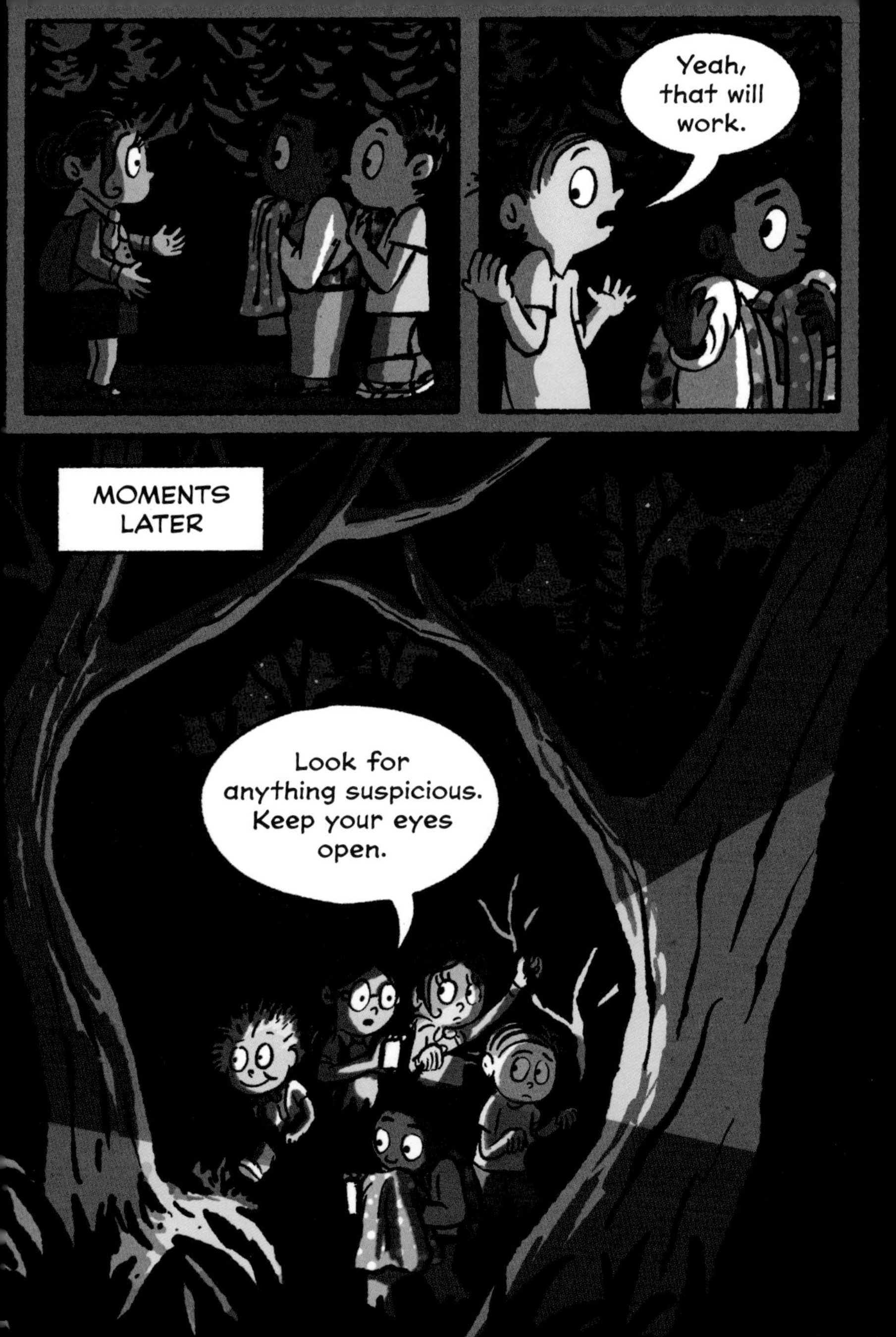
Yeah, that will work.
MOMENTS LATER
Look for anything suspicious. Keep your eyes open.

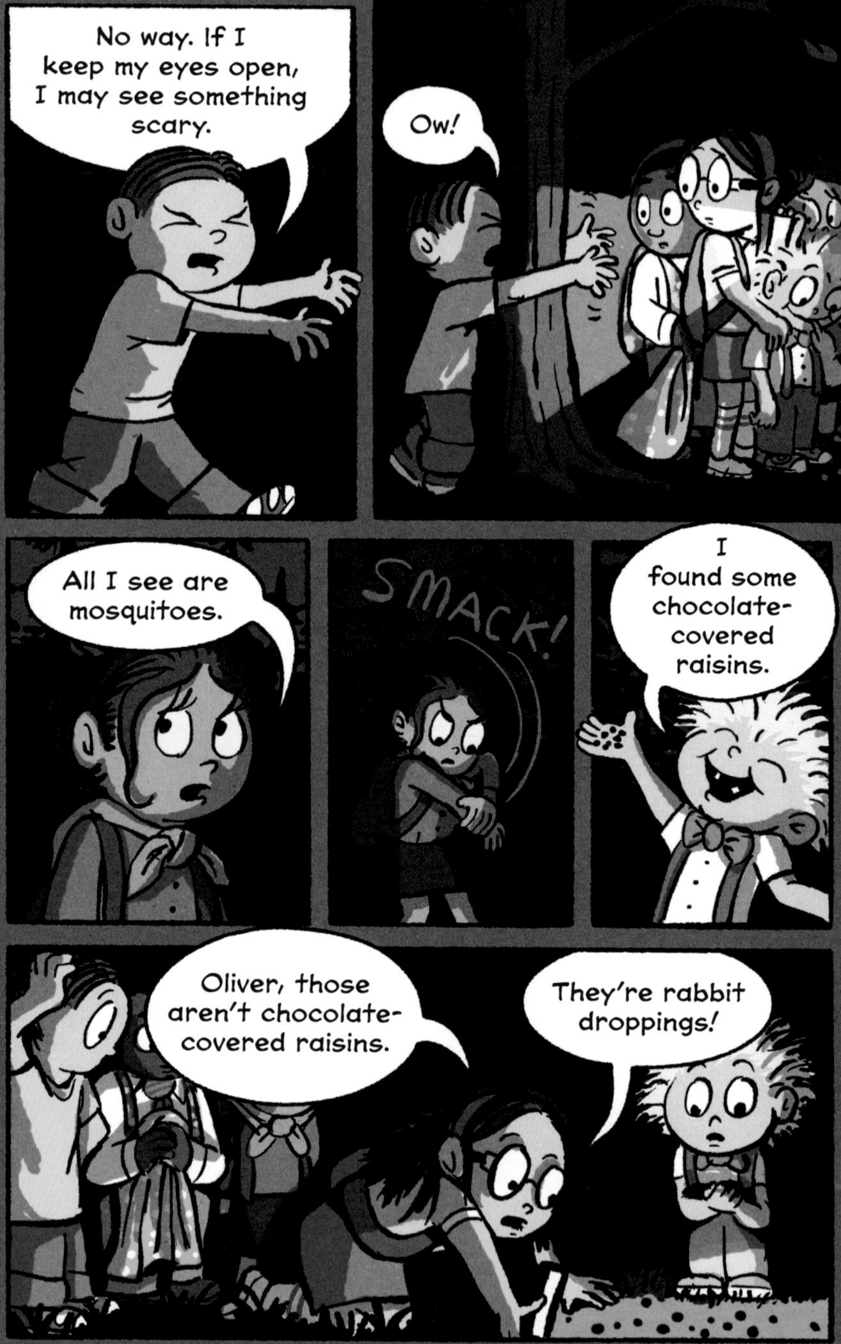
No way. If I keep my eyes open, I may see something scary.
Ow!
All I see are mosquitoes.
SMACK!
I found some chocolate-covered raisins.
Oliver, those aren't chocolate-covered raisins.
They're rabbit droppings!

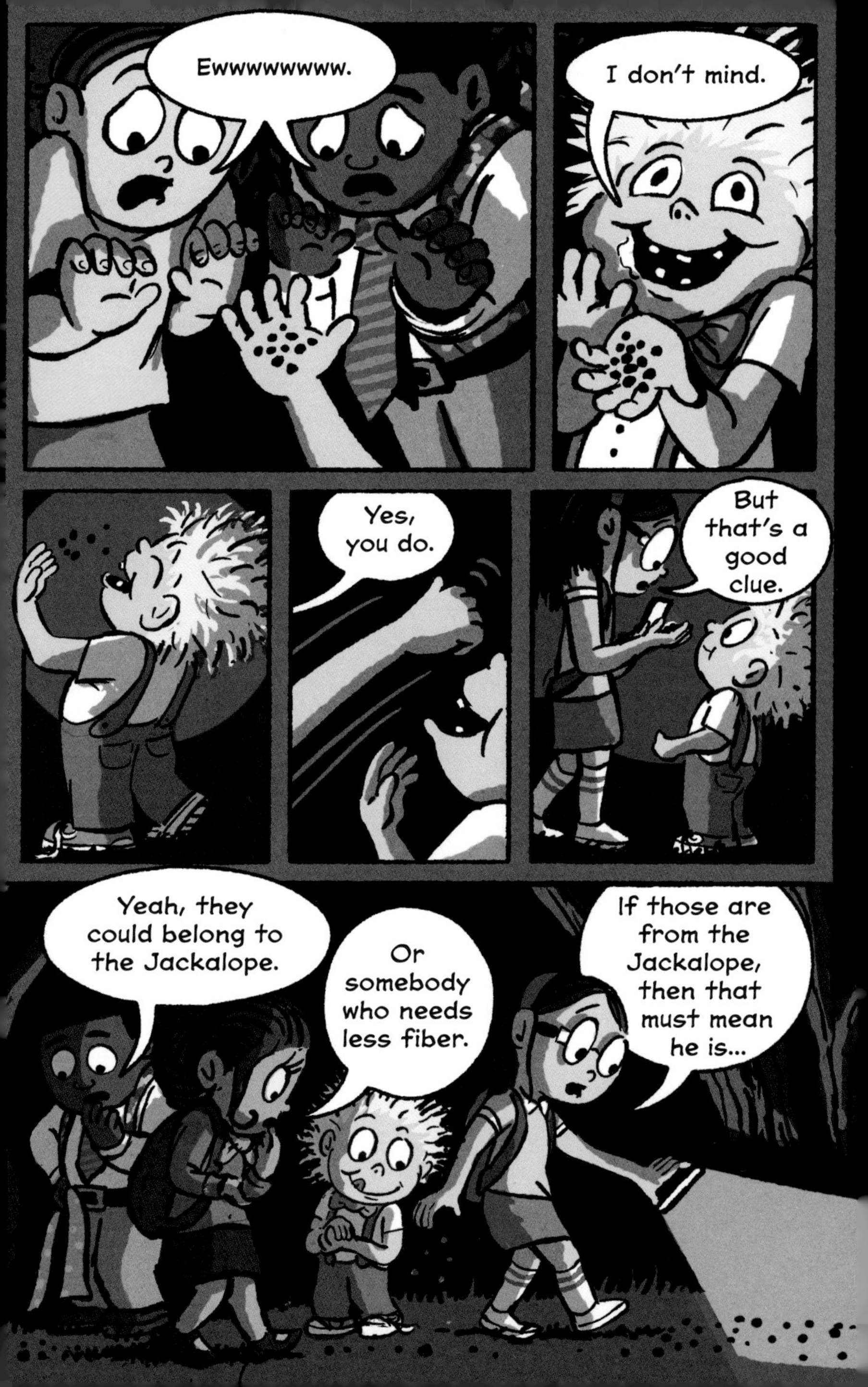
Ewwwwwwww.
I don't mind.
Yes, you do.
But that's a good clue.
Yeah, they could belong to the Jackalope.
Or somebody who needs less fiber.
If those are from the Jackalope, then that must mean he is...

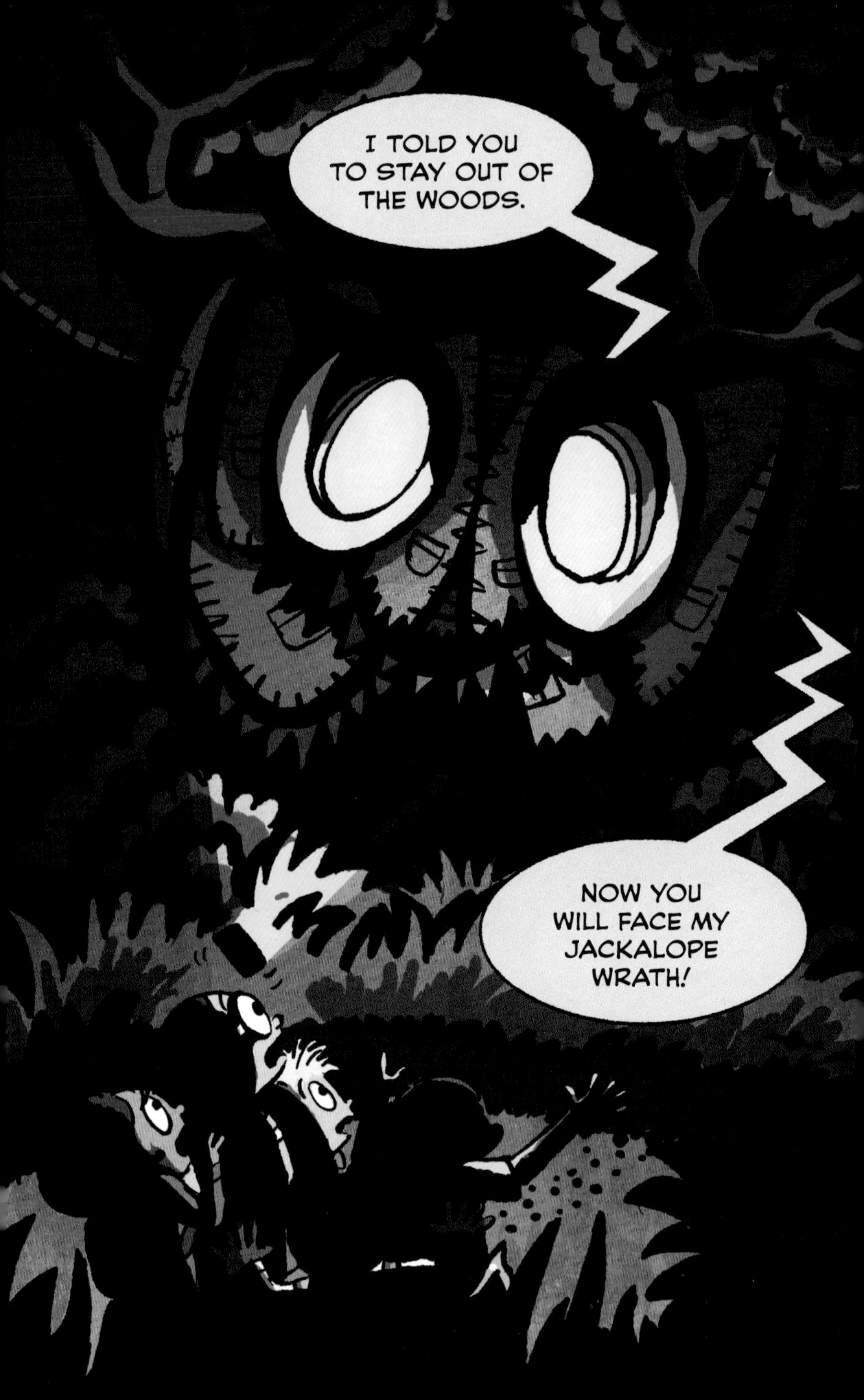
I TOLD YOU TO STAY OUT OF THE WOODS.
NOW YOU WILL FACE MY JACKALOPE WRATH!

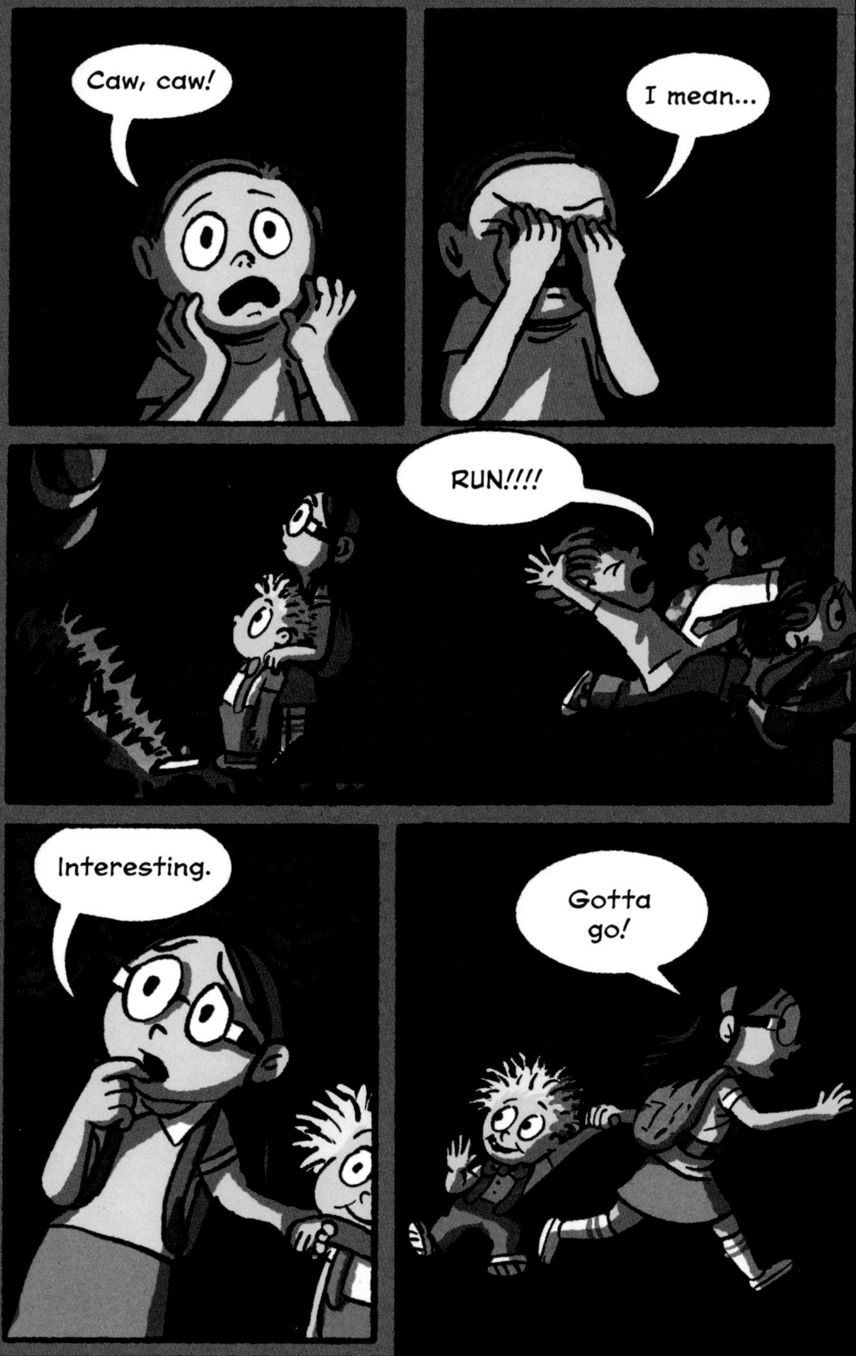

Caw, caw!
I mean...
RUN!!!!
Interesting.
Gotta go!

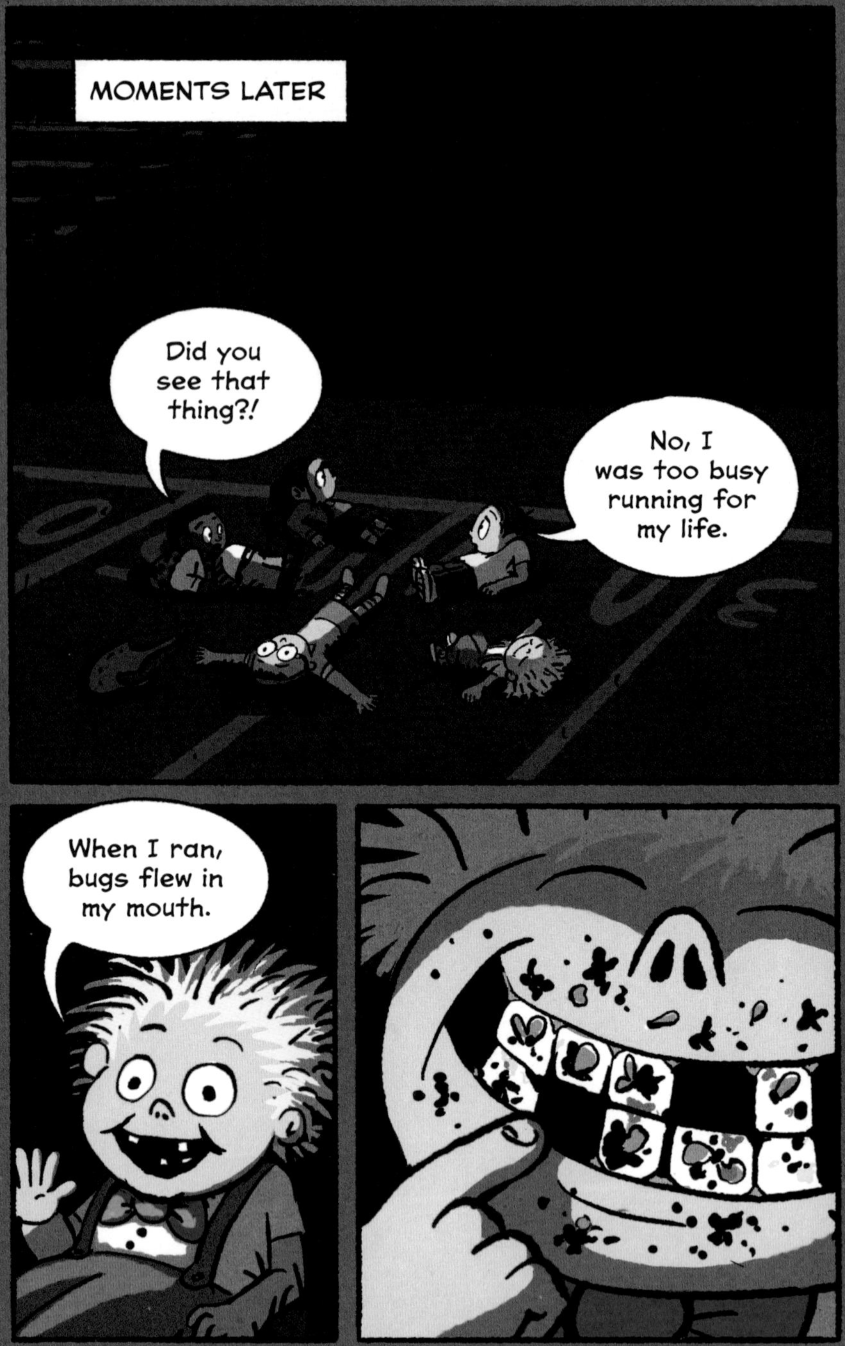
MOMENTS LATER
Did you see that thing?!
No, I was too busy running for my life.
When I ran, bugs flew in my mouth.

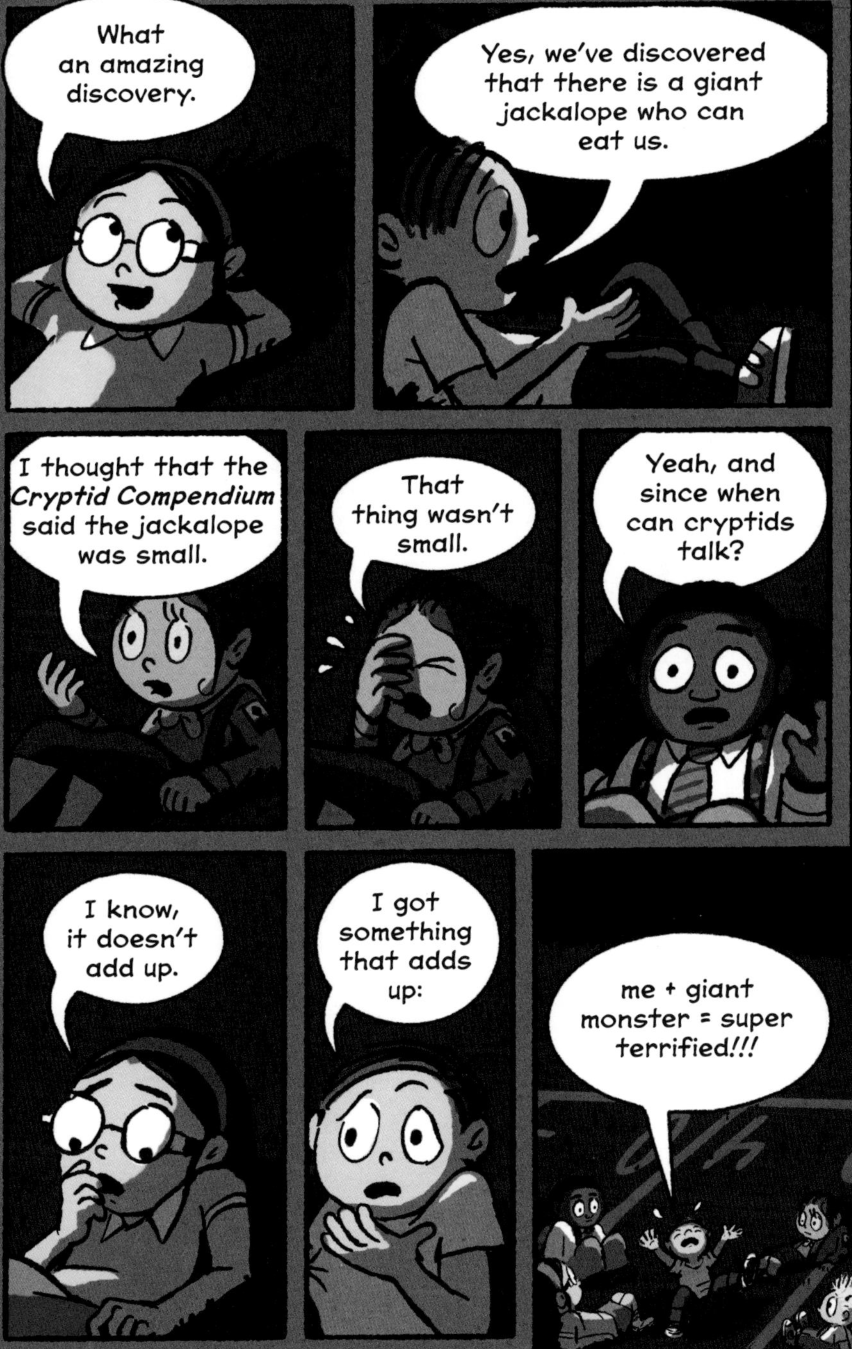
What an amazing discovery.
Yes, we've discovered that there is a giant jackalope who can eat us.
I thought that the *Cryptid Compendium* said the jackalope was small.
That thing wasn't small.
Yeah, and since when can cryptids talk?
I know, it doesn't add up.
I got something that adds up:
me + giant monster = super terrified!!!

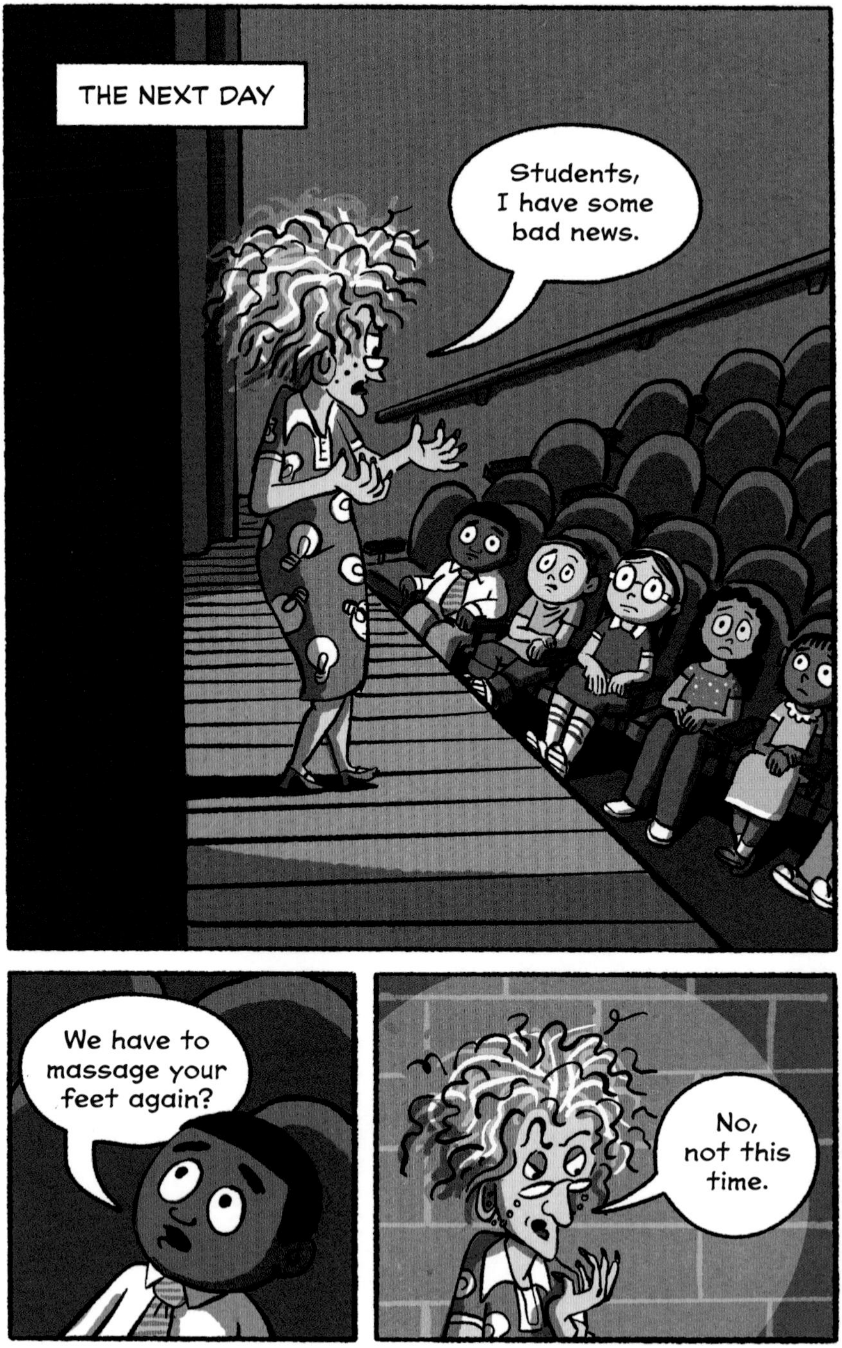
THE NEXT DAY
Students, I have some bad news.
We have to massage your feet again?
No, not this time.

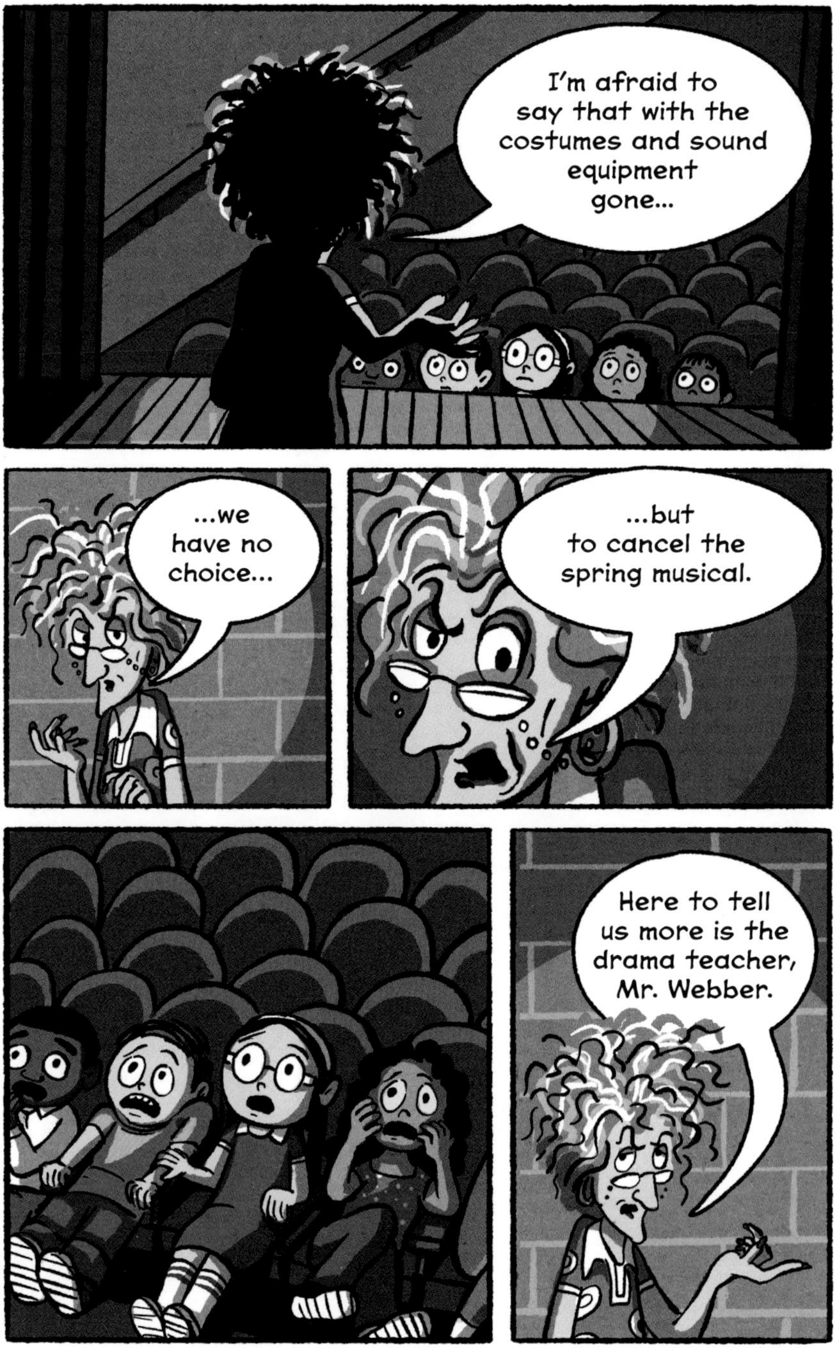
I'm afraid to say that with the costumes and sound equipment gone...
...we have no choice...
...but to cancel the spring musical.
Here to tell us more is the drama teacher, Mr. Webber.

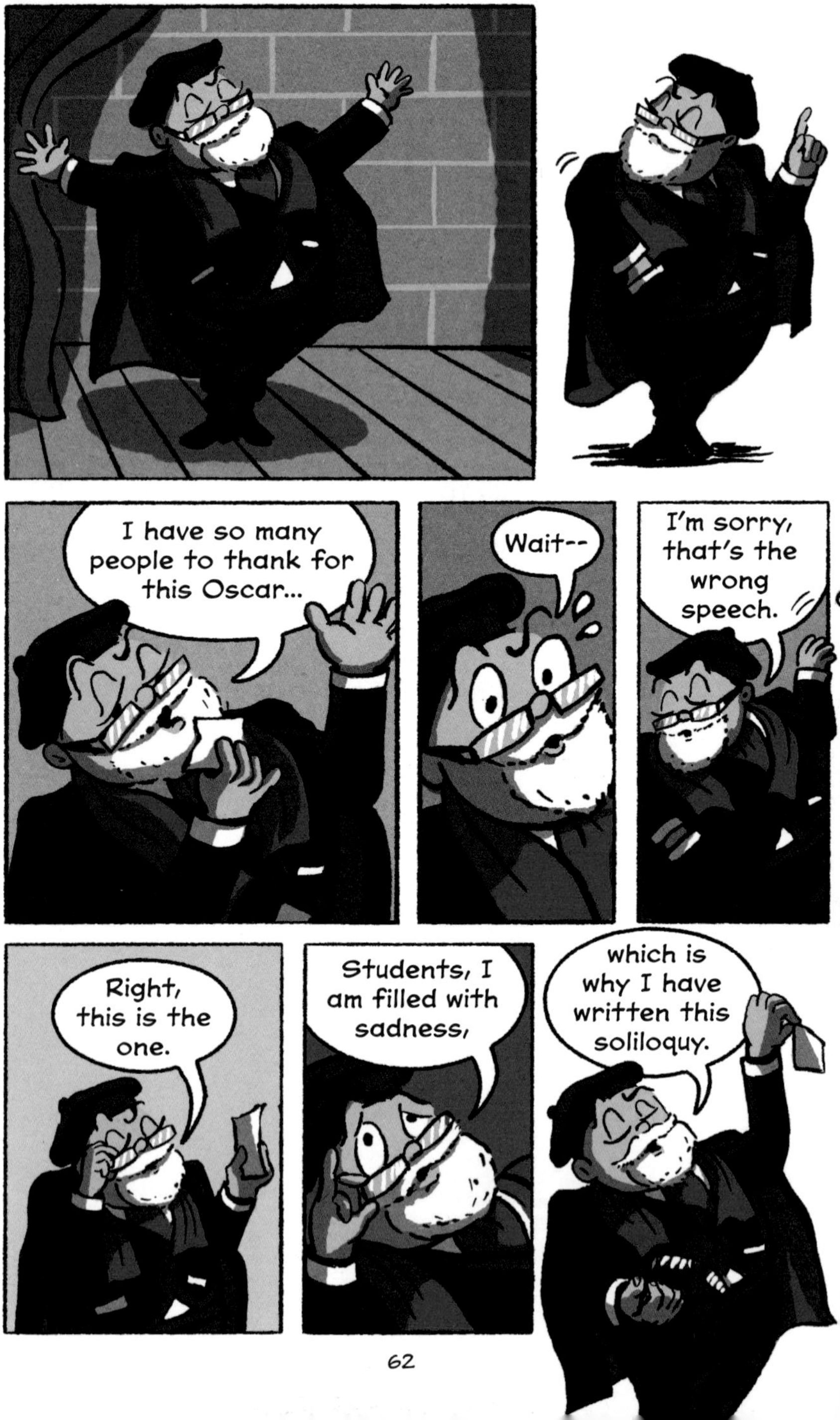
I have so many people to thank for this Oscar...
Wait--
I'm sorry, that's the wrong speech.
Right, this is the one.
Students, I am filled with sadness,
which is why I have written this soliloquy.

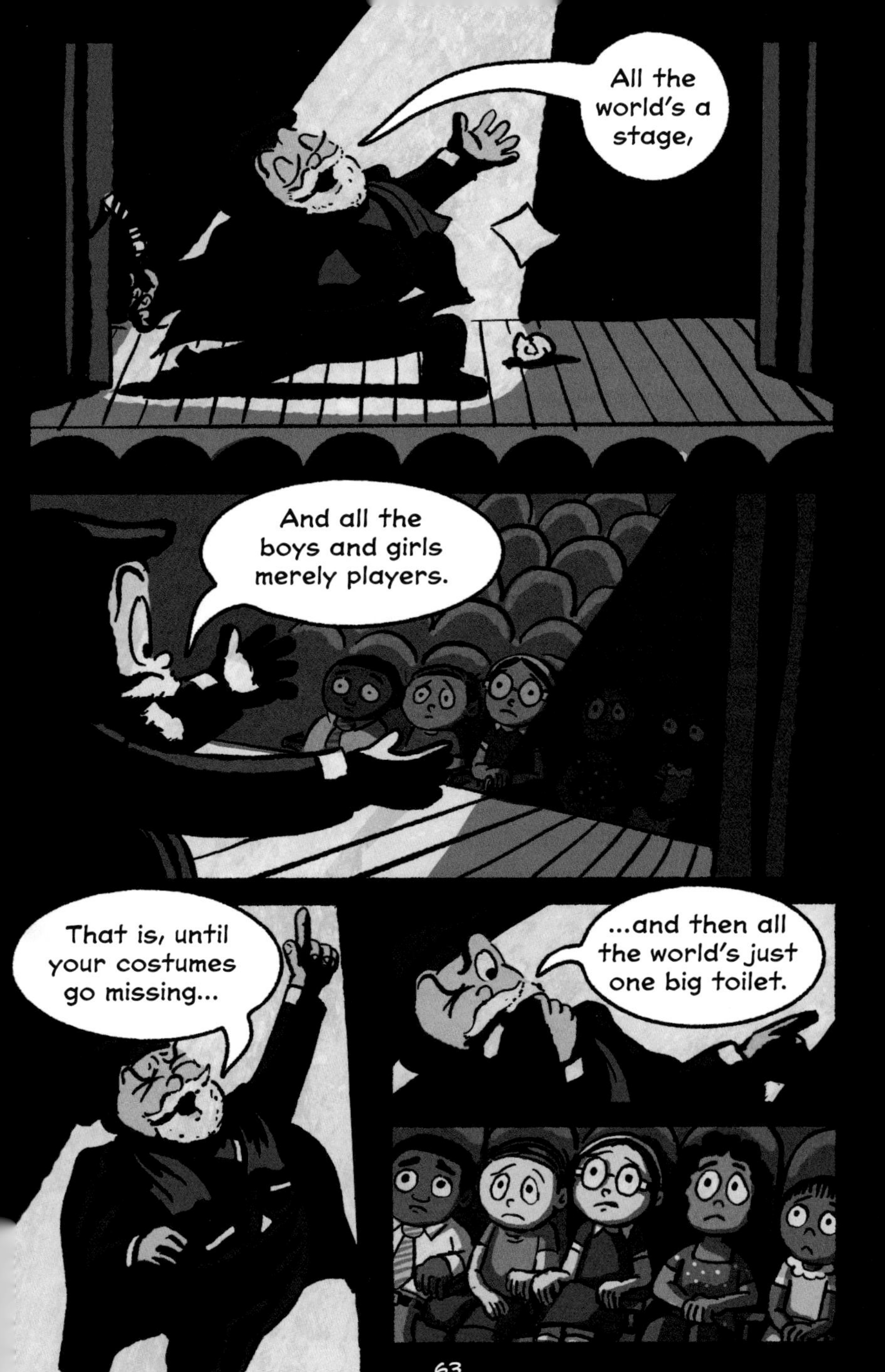
All the world's a stage,
And all the boys and girls merely players.
That is, until your costumes go missing...
...and then all the world's just one big toilet.

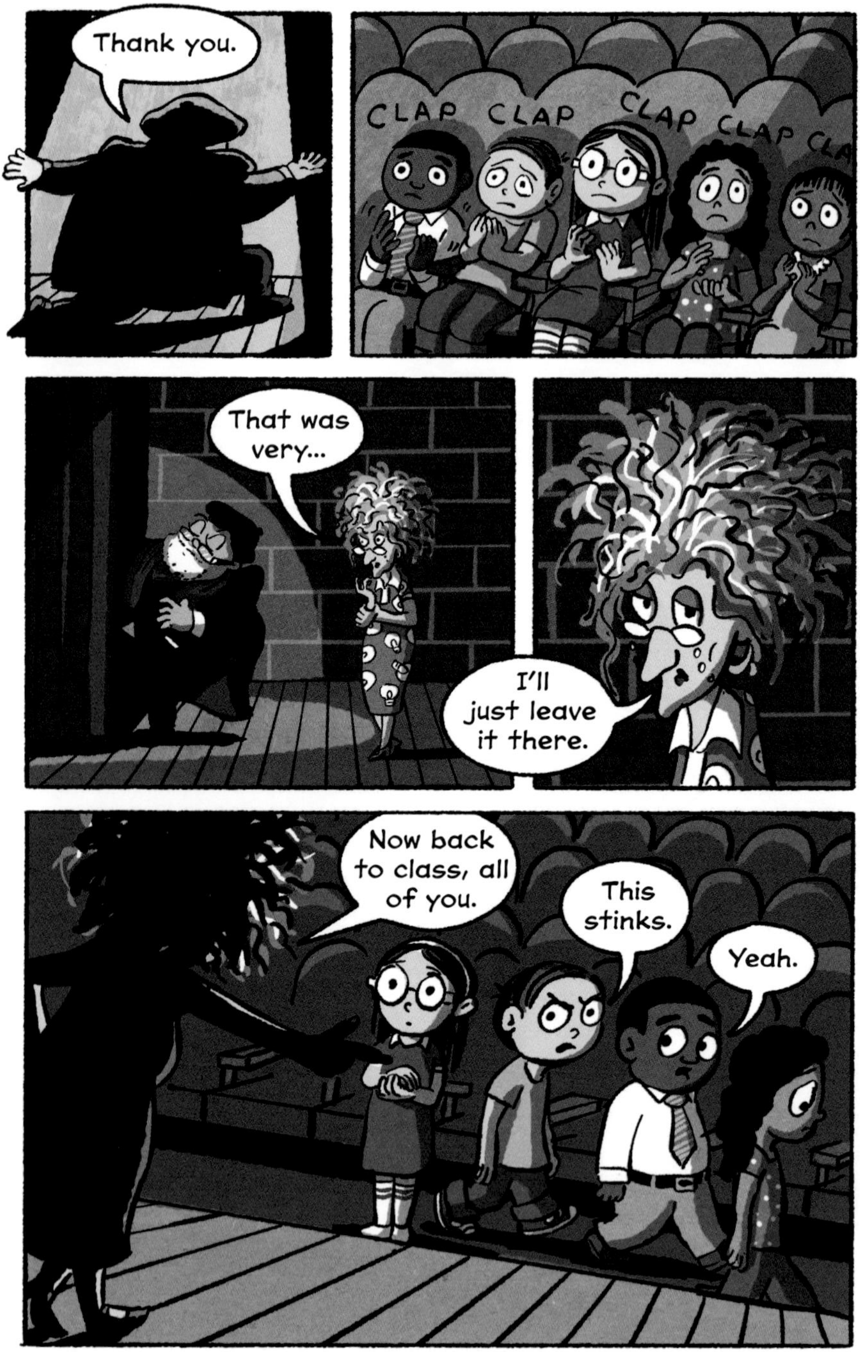
Thank you.
CLAP CLAP CLAP CLAP
That was very...
I'll just leave it there.
Now back to class, all of you.
This stinks.
Yeah.

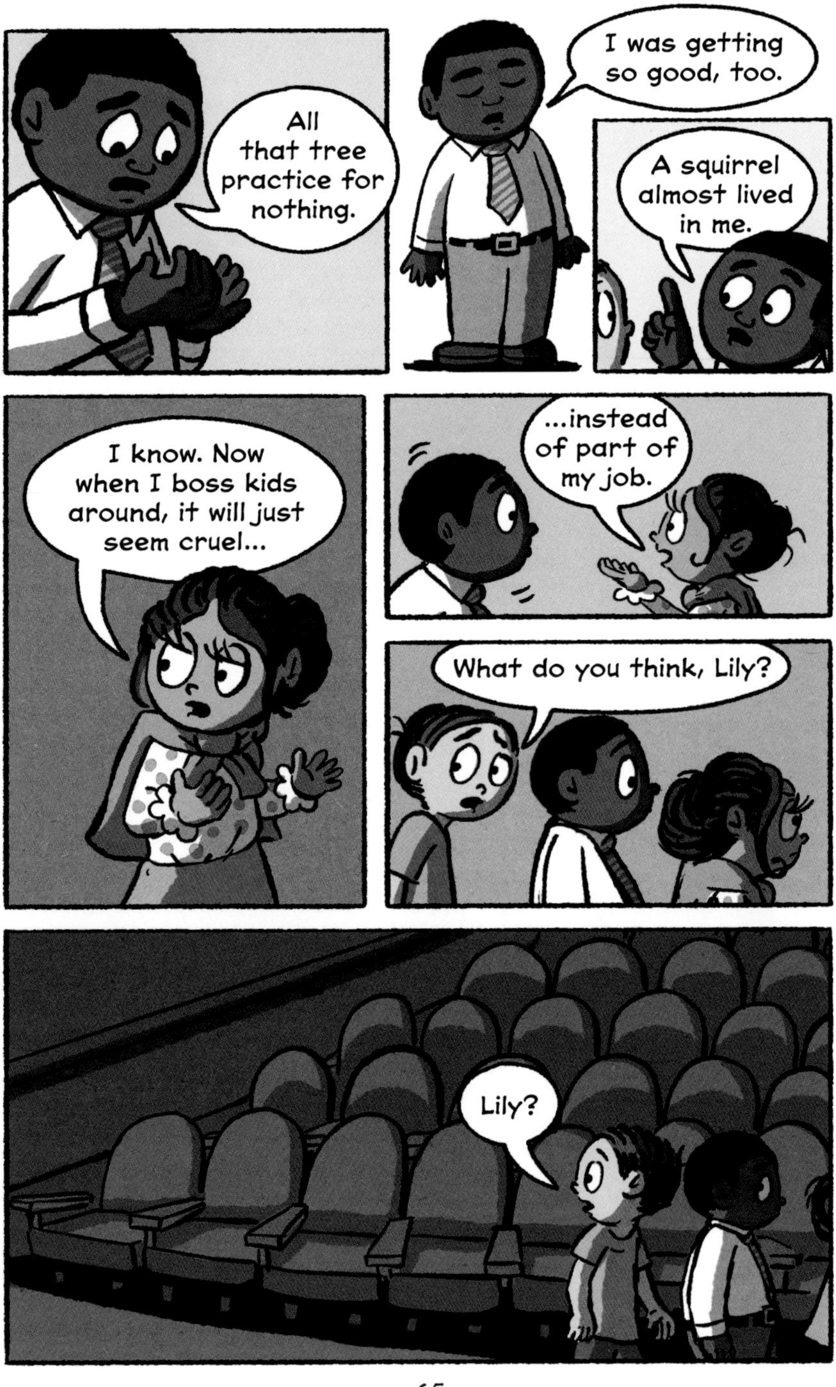
All that tree practice for nothing.
I was getting so good, too.
A squirrel almost lived in me.
I know. Now when I boss kids around, it will just seem cruel...
...instead of part of my job.
What do you think, Lily?
Lily?

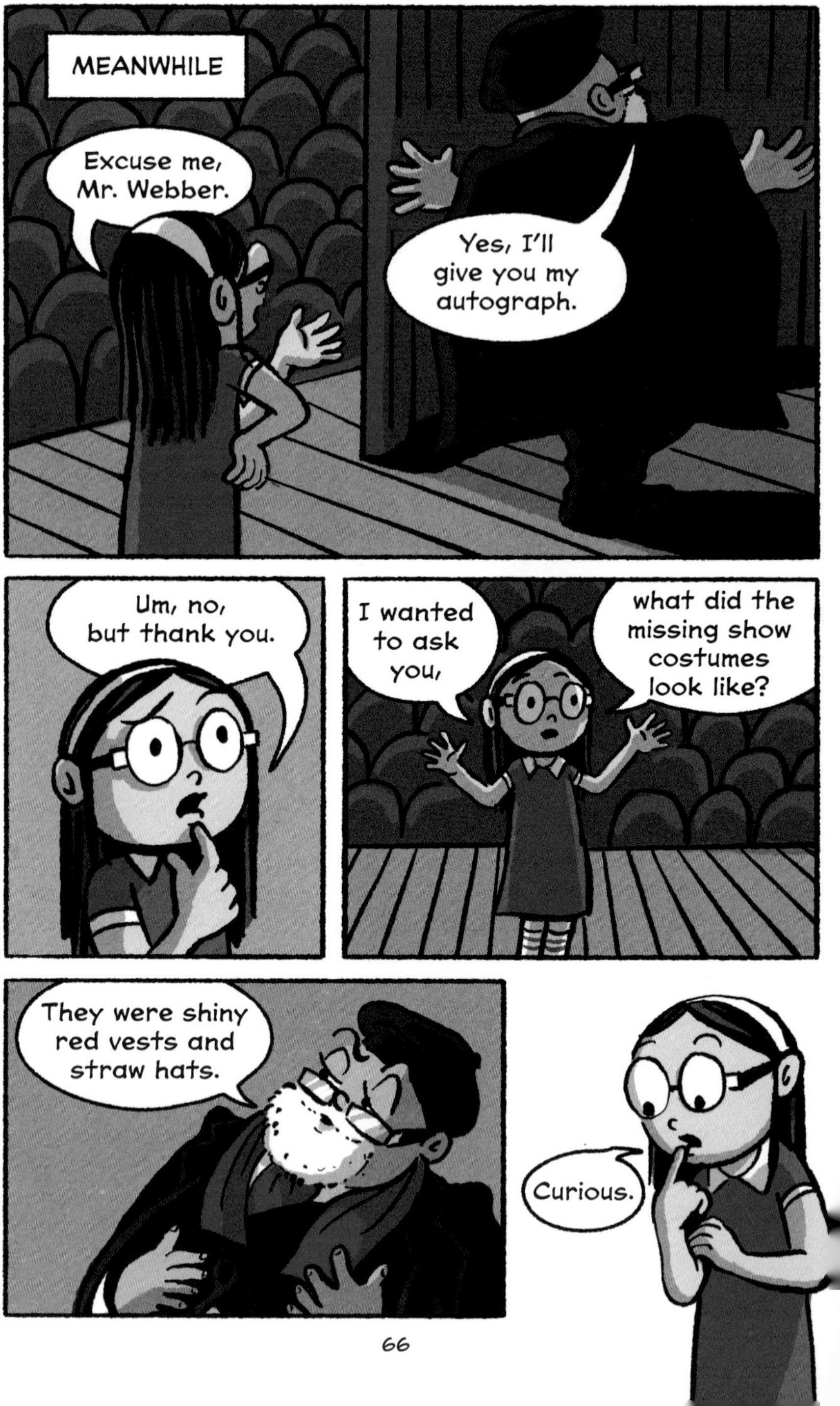
MEANWHILE
Excuse me, Mr. Webber.
Yes, I'll give you my autograph.
Um, no, but thank you.
I wanted to ask you,
what did the missing show costumes look like?
They were shiny red vests and straw hats.
Curious.

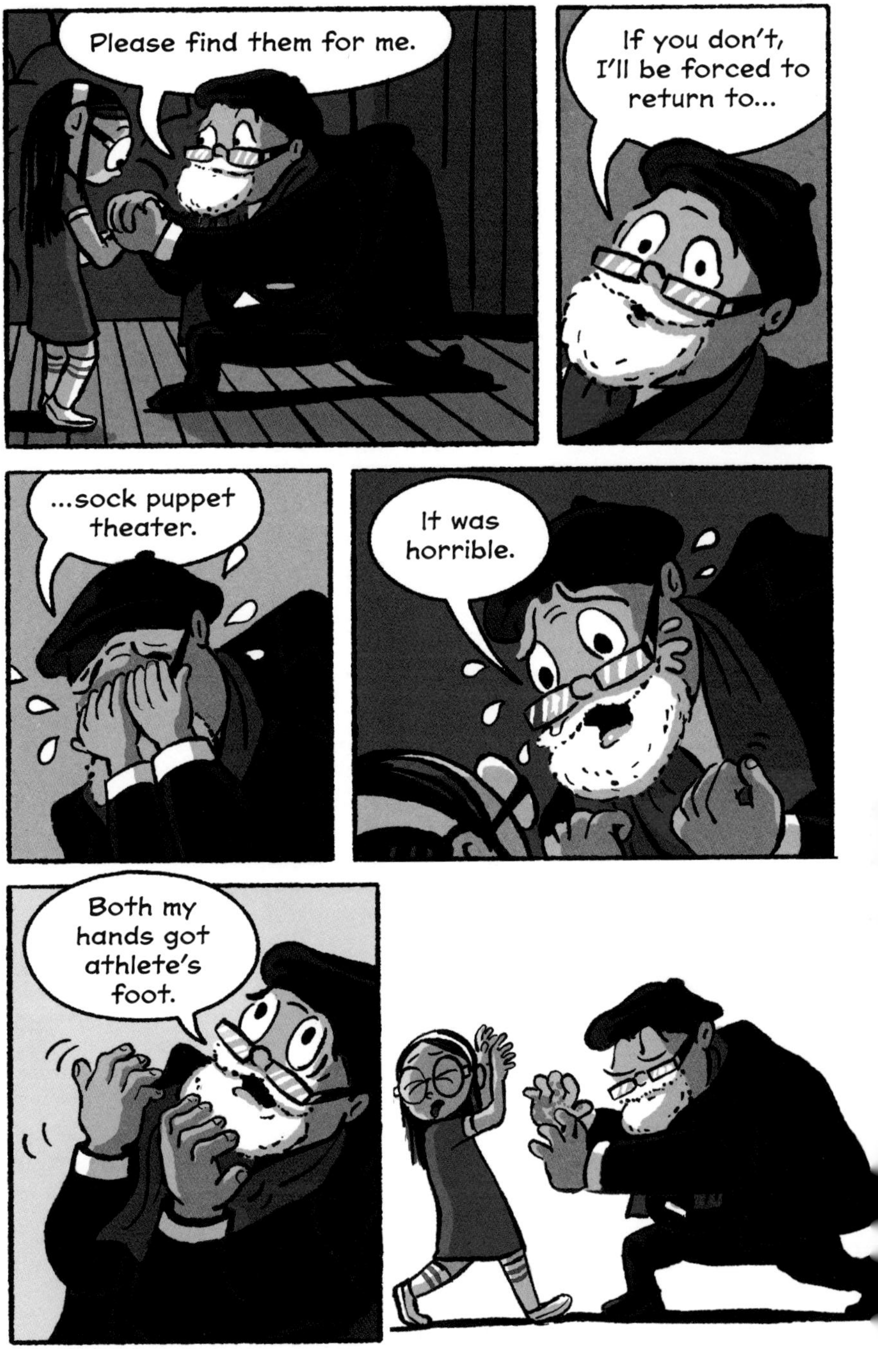
Please find them for me.
If you don't, I'll be forced to return to...
...sock puppet theater.
It was horrible.
Both my hands got athlete's foot.

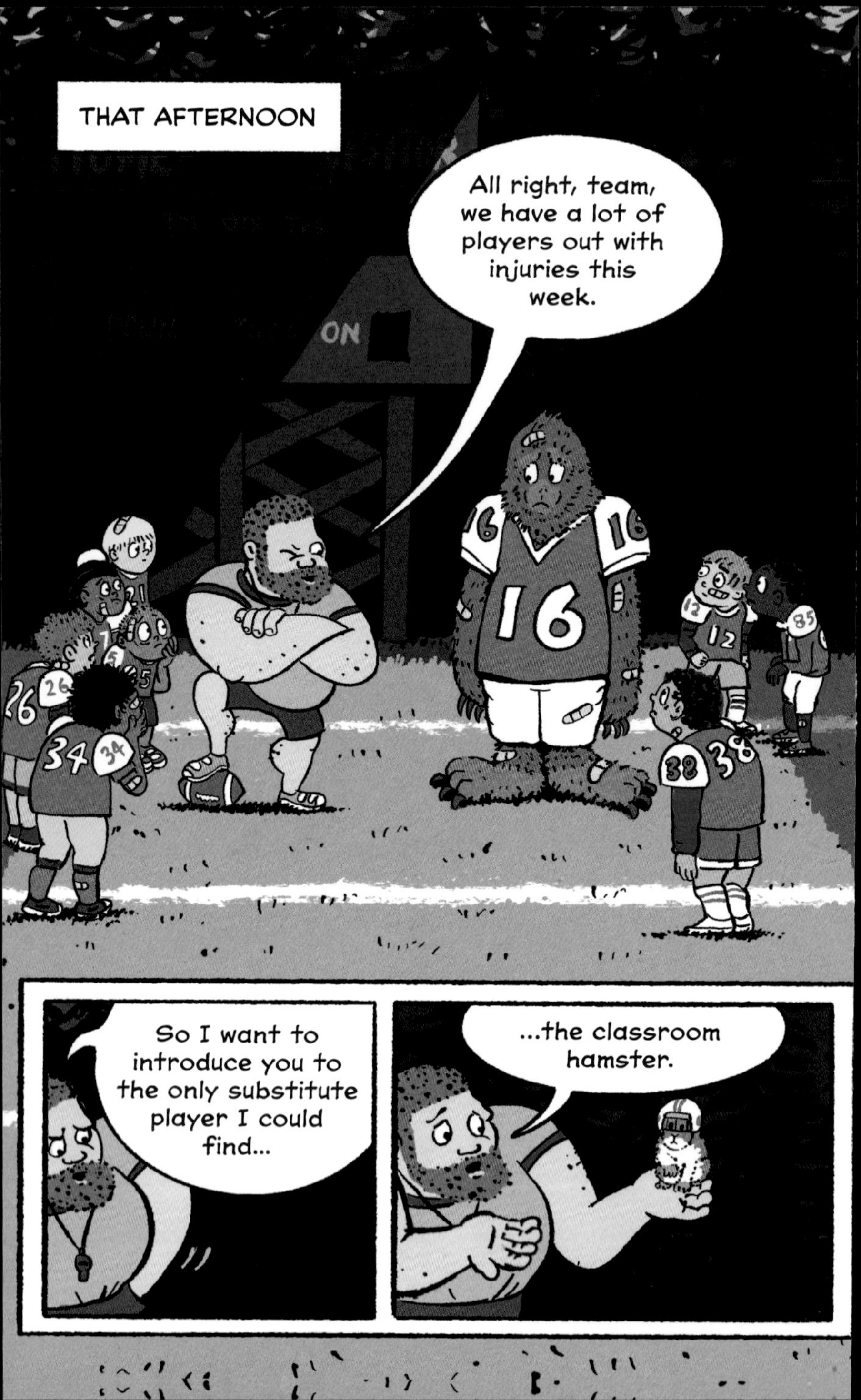
THAT AFTERNOON
All right, team, we have a lot of players out with injuries this week.
So I want to introduce you to the only substitute player I could find...
...the classroom hamster.

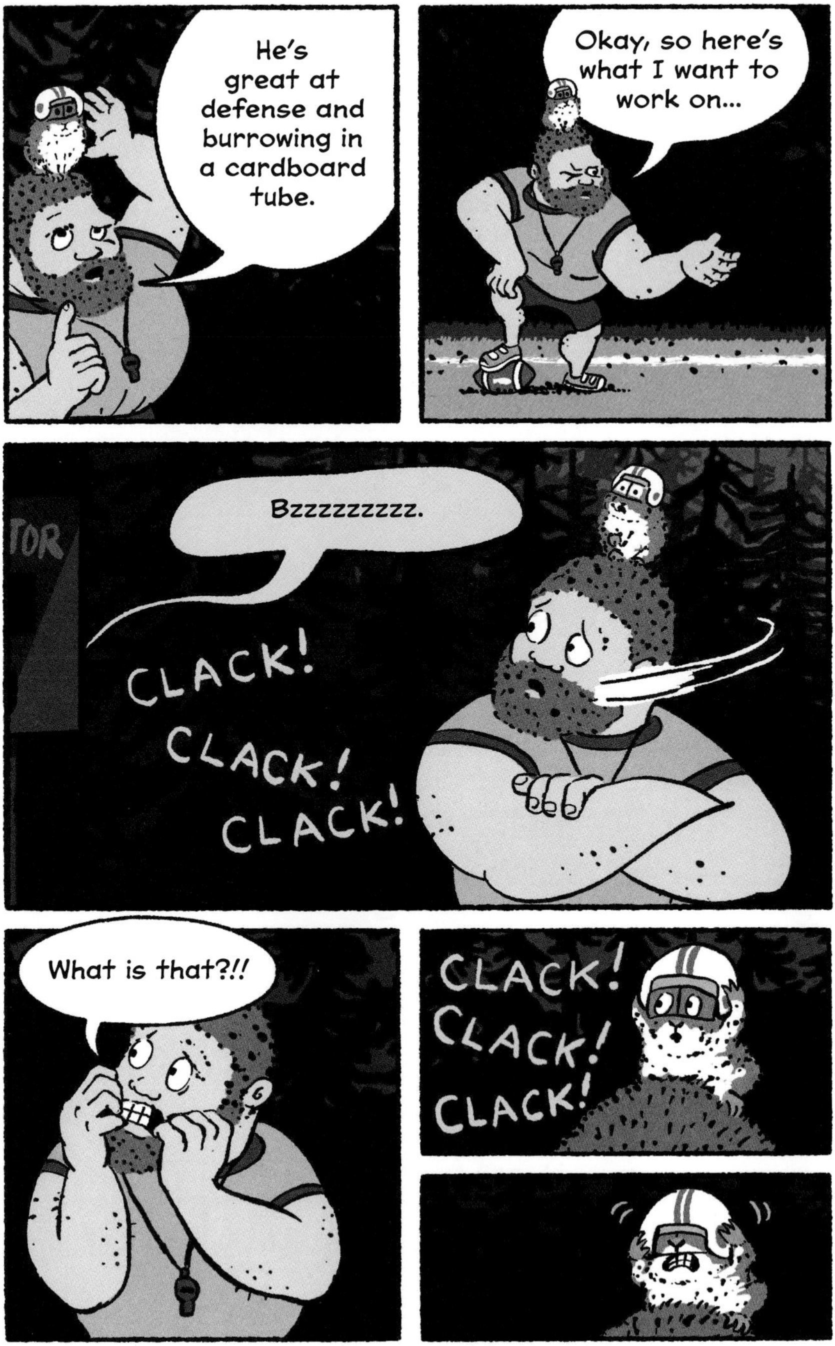
He's great at defense and burrowing in a cardboard tube.
Okay, so here's what I want to work on...
Bzzzzzzzzz.
TOR
CLACK!
CLACK!
CLACK!
What is that?!!
CLACK!
CLACK!
CLACK!

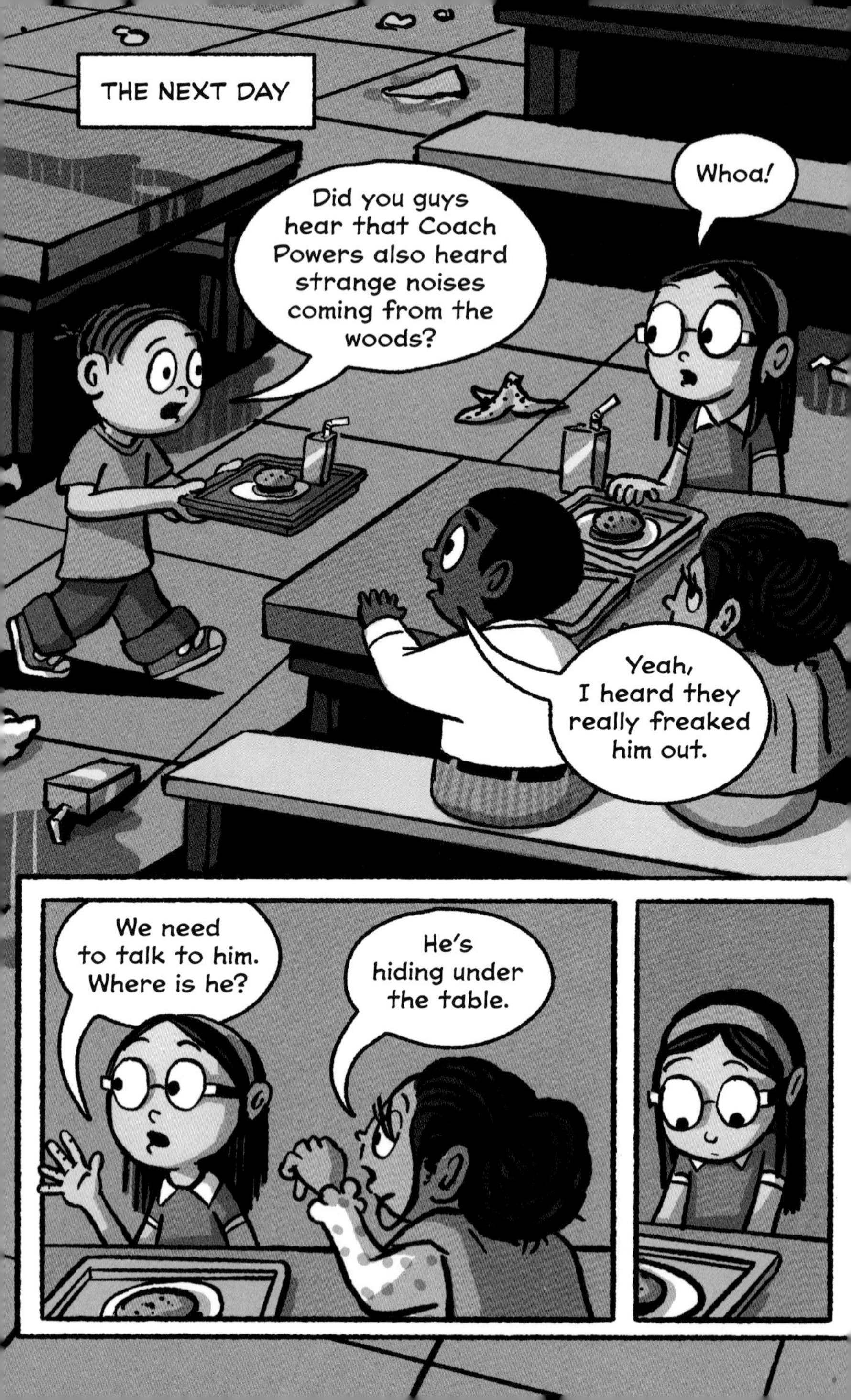
THE NEXT DAY
Did you guys hear that Coach Powers also heard strange noises coming from the woods?
Whoa!
Yeah, I heard they really freaked him out.
We need to talk to him. Where is he?
He's hiding under the table.

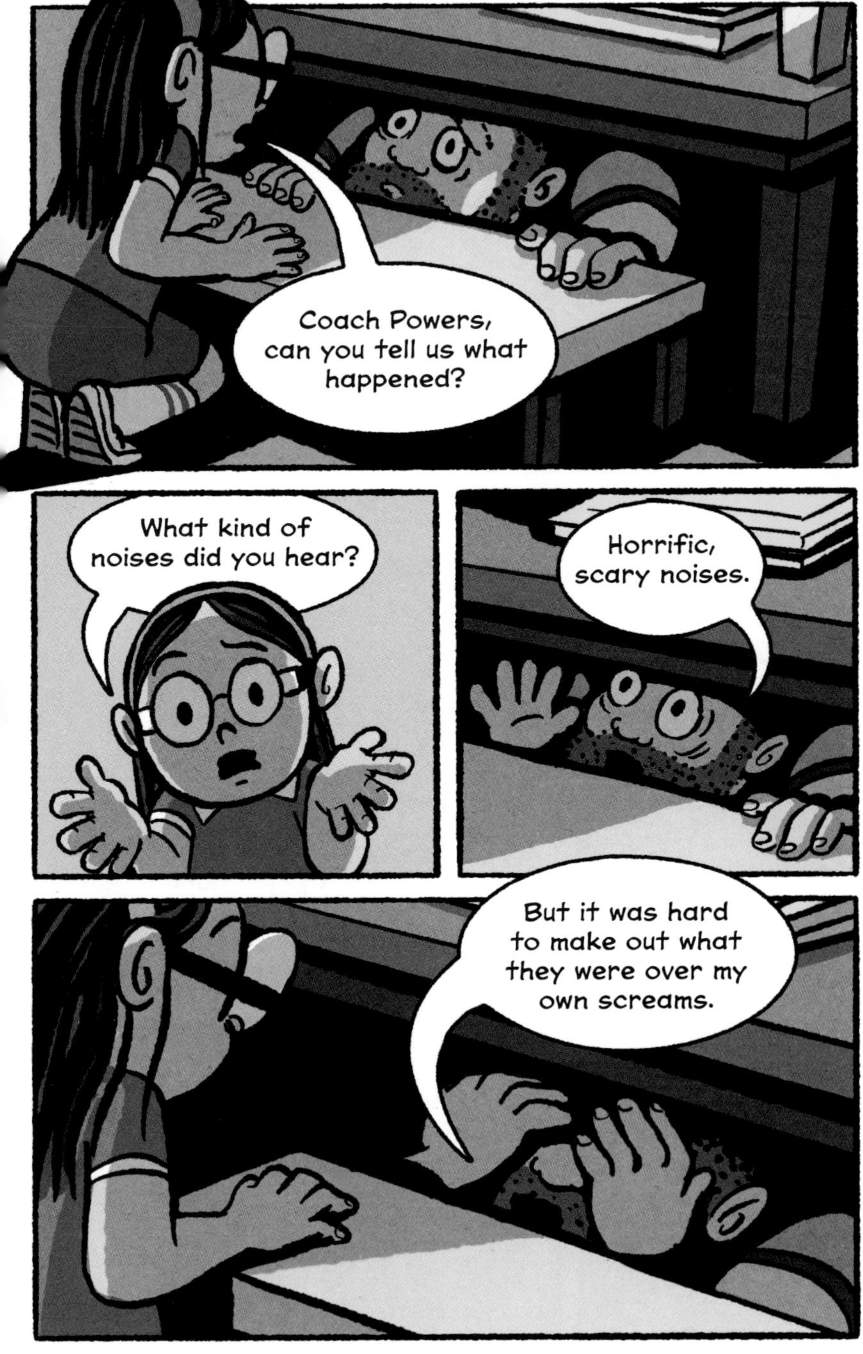
Coach Powers, can you tell us what happened?
What kind of noises did you hear?
Horrific, scary noises.
But it was hard to make out what they were over my own screams.

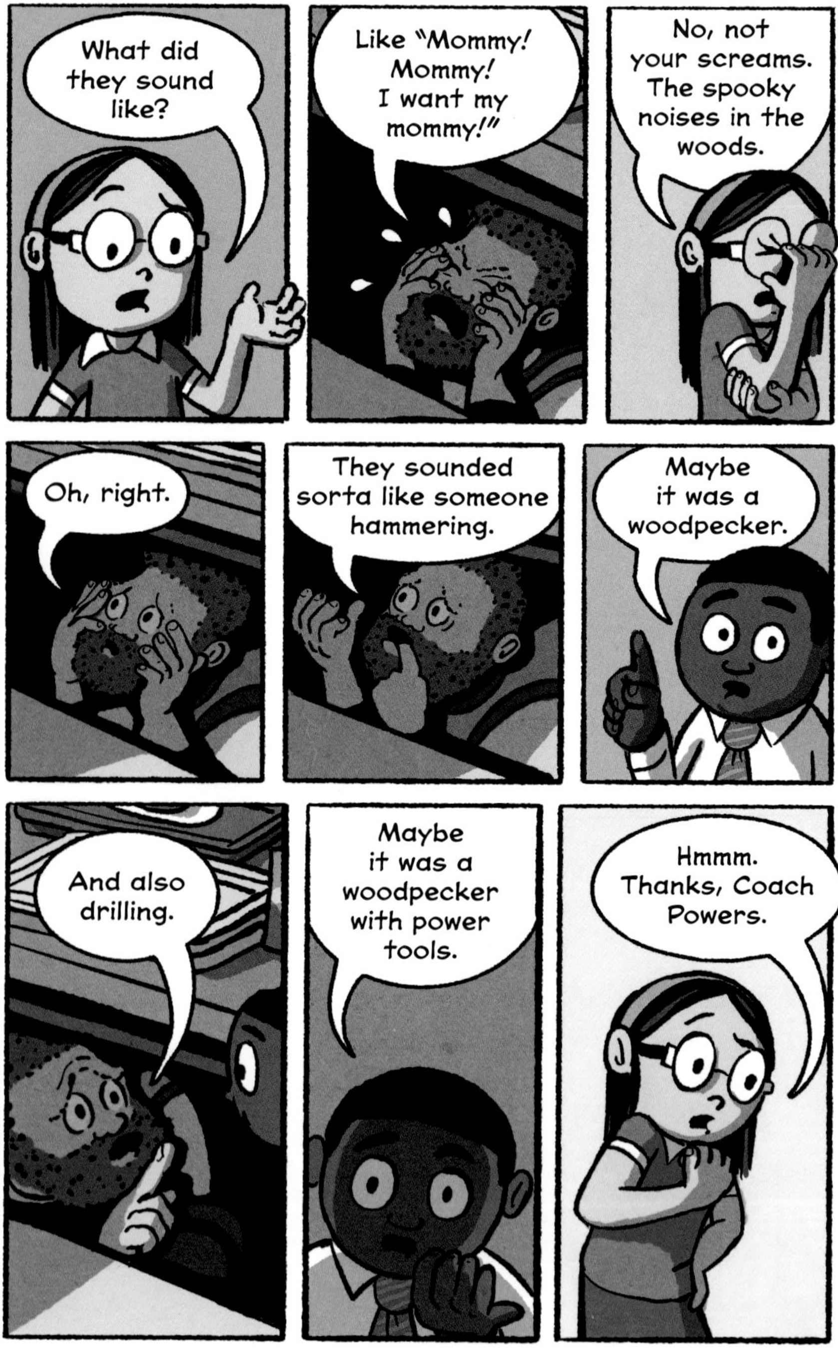
What did they sound like?
Like "Mommy! Mommy! I want my mommy!"
No, not your screams. The spooky noises in the woods.
Oh, right.
They sounded sorta like someone hammering.
Maybe it was a woodpecker.
And also drilling.
Maybe it was a woodpecker with power tools.
Hmmm. Thanks, Coach Powers.

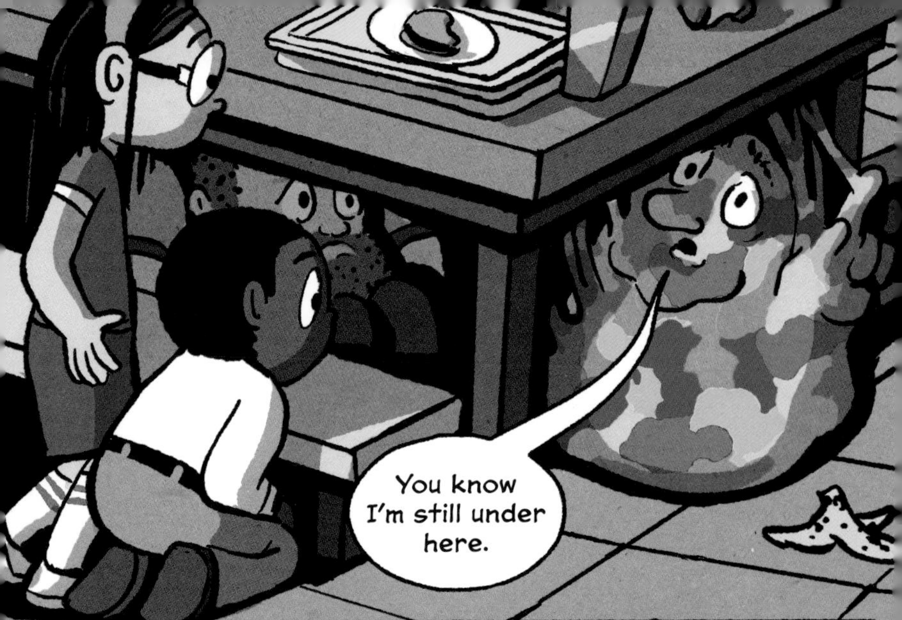
You know I'm still under here.

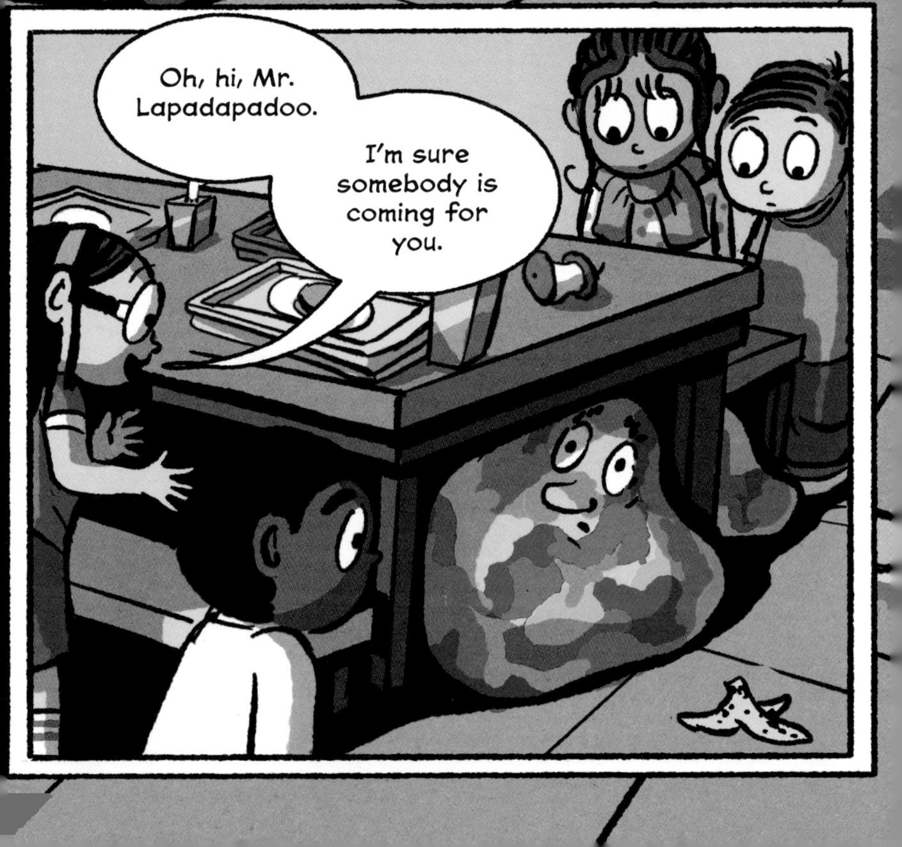
Oh, hi, Mr. Lapadapadoo.
I'm sure somebody is coming for you.

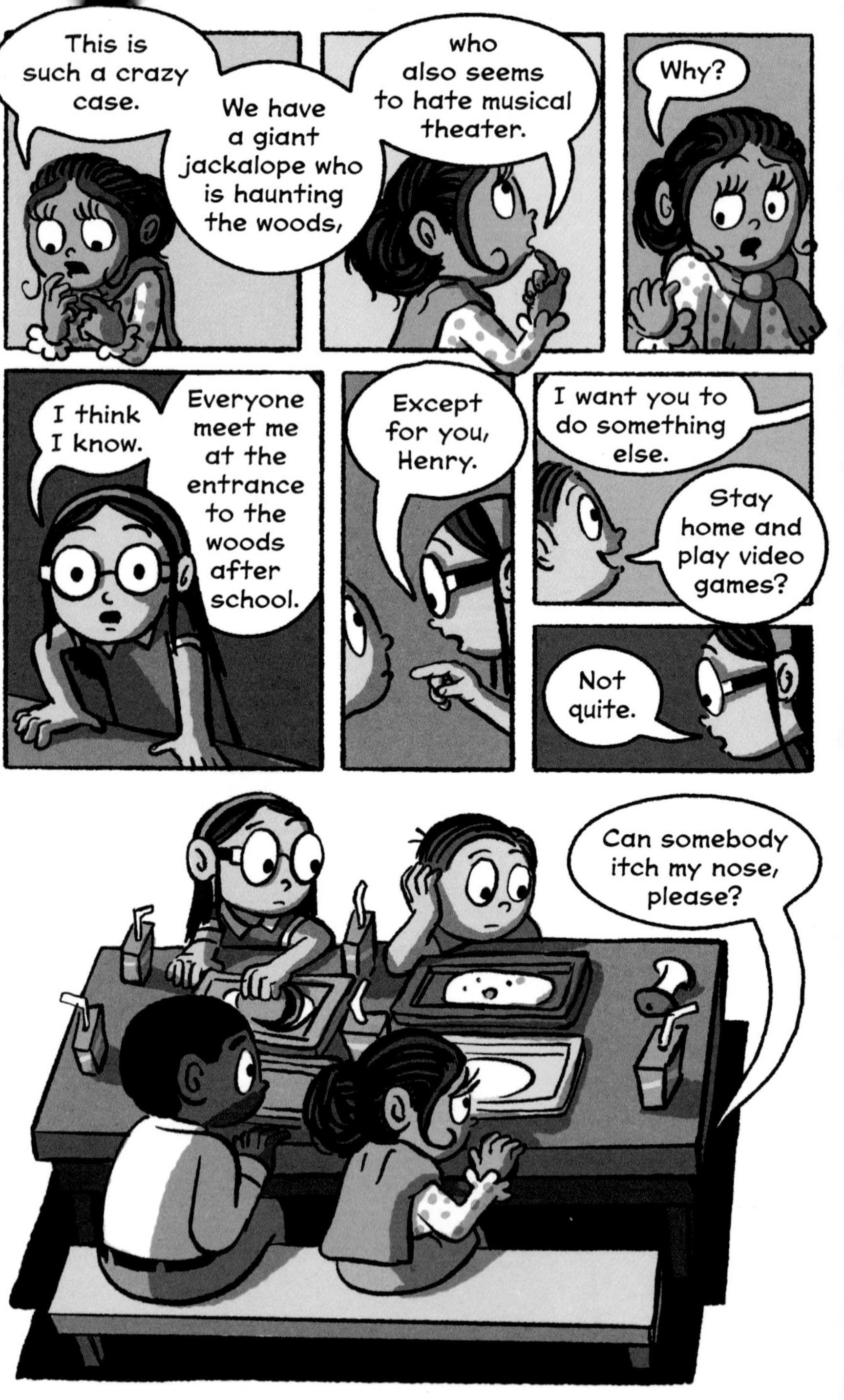

This is such a crazy case.
We have a giant jackalope who is haunting the woods,
who also seems to hate musical theater.
Why?
I think I know.
Everyone meet me at the entrance to the woods after school.
Except for you, Henry.
I want you to do something else.
Stay home and play video games?
Not quite.
Can somebody itch my nose, please?

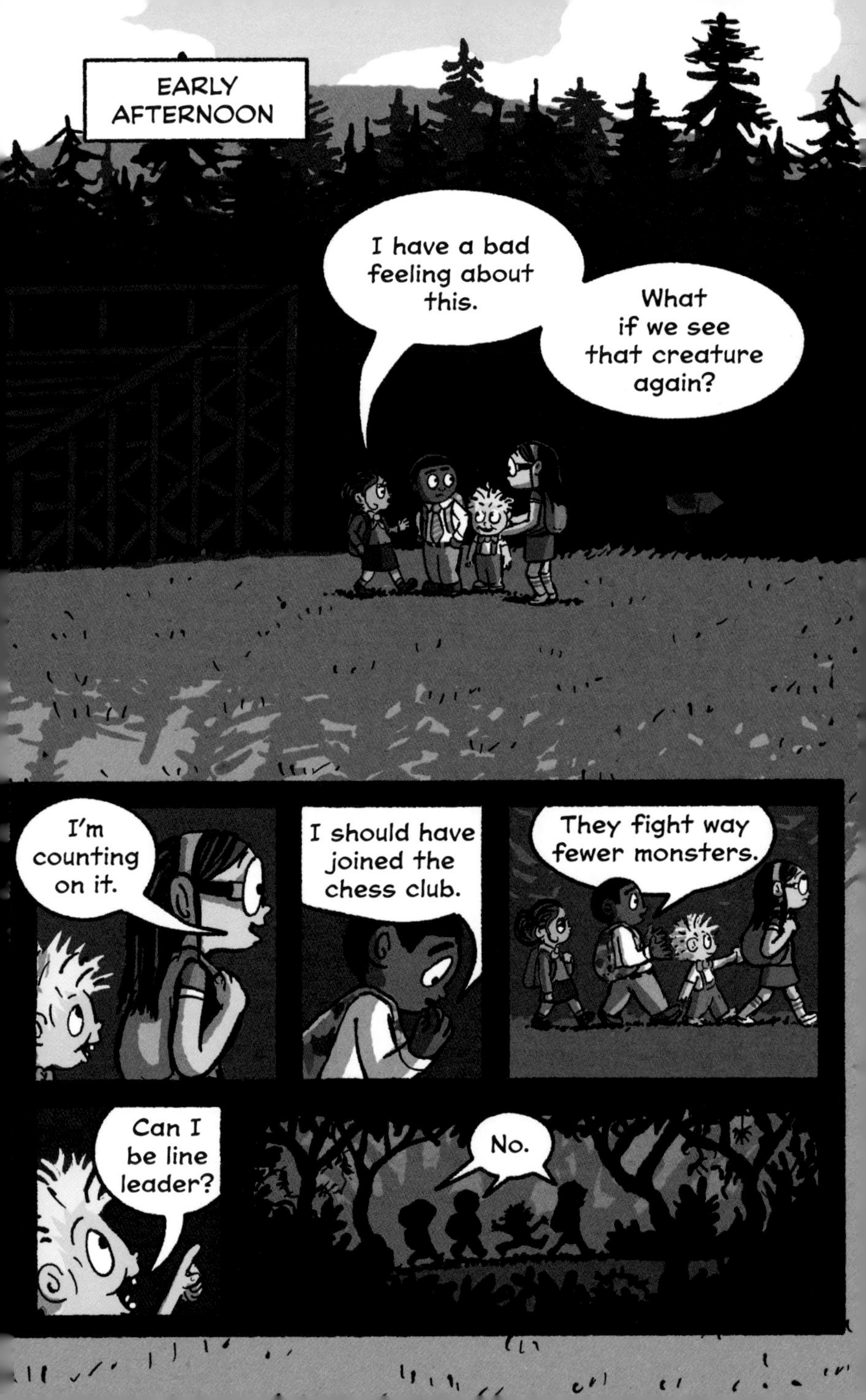
EARLY AFTERNOON
I have a bad feeling about this.
What if we see that creature again?
I'm counting on it.
I should have joined the chess club.
They fight way fewer monsters.
Can I be line leader?
No.

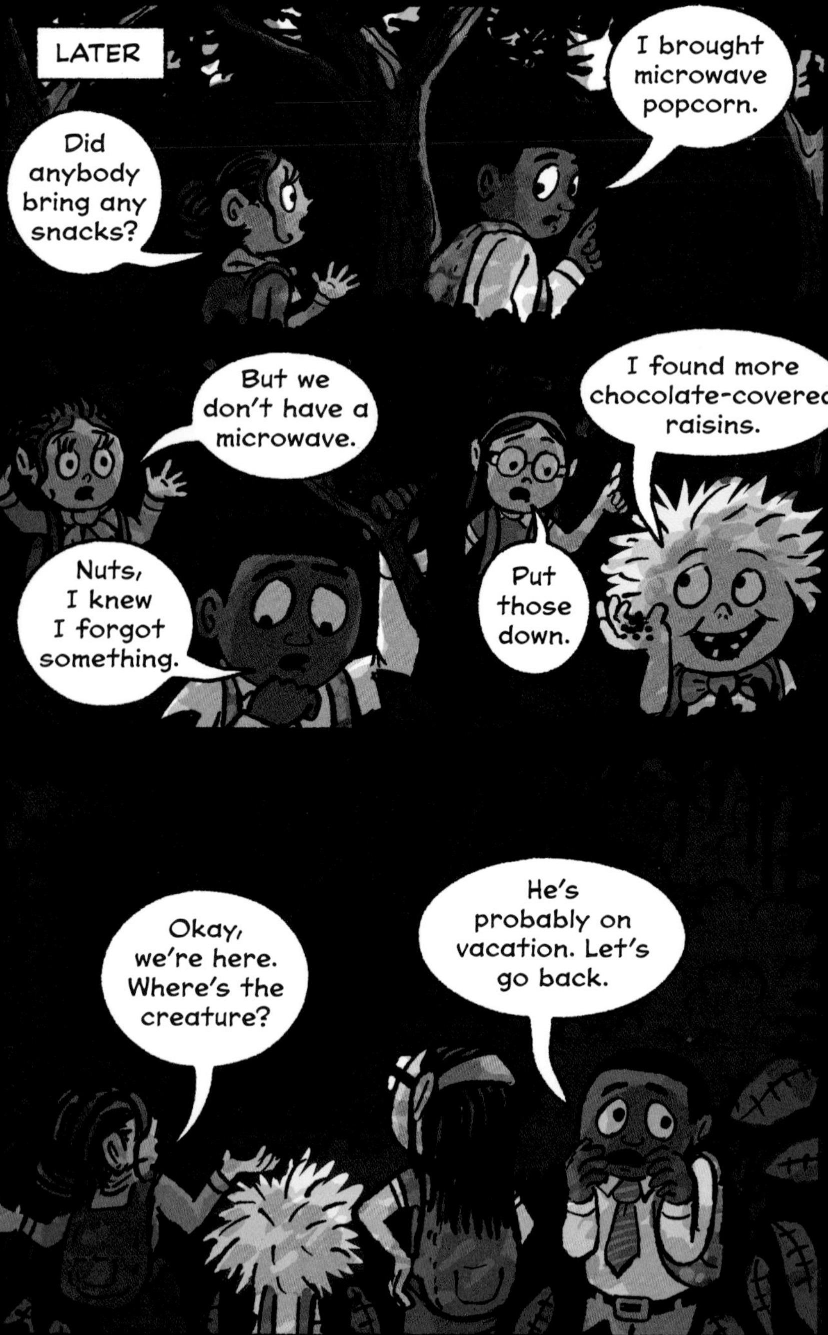
LATER
Did anybody bring any snacks?
I brought microwave popcorn.
But we don't have a microwave.
Nuts, I knew I forgot something.
I found more chocolate-covered raisins.
Put those down.
Okay, we're here. Where's the creature?
He's probably on vacation. Let's go back.

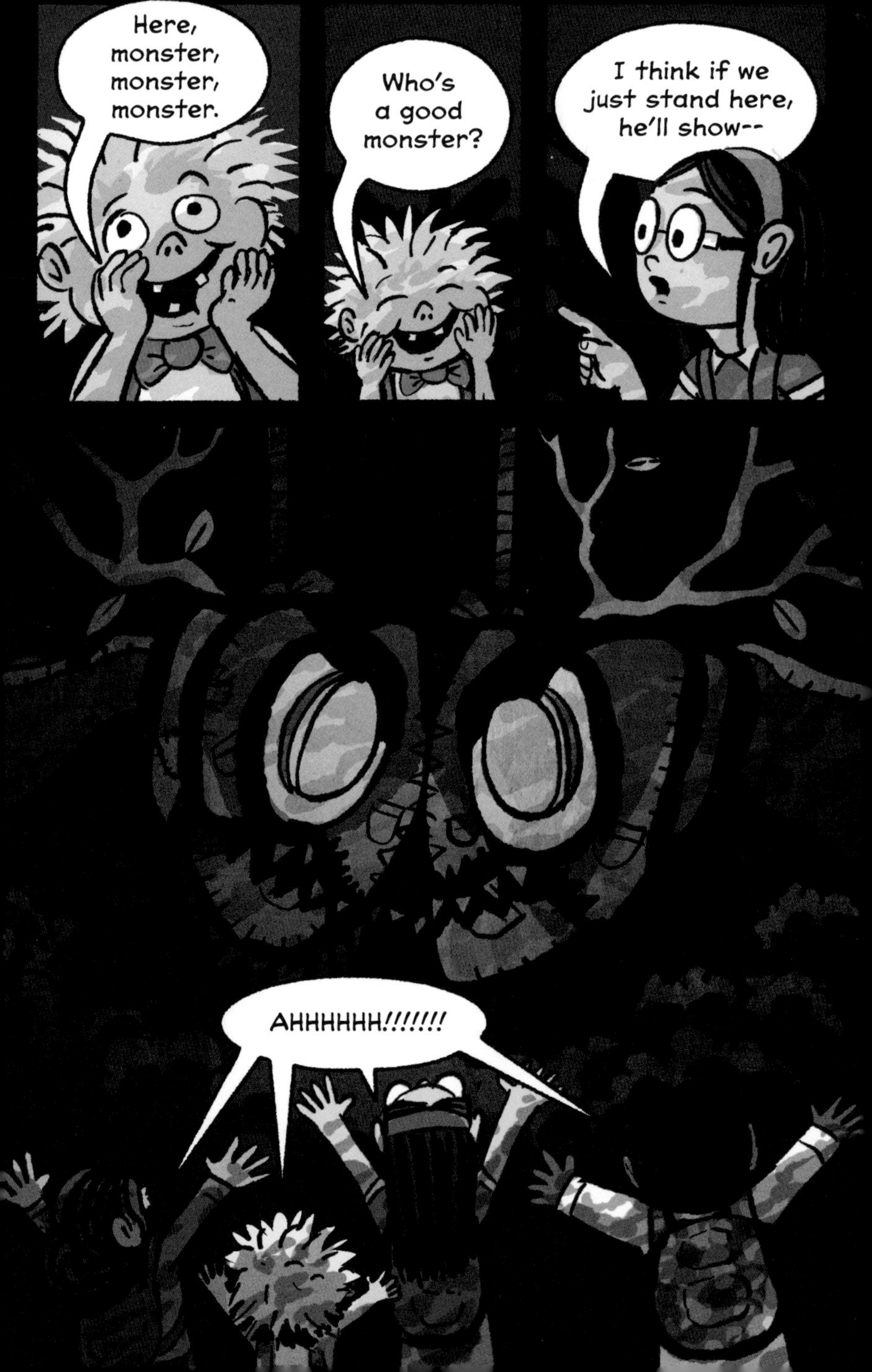
Here, monster, monster, monster.
Who's a good monster?
I think if we just stand here, he'll show--
AHHHHHH!!!!!!!

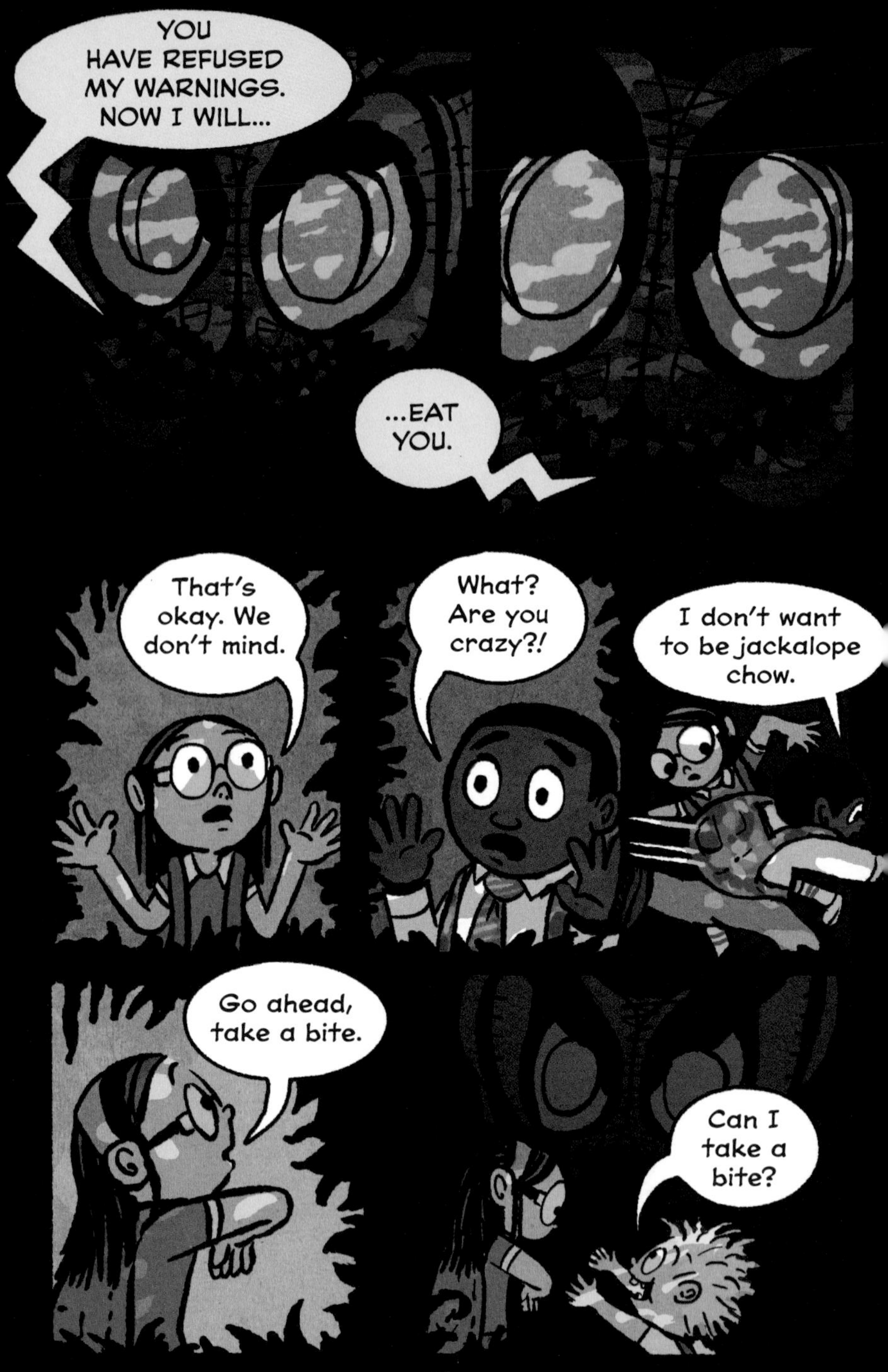
YOU HAVE REFUSED MY WARNINGS. NOW I WILL...
...EAT YOU.
That's okay. We don't mind.
What? Are you crazy?!
I don't want to be jackalope chow.
Go ahead, take a bite.
Can I take a bite?

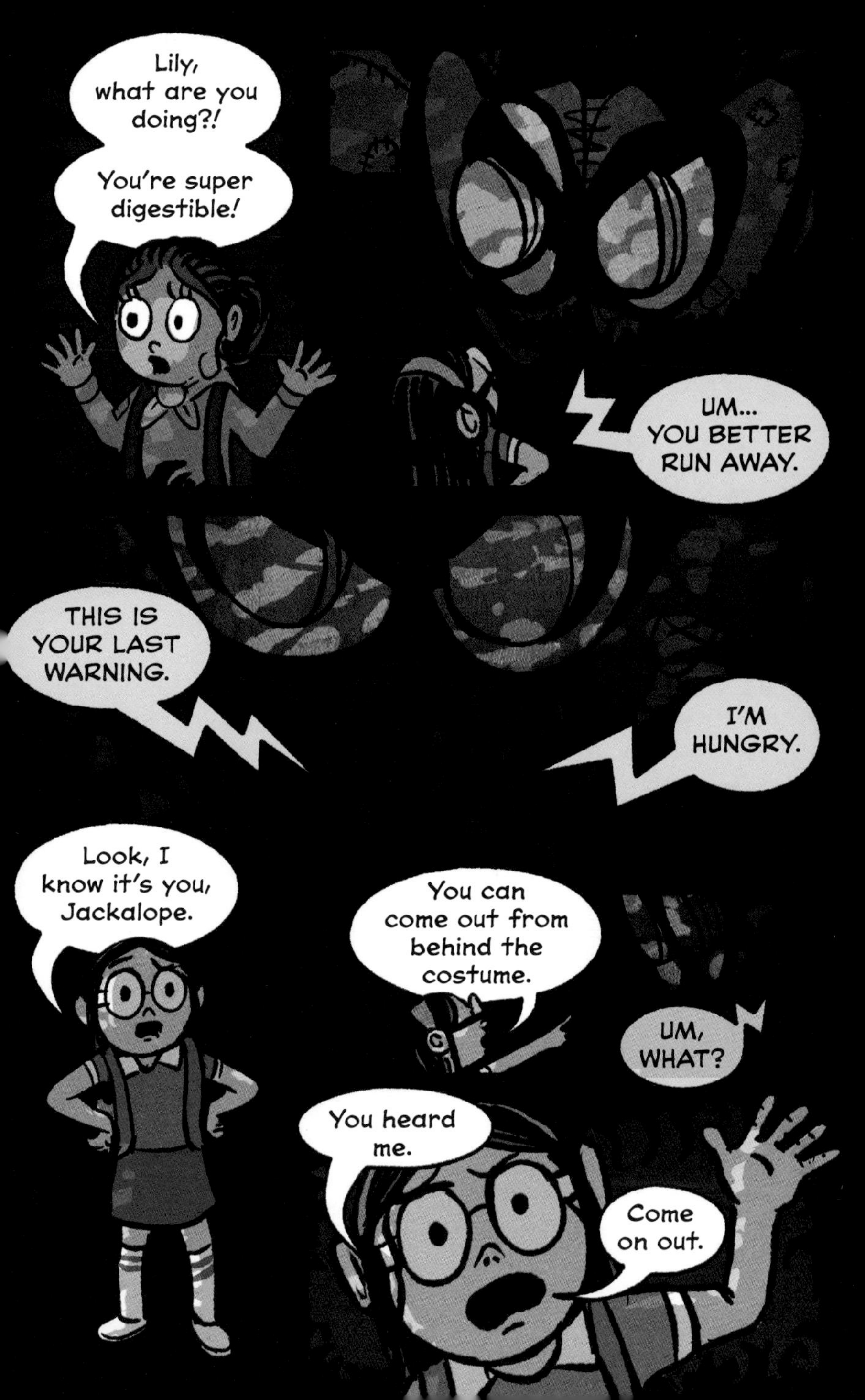
Lily, what are you doing?!
You're super digestible!
UM... YOU BETTER RUN AWAY.
THIS IS YOUR LAST WARNING.
I'M HUNGRY.
Look, I know it's you, Jackalope.
You can come out from behind the costume.
UM, WHAT?
You heard me.
Come on out.

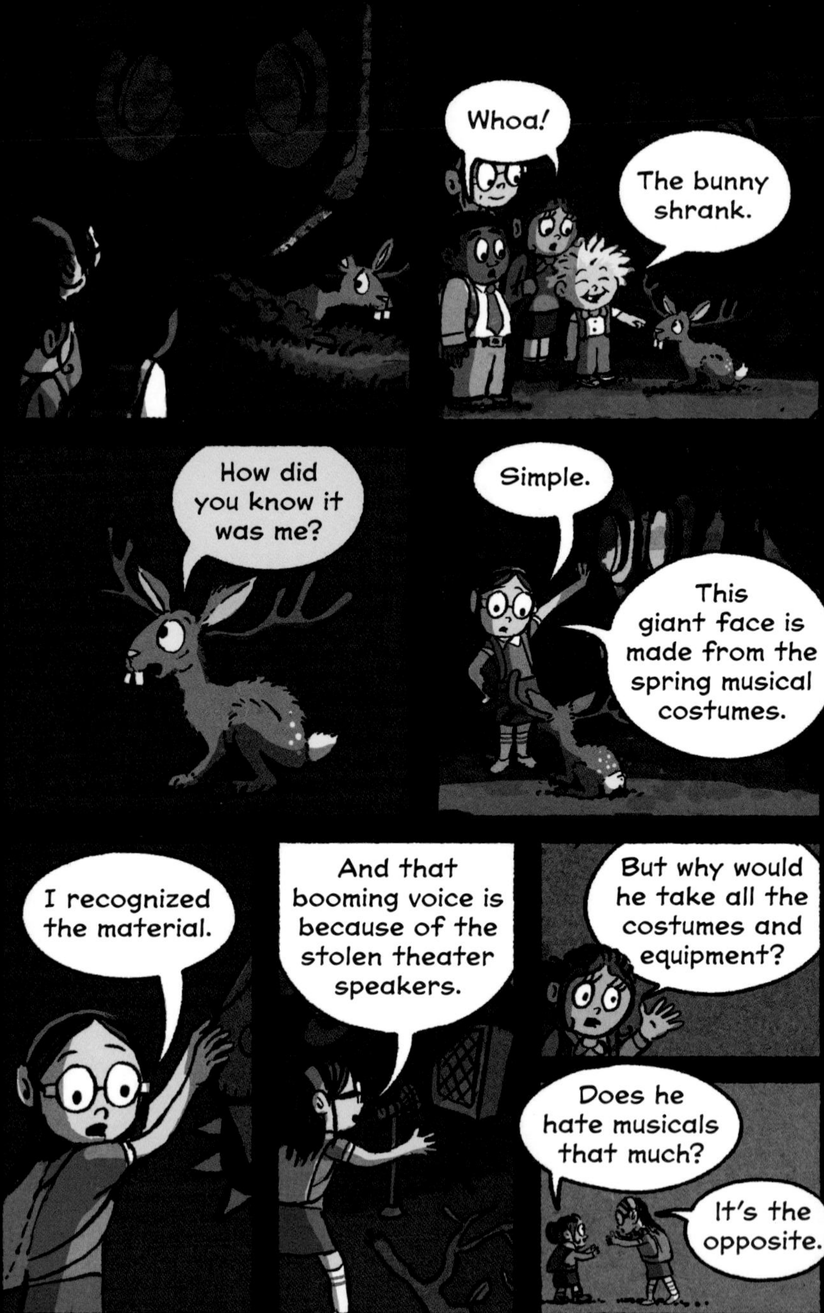

Whoa!
The bunny shrank.
How did you know it was me?
Simple.
This giant face is made from the spring musical costumes.
I recognized the material.
And that booming voice is because of the stolen theater speakers.
But why would he take all the costumes and equipment?
Does he hate musicals that much?
It's the opposite.

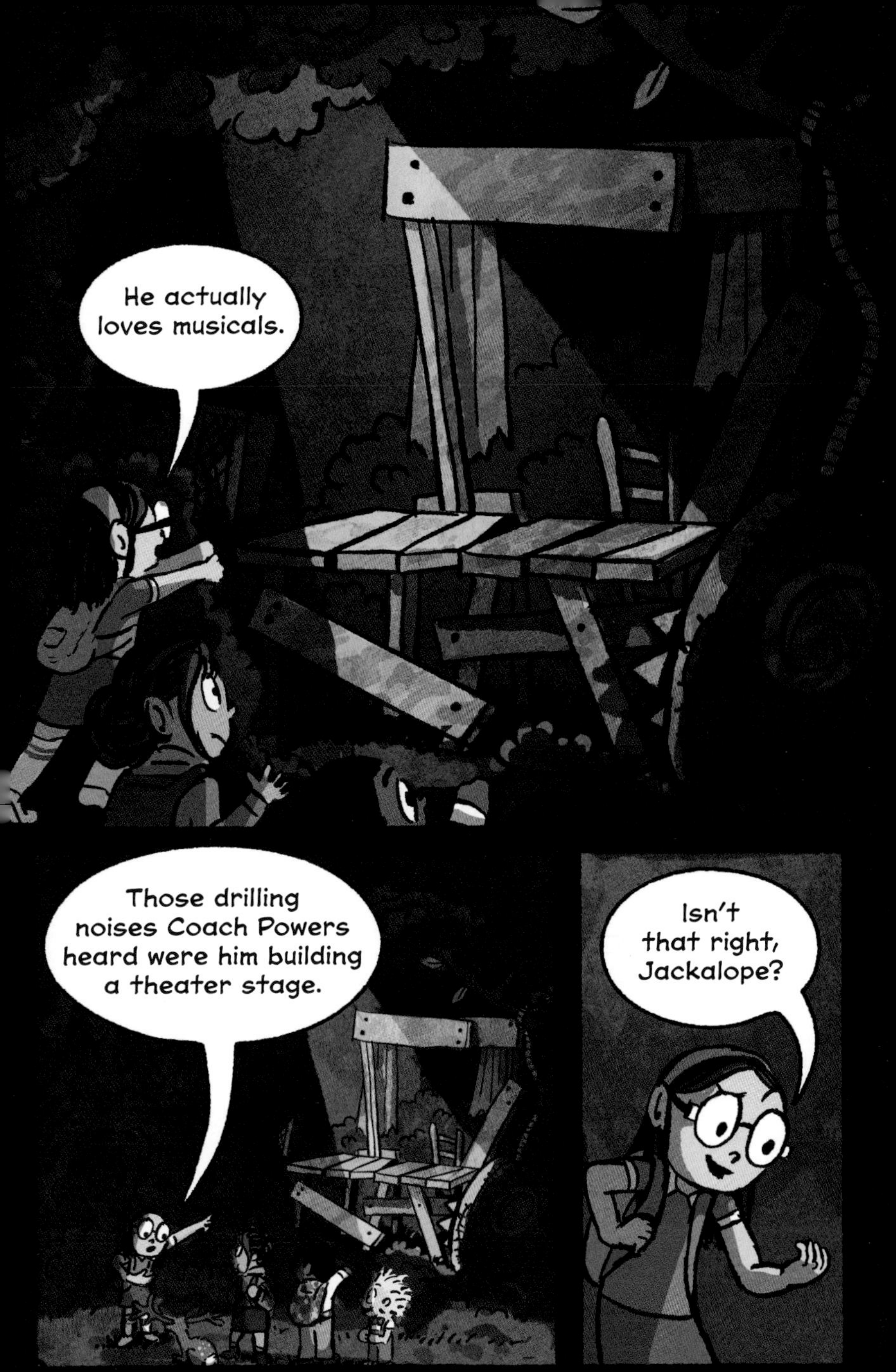
He actually loves musicals.
Those drilling noises Coach Powers heard were him building a theater stage.
Isn't that right, Jackalope?

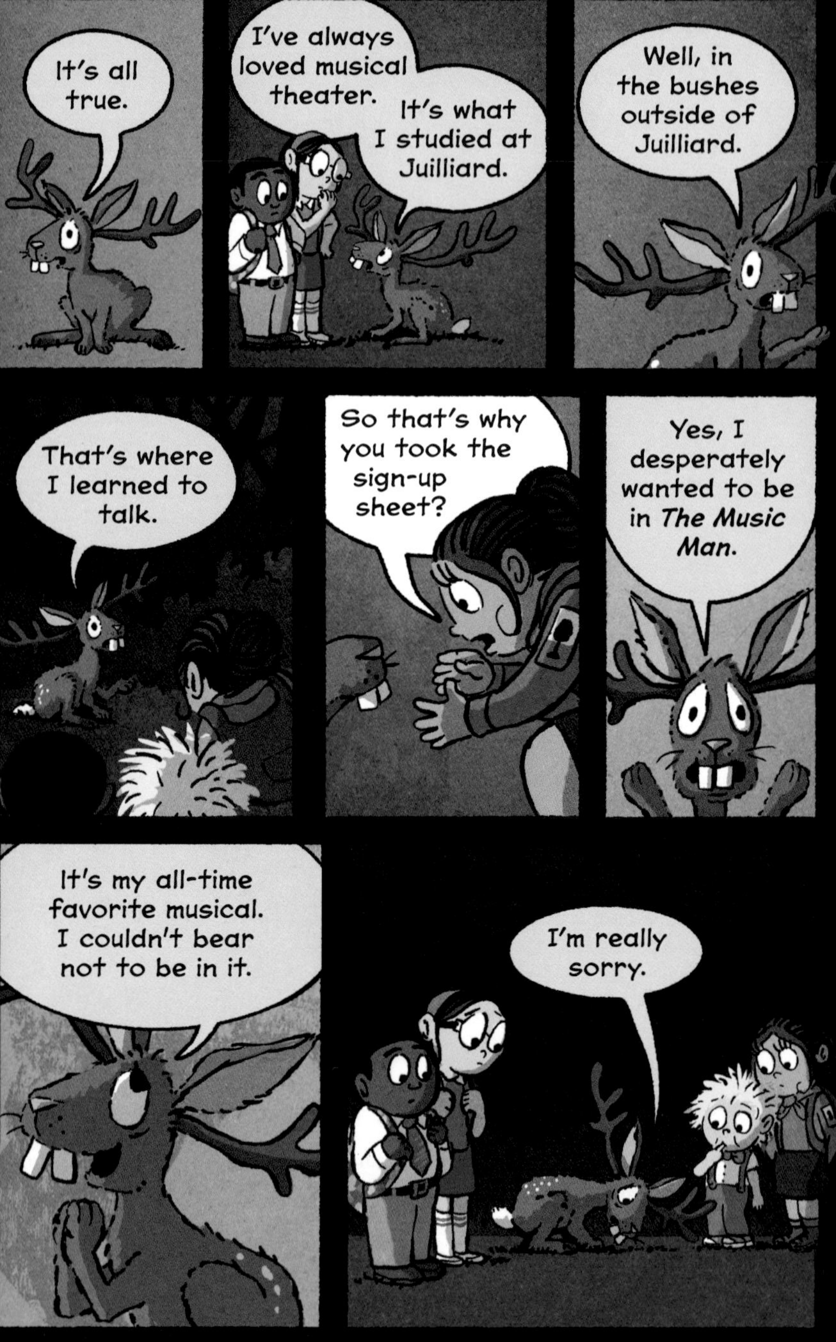
It's all true.
I've always loved musical theater.
It's what I studied at Juilliard.
Well, in the bushes outside of Juilliard.
That's where I learned to talk.
So that's why you took the sign-up sheet?
Yes, I desperately wanted to be in *The Music Man*.
It's my all-time favorite musical. I couldn't bear not to be in it.
I'm really sorry.

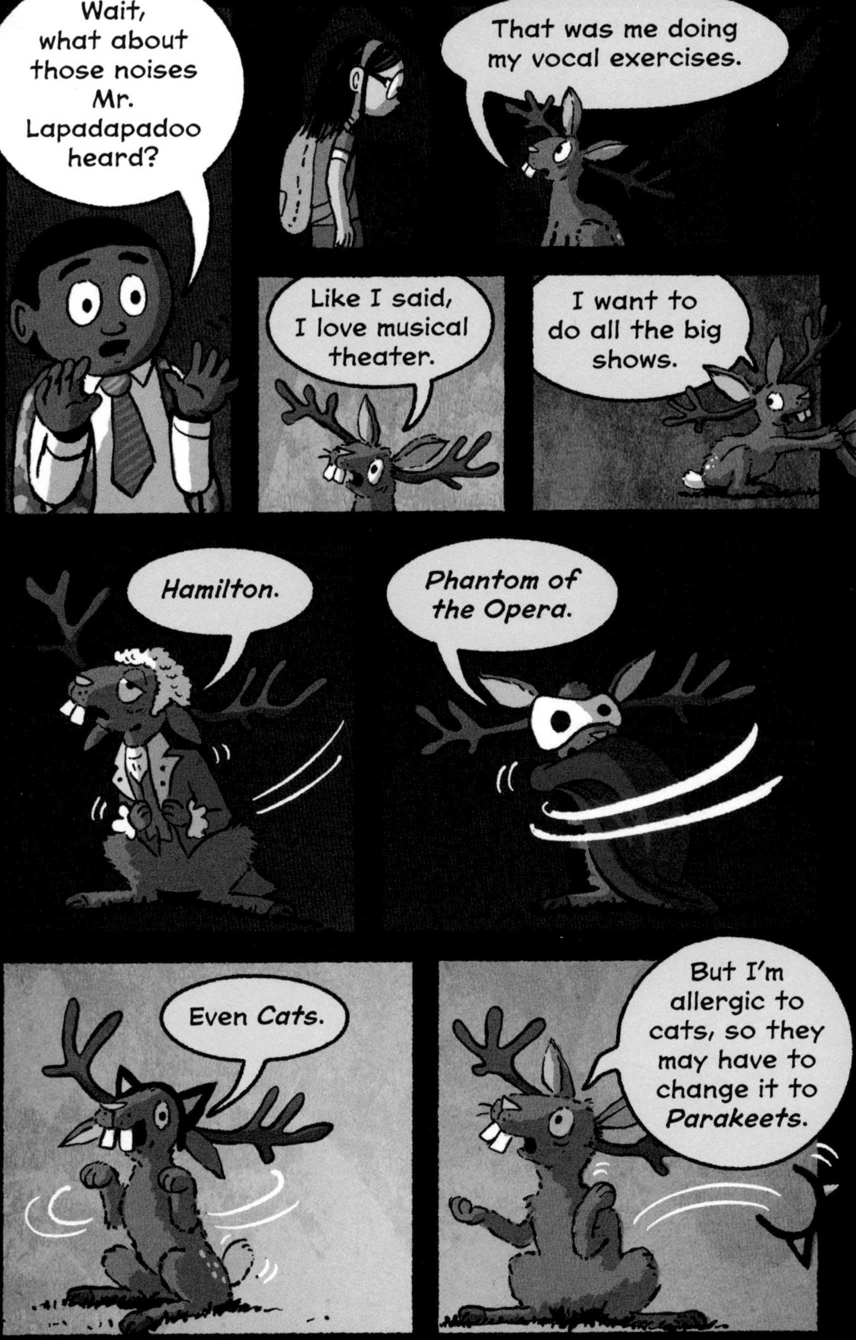
Wait, what about those noises Mr. Lapadapadoo heard?
That was me doing my vocal exercises.
Like I said, I love musical theater.
I want to do all the big shows.
Hamilton.
Phantom of the Opera.
Even *Cats.*
But I'm allergic to cats, so they may have to change it to *Parakeets.*

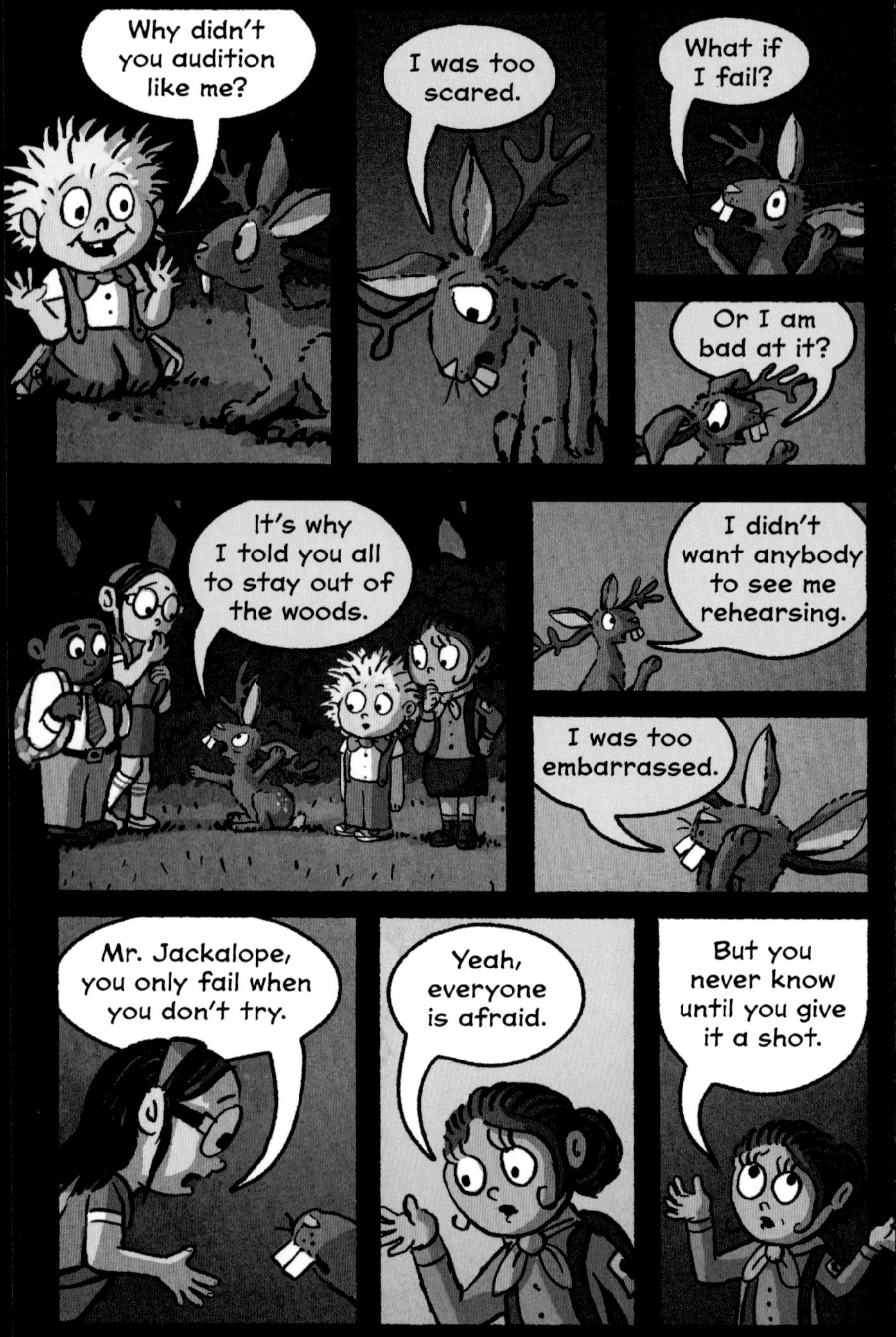
Why didn't you audition like me?
I was too scared.
What if I fail?
Or I am bad at it?
It's why I told you all to stay out of the woods.
I didn't want anybody to see me rehearsing.
I was too embarrassed.
Mr. Jackalope, you only fail when you don't try.
Yeah, everyone is afraid.
But you never know until you give it a shot.

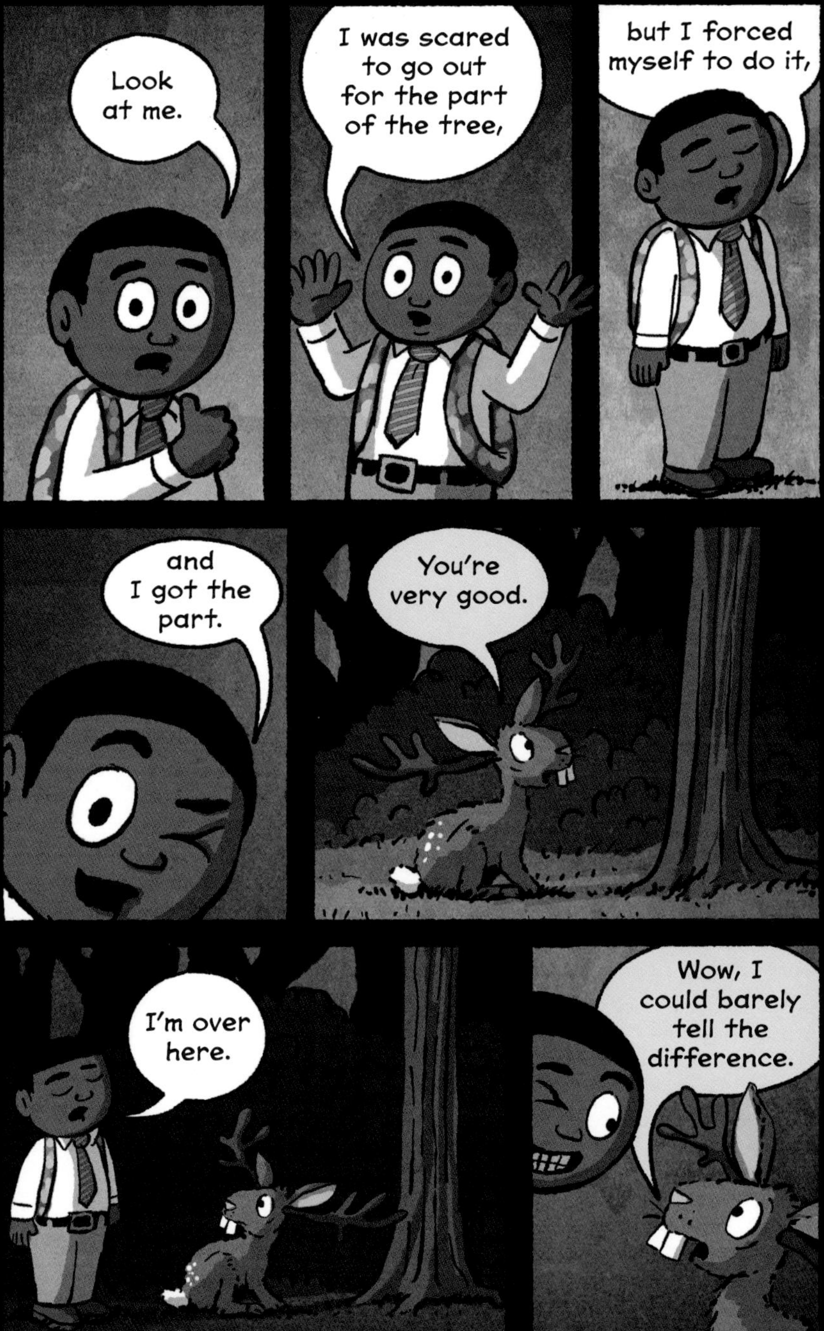
Look at me.
I was scared to go out for the part of the tree,
but I forced myself to do it,
and I got the part.
You're very good.
I'm over here.
Wow, I could barely tell the difference.

Mr. Jackalope, we'd love to hear you sing.

I don't know. What if I can't do it?

Then at least you've tried.

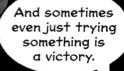

And sometimes even just trying something is a victory.

You're right.

I've been scared for too long.

Here goes nothing...

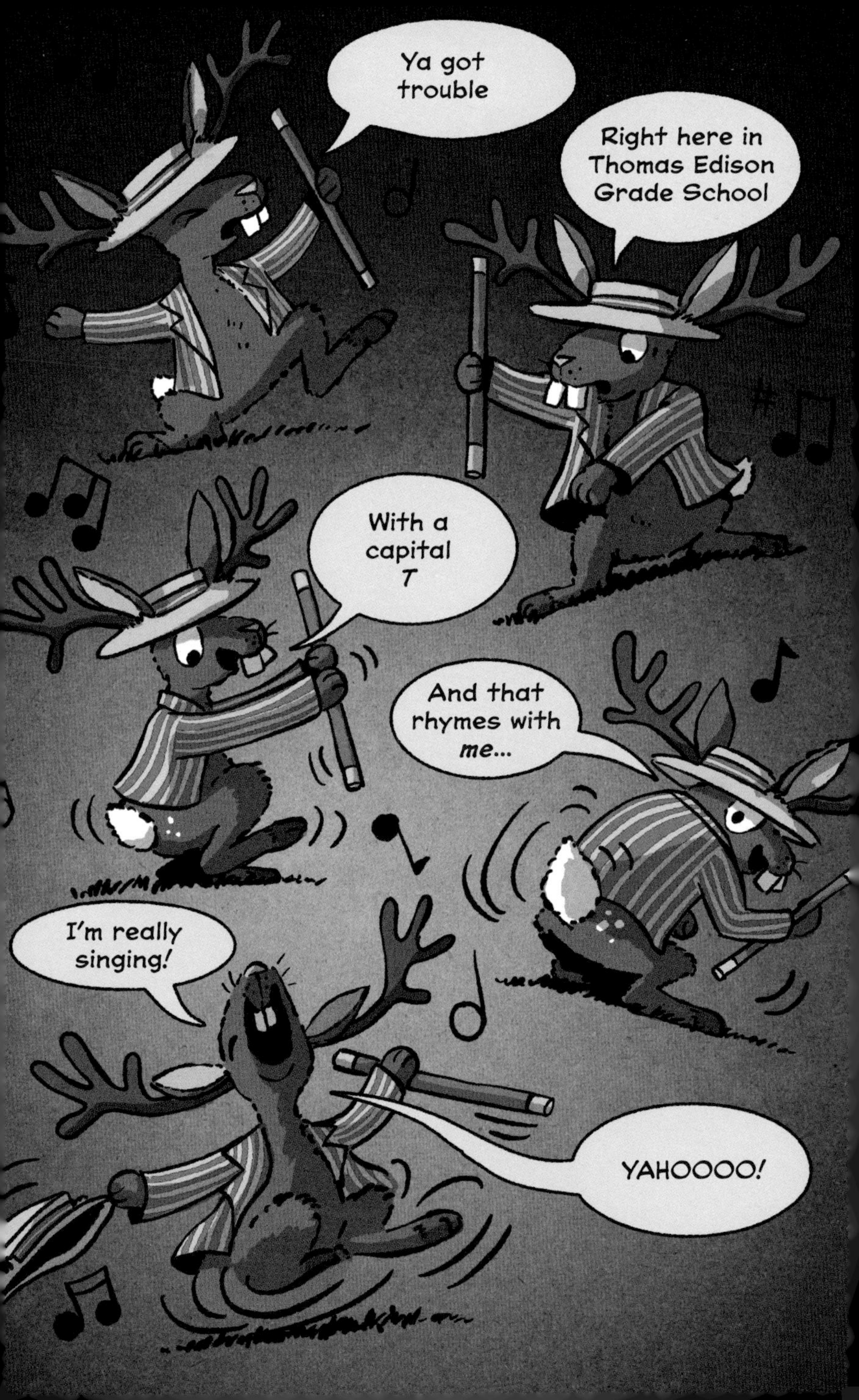
Ya got trouble
Right here in Thomas Edison Grade School
With a capital *T*
And that rhymes with *me*...
I'm really singing!
YAHOOOO!

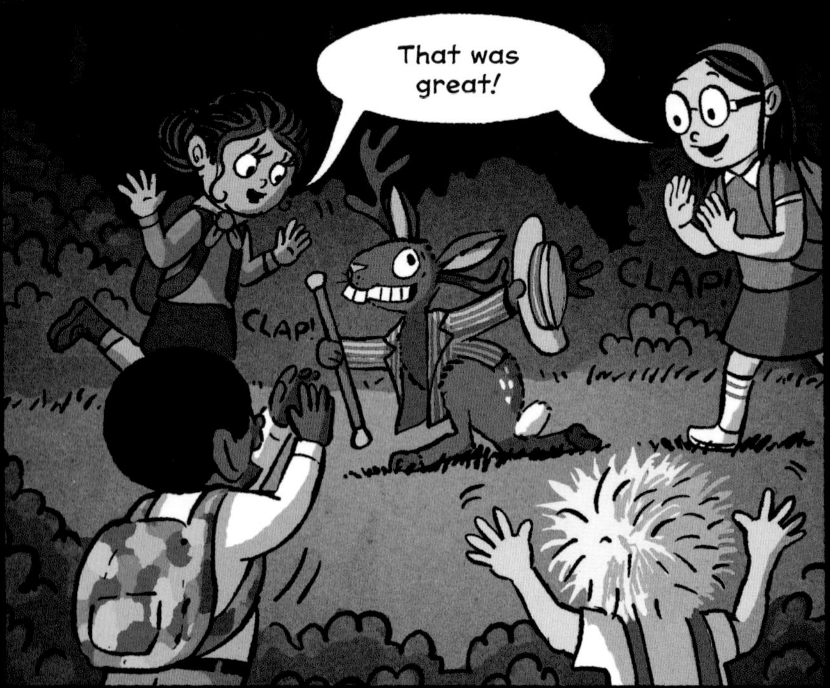
That was great!
CLAP!
CLAP!

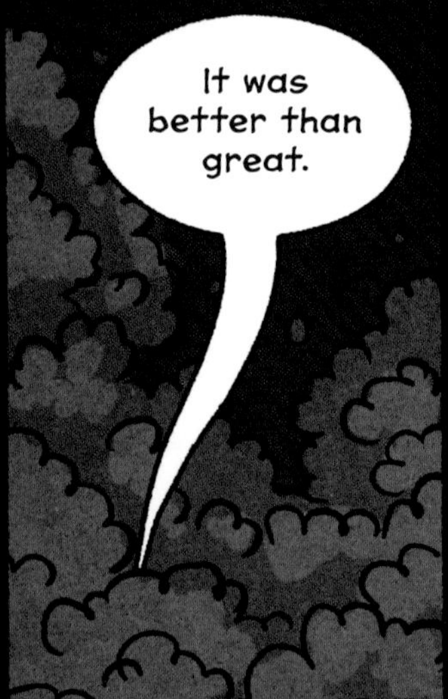
It was better than great.

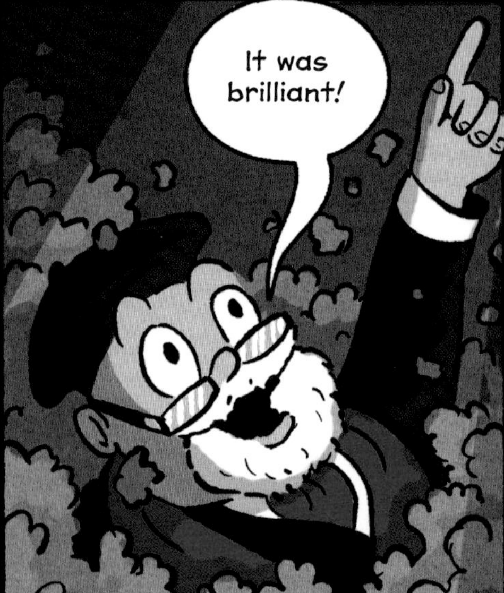
It was brilliant!

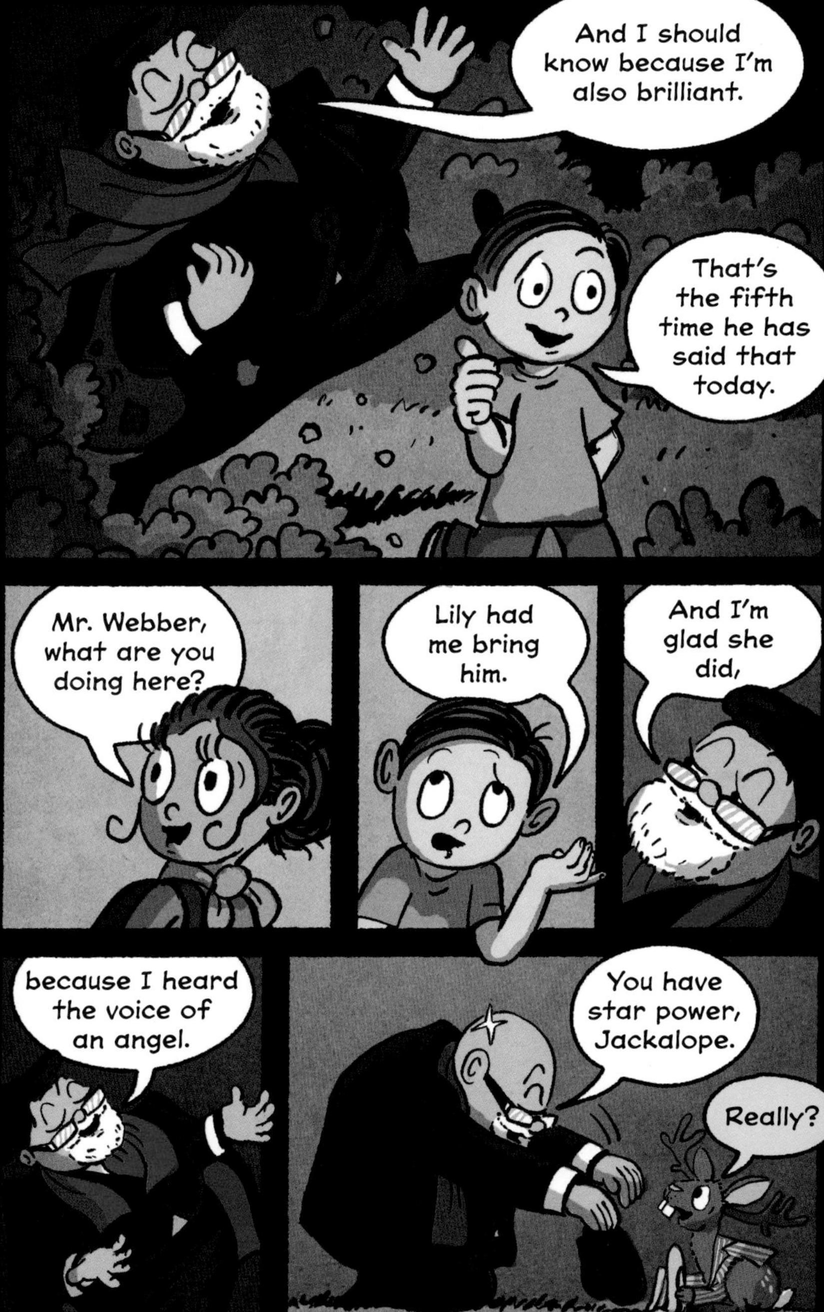

And I should know because I'm also brilliant.
That's the fifth time he has said that today.
Mr. Webber, what are you doing here?
Lily had me bring him.
And I'm glad she did,
because I heard the voice of an angel.
You have star power, Jackalope.
Really?

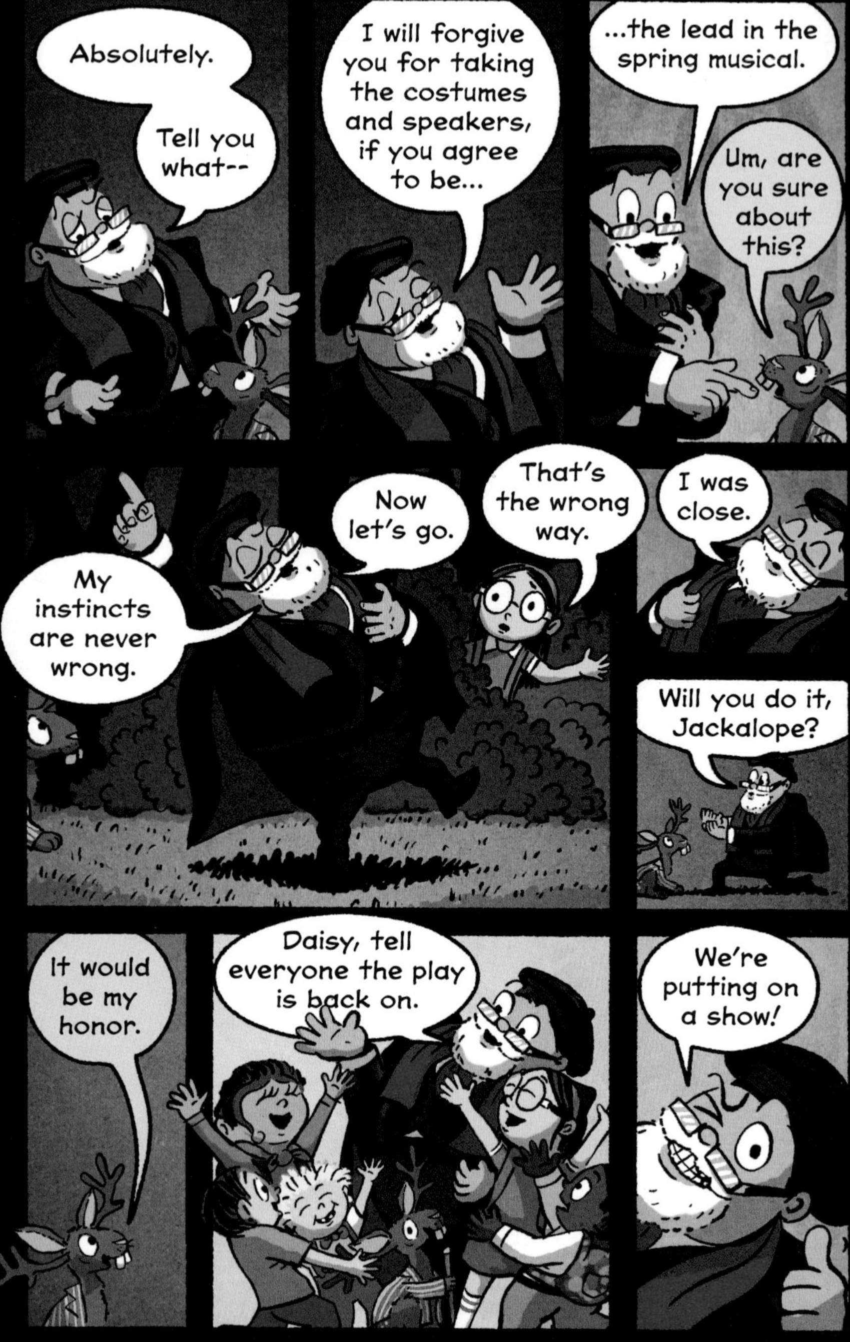
Absolutely.
Tell you what--
I will forgive you for taking the costumes and speakers, if you agree to be...
...the lead in the spring musical.
Um, are you sure about this?
My instincts are never wrong.
Now let's go.
That's the wrong way.
I was close.
Will you do it, Jackalope?
It would be my honor.
Daisy, tell everyone the play is back on.
We're putting on a show!

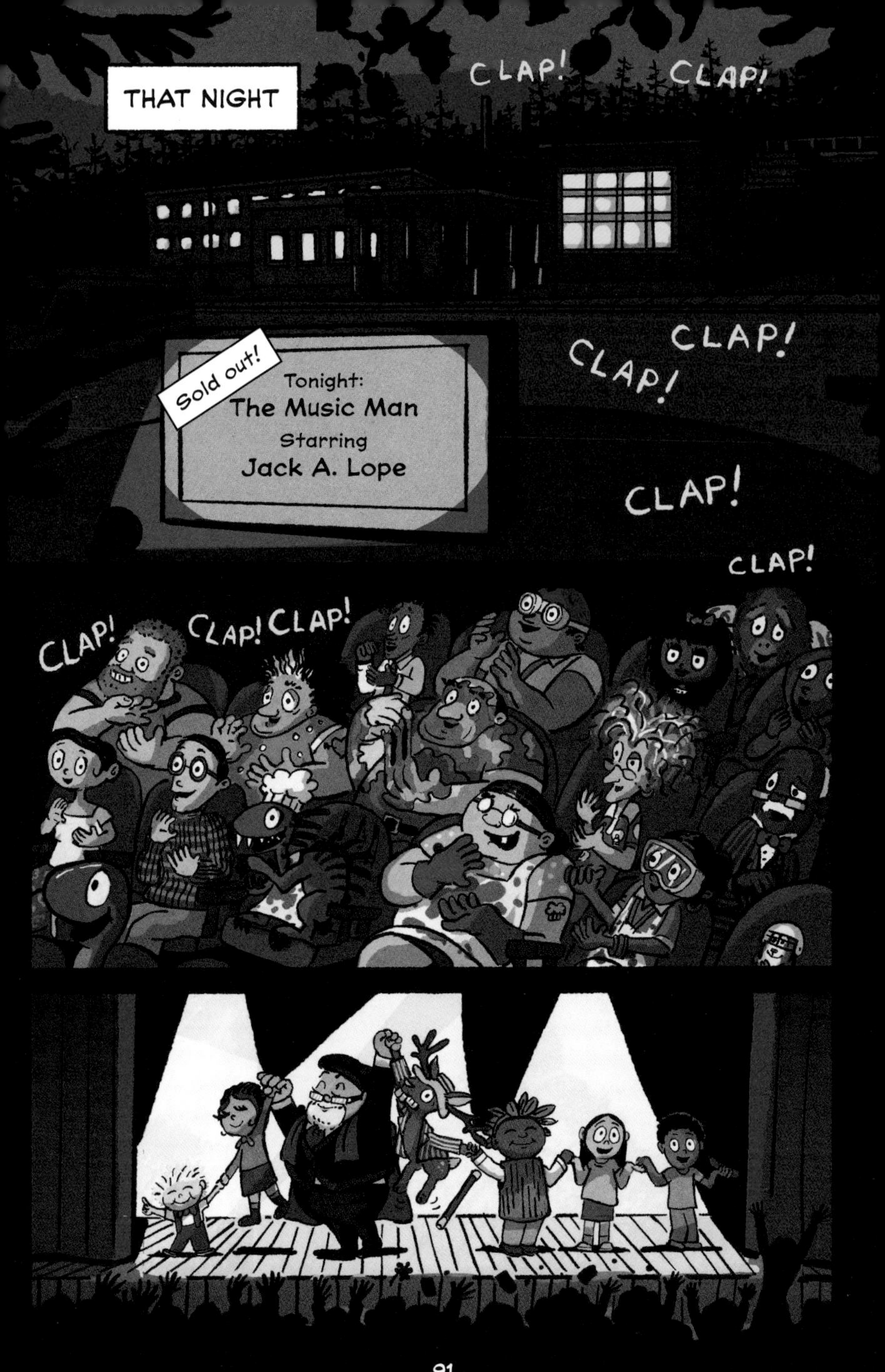
THAT NIGHT
CLAP!
CLAP!
Sold out!
Tonight:
The Music Man
Starring
Jack A. Lope
CLAP!
CLAP!
CLAP!
CLAP!
CLAP!
CLAP! CLAP!

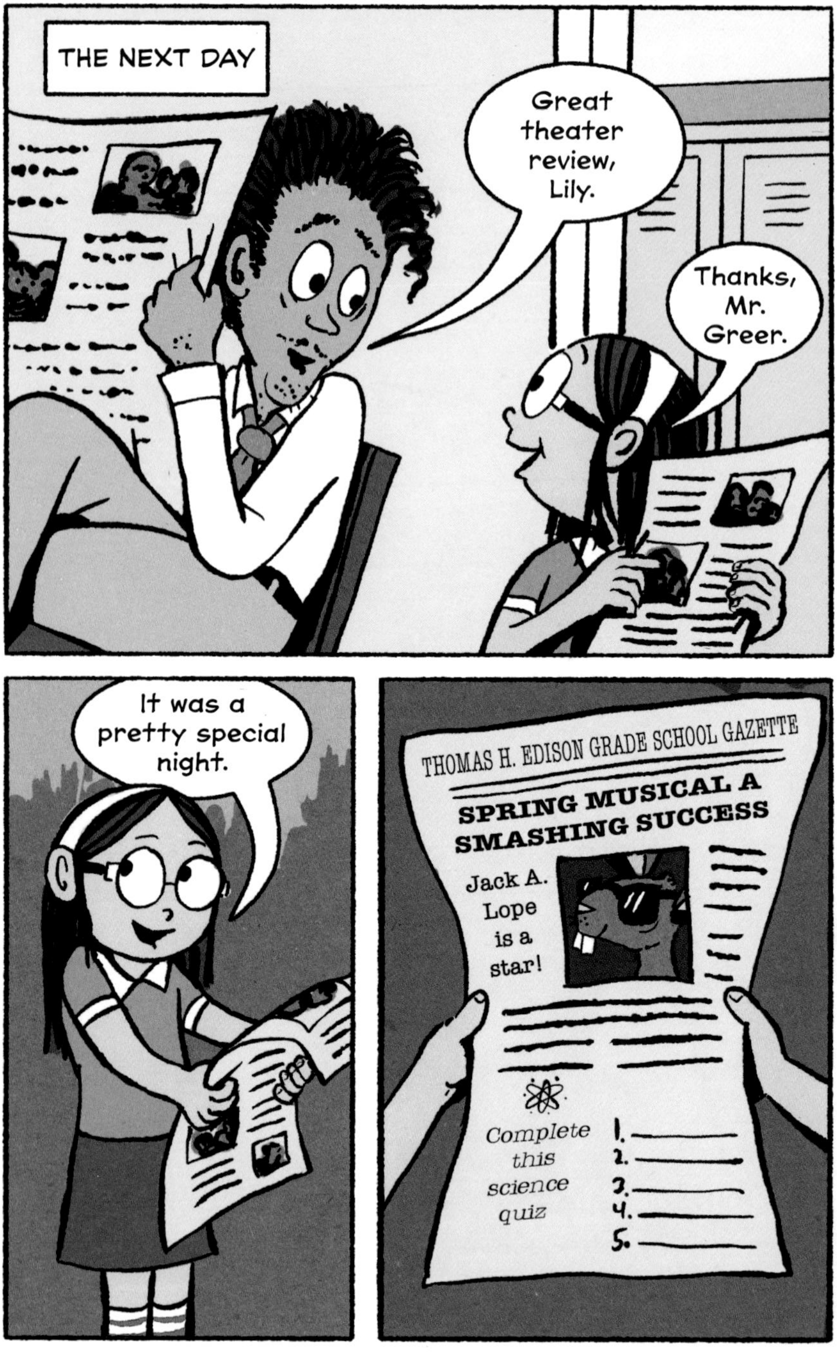
THE NEXT DAY
Great theater review, Lily.
Thanks, Mr. Greer.
It was a pretty special night.
THOMAS H. EDISON GRADE SCHOOL GAZETTE
SPRING MUSICAL A SMASHING SUCCESS
Jack A. Lope is a star!
Complete this science quiz
1.
2.
3.
4.
5.

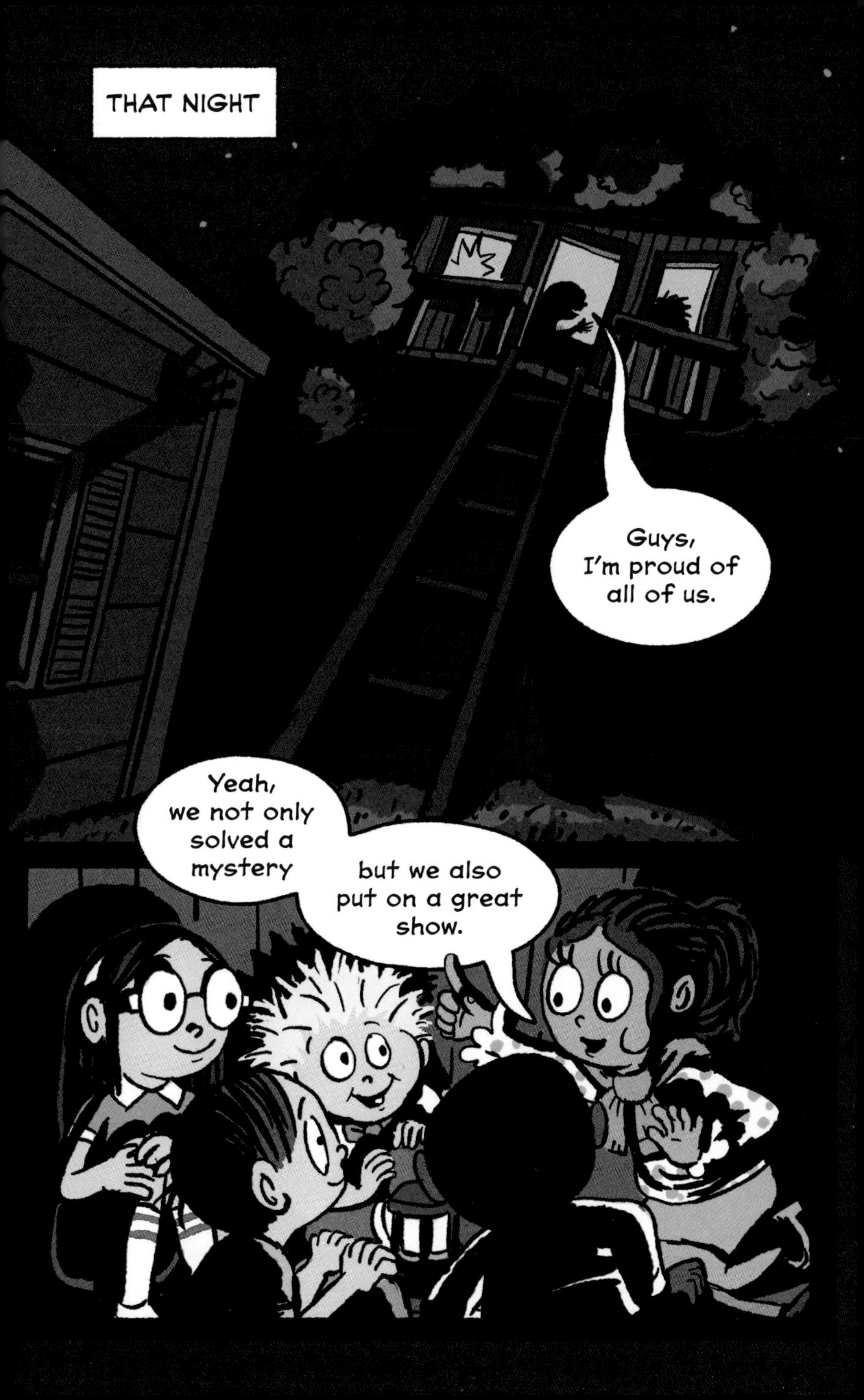
THAT NIGHT
Guys, I'm proud of all of us.
Yeah, we not only solved a mystery
but we also put on a great show.

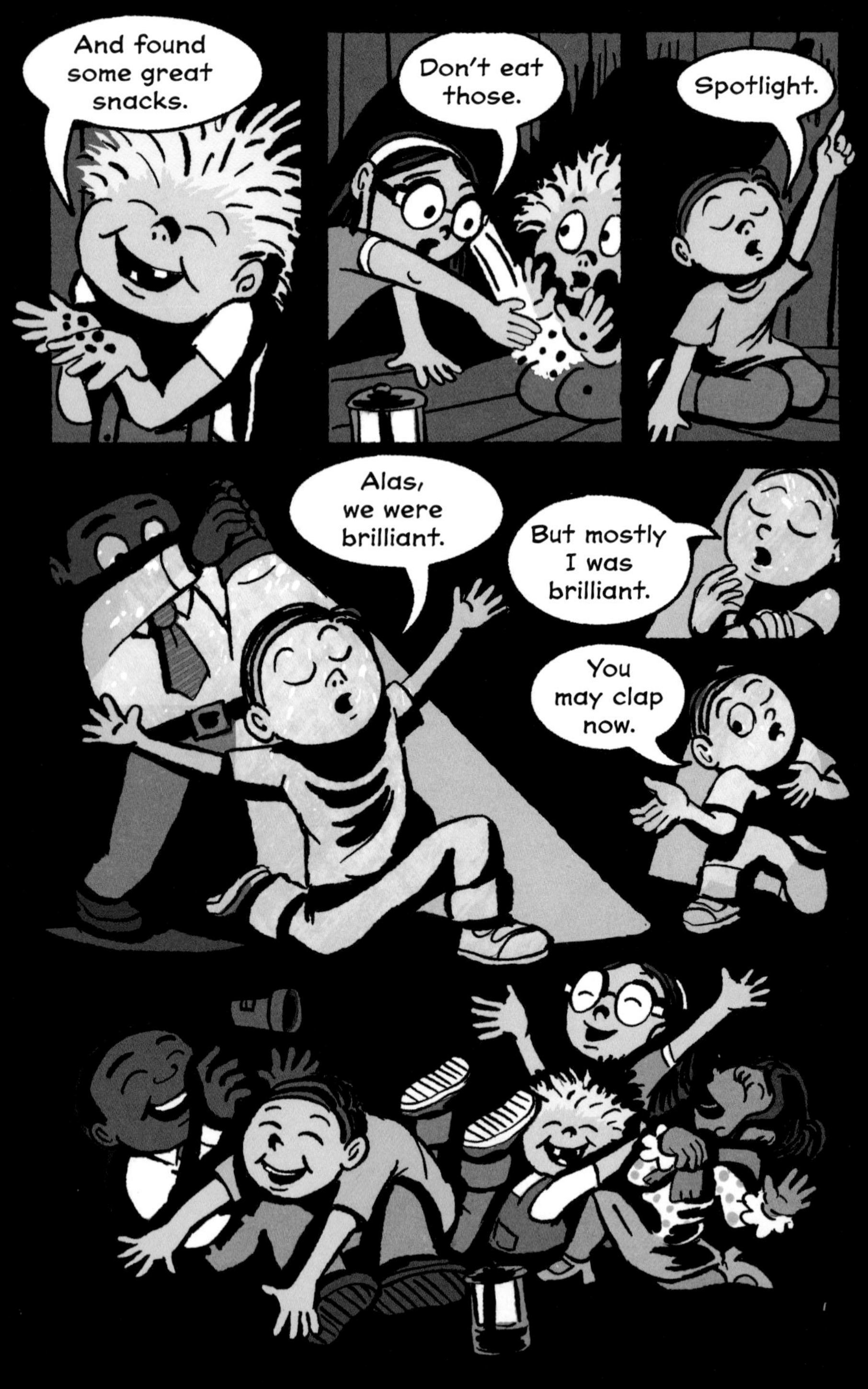
And found some great snacks.
Don't eat those.
Spotlight.
Alas, we were brilliant.
But mostly I was brilliant.
You may clap now.

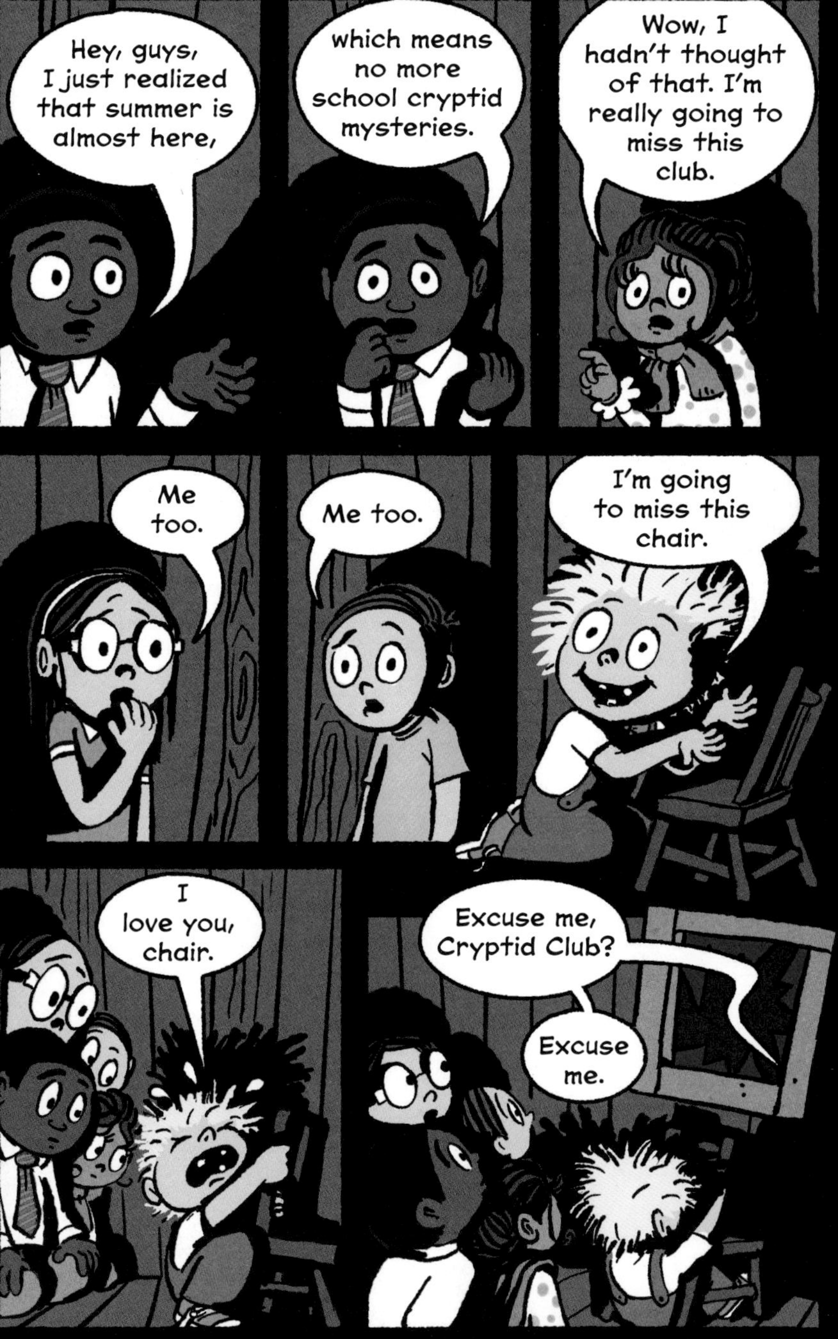
Hey, guys, I just realized that summer is almost here,
which means no more school cryptid mysteries.
Wow, I hadn't thought of that. I'm really going to miss this club.
Me too.
Me too.
I'm going to miss this chair.
I love you, chair.
Excuse me, Cryptid Club?
Excuse me.

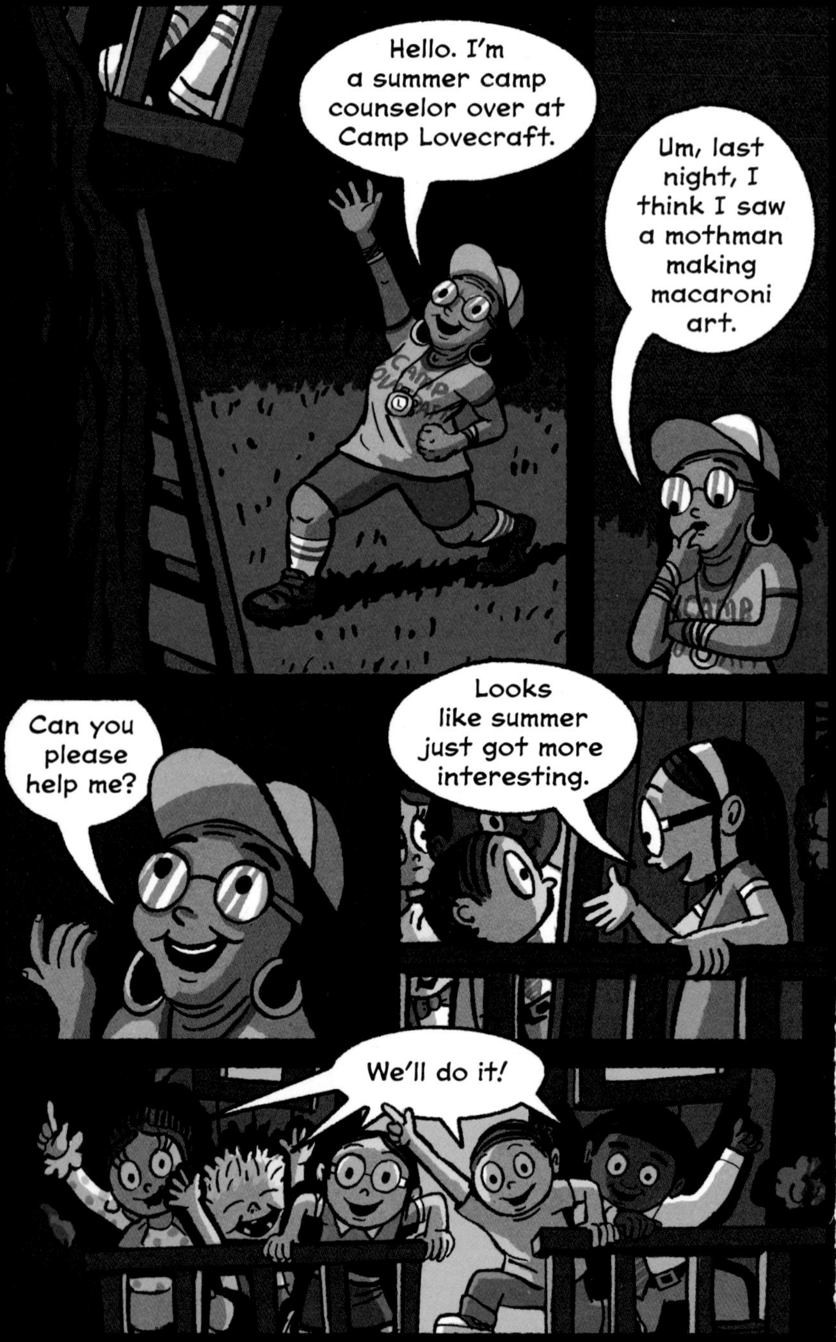
Hello. I'm a summer camp counselor over at Camp Lovecraft.
Um, last night, I think I saw a mothman making macaroni art.
Can you please help me?
Looks like summer just got more interesting.
We'll do it!